I'm Afraid You've Got Dragons

ALSO BY PETER S. BEAGLE

NOVELS

A Fine and Private Place

The Last Unicorn

Lila the Werewolf

The Folk of the Air

The Innkeeper's Song

The Unicorn Sonata

Tamsin

A Dance for Emilia

Return

Summerlong

In Calabria

The Last Unicorn: The Lost Journey

NONFICTION

I See by My Outfit

The California Feeling
(with Michael Bry)

American Denim

The Lady and Her Tiger
(with Pat Derby)

The Garden of Earthly Delights

In the Presence of Elephants

COLLECTIONS

The Fantasy Worlds of Peter S. Beagle

Giant Bones

The Rhinoceros Who Quoted Nietzsche and other Odd Acquaintances

The Line Between

Your Friendly Neighborhood Magician

We Never Talk About My Brother

Strange Roads
(with Lisa Snellings-Clark)

Four Years, Five Seasons (Audiobook Only)

Mirror Kingdoms: The Best of Peter S. Beagle

Sleight of Hand

The Overneath

The Karkadann Triangle
(with Patricia A. McKillip)

ANTHOLOGIES

Peter S. Beagle's Immortal Unicorn
Edited by Peter S. Beagle, Janet Berliner, and Martin Greenberg

The Secret History of Fantasy
Edited by Peter S. Beagle

The Urban Fantasy Anthology
Edited by Peter S. Beagle and Joe Lansdale

The New Voices of Fantasy
Edited by Peter S. Beagle and Jacob Weisman

The Unicorn Anthology
Edited by Peter S. Beagle and Jacob Weisman

I'm Afraid You've Got Dragons

PETER S. BEAGLE

LONDON SYDNEY NEW YORK TORONTO NEW DELHI

1230 Avenue of the Americas
New York, NY 10020

First Saga Press hardcover edition May 2024

SAGA PRESS and colophon are trademarks of Simon & Schuster, LLC

Simon & Schuster: Celebrating 100 Years of Publishing in 2024

For information about special discounts for bulk purchases, please contact Simon & Schuster Special Sales at 1-866-506-1949 or business@simonandschuster.com.

The Simon & Schuster Speakers Bureau can bring authors to your live event. For more information or to book an event, contact the Simon & Schuster Speakers Bureau at 1-866-248-3049 or visit our website at www.simonspeakers.com.

Interior design by Esther Paradelo
Cover and endpaper artwork by Justin and Annie Gerard

Manufactured in the United States of America

1 3 5 7 9 10 8 6 4 2

Library of Congress Control Number: 2024931399

ISBN 978-1-6680-2527-7
ISBN 978-1-6680-2529-1 (ebook)

This story is for Jenella DuRousseau,
wherever she is,
for always and always.

But since, for so many reasons,
it would never have reached anyone at all
without the aid of my beloved friend Kathleen Hunt,
this story is also for her.

PROLOGUE

The warning came in the form of a great wind, sudden and cold, sweeping out of the western mountains on a perfectly bland and cloudless summer day. Along with it came the charcoal-burners, the trappers, and the rest of the forest folk—woodcutters, swineherds, herbwives, even the occasional hermit and more occasional outlaw—rushing to seek shelter in the nearby village. The villagers eagerly took them all in, glad of more hands to share in hastily battening down doors, windows, shelves, and cellars, and hanging stones from the eaves and edges of thatched roofs, in hopes of holding their houses together against the rising wind. As they worked, they prayed it might indeed be only wind.

The village's three Wise Women—a larger town would have had as many as seven—were the only inhabitants bold enough to stand exposed in the fields on the mountain-facing side of the village. Their hair and garments whipped behind them as they watched the forest bend and twist as if wrenched between invisible hands. The air was thick now with dust and twigs and torn leaves, and over the growing howl they could hear tree limbs snap and splinter with a sound like cracking bones.

The Wise Women watched, and worried, and debated.

"This is no storm," said Uska, youngest of the three, her one good eye searching the oddly clear sky. "The Kings return."

"Nonsense," replied Yairi. At sixty-three, she was Uska's elder by thirty years. She never missed a chance to hint that Uska had attained her place too soon, and with insufficient testing. "The Kings passed before you were born, and none of their progeny could do this. Besides, this wind is cold. I remember the Kings. The wind of their passage was always hot, almost too hot to breathe, as if their wings were made of stolen sun. This fury is another matter altogether. Some faraway shift in the land or sea, perhaps, echoing its way to us across the distance. Watch. It will shake itself out and fade."

"What great lurch or tide, no matter how distant, moves trees without touching the sky? It *is* the Kings. We must light the beacons, so we might yet be noticed and avoided. We must prepare the rune arrows, to ask forgiveness and beg them pass us by."

"You are young and coarse, and lack understanding." Yairi made no attempt to hide her condescension. "The world has many mysteries. Is that not so, Brugge?"

The oldest of the Wise Women held her bony right hand out flat, wobbling it slightly this way and that: *maybe yes, maybe no*. Her skin was almost transparent with age. She frowned at her companions and breathed in twice, preparing to speak, but before she could begin, a tangle of crosscurrents stilled the air for a moment. In the sudden hush a new sound came to them from the forest: a low, dark rumble that rose and fell in waves, and seemed to be made of many other noises all blurred and jumbled together. When the wind rose again the sound was dulled, but they could still hear it, growing louder. It was as if all the lightning in the world had been bridled and *something* now rode it toward their village.

Brugge's sure stance and undimmed eyes belied the count of her years, which only she remembered. But uncertainty colored her voice, and this change in the fixed star of their hierarchy frightened her listeners more than either could admit in the other's company.

"Shoot your arrows at will, sister, for whatever you think they are worth. Light your beacons as you choose. And you, Yairi, so quick to dismiss strangeness, so anxious to quell your own troubled thoughts: I do not believe we will be laughing about this tonight, or tomorrow, or at any time to come."

The gale grew steadily wilder, and for a moment all three women peered keenly back at the village, dreading to see a hearth fire drawn up even one chimney, to leap from housetop to housetop, setting the whole village ablaze. But there was no sign of that disaster, at least.

"The world has turned noisily in its sleep, like some babe disturbed in the cradle, fussing and crying until it forgets the dreams that troubled it. The Kings do not come now to harm us in their vast indifference. Something else is loosed, something that stinks of magic."

"Aye? And what will *he* do?"

As venerable as she insisted on being regarded by her companions, it was extremely rare for Yairi ever to challenge Brugge's authority so directly; she had always been far more likely to snap sideways at her, and then to back away with a quick, inaudible mumble. "When *that one* comes once again to challenge our supposed wisdom, our legendary power for the very last time . . . how do you imagine we will face him then, my sister?" The last two words flashed and bit with contempt, as they were precisely meant to do.

The oldest of the three Wise was silent for such a long moment that Yairi began to shrink hard away from her, while trying her best not to show fear. None of the other Wise had ever seen Brugge in a rage; and Yairi suddenly became utterly aware that she did not ever want to be the first. But the older woman's voice was quite calm when she spoke again, which young Uska thought was quite the most terrible thing of all. Brugge finally shook her white head in distaste. "What *we* will do," she said at last, "is what we Wise always do when wisdom fails. We will chant and charm in all the languages we know, using every prayer, every incantation at our disposal, conjuring to make what approaches leave us in peace. And it . . . it will do whatever *it* will do. Begin."

They knelt together, Brugge's authority still strong enough to bind them. And where else, in truth, could they go? What else, in fact, might they possibly do?

Hours of chanting passed without effect. The sky was still far too clear come nightfall; beneath its dark ceiling the air raged, and the noise from the woods grew harsher and louder than the world might possibly contain. Though the three women screamed their secrets into the onrushing wind, seeking to blunt its fury, they could no longer hear each other or themselves. Their words were torn and scattered as if they had never had form or meaning.

And then there were no words at all.

ONE

R*obert dreamed . . .*

It was The Dream—the one that visited him so often that it had long since lost any terrifying aspect and become as drearily predictable as the ones in which he was being driven out of town by a jeering, laughing mob, or found himself suddenly naked and pink as a shrimp while kneeling to court Violette-Elisabeth, the baker's daughter. Even so, The Dream left him feeling strangely thrilled—in a shivery sort of way—when he woke to his mother's call from downstairs: "Gaius Aurelius! Gaius Aurelius Constantine!"

"Not now, not now," he muttered into his pillow, turning over in forlorn pursuit of a few last fragments of sleep. But Adelise was on the bed already, pulling the coverlet back with her tiny fangs and tickling his ear with her forked tongue. He could hear clumsy Fernand scrabbling for purchase on the shaky bedstead, which meant that Lux would be next, and then Reynald—poor little Reynald, always last in everything.

The call came again. "Gaius Aurelius Constantine Heliogabalus!"

He tried to shout, "I'm awake!" but only managed a croak this time, as he forced himself to sit up. *What was in that new batch at Jarold's last night?* "Get away, Adelise, I'm awake, I'm awake. . . . Oh dear God, I'm dead but I'm awake." Reynald's long scarlet head appeared above the edge of the bed, accompanied by a piercing cry for attention. "Reynald, keep it *down*, I'm not well."

"Gaius Aurelius Constantine Heliogabalus *Thrax*, it's chestnut pancakes—and if you're not here in the kitchen in two minutes, it'll be hog slop!" The three pigs rooting disconsolately in the small pasture out back could no more have passed as hogs than Robert could have, but Odelette Thrax was an optimist in all things. "And there's a job waiting, Gaius Aurelius—"

"Don't call me that!" It was enough of a bellow to send all four of the dragons scurrying as he lurched out of bed and began stiffly fumbling his way into his heavy working clothes. Robert's mother alternated between being his best friend and a headache to dwarf the one he already had—sometimes she filled both positions simultaneously—but at all times he was extremely fond of her cooking.

Adelise leaped to his shoulder as he clumped down the stair, her claws skidding on the dragonskin vest that he always wore to a job, and whose origins she and the others never seemed to sense. He hated the vest and all the rest of the armor of his trade as he had never hated any item of clothing—all right, except for the silly green forester's cap that his mother had made him wear as a boy—but his customers took confidence in his appearance, as some kind of emblem of his expertise, and it did have practical benefits in a day's work, for all its uncomfortable stiffness. He reached up awkwardly to pet the carefully balanced dragonlet, feeling the feather softness of her deep green scales, which would not turn tough, almost impermeable, for another year yet. *The women like them just like this at Dragon Market. The men want the yearlings.*

The thought of Dragon Market roiled his empty stomach as he sat down at his mother's table. She was at the stove with her back to him, cooking what amounted to her third breakfast of the morning. Robert's younger brothers, Caralos and Hector, were of course already out and at work behind a neighboring farmer's oxen, having left at dawn. Now Patience and Rosamonde were racing through their own meal, late for lessons as usual, too hurried even to greet him.

Robert loved his younger sisters, but he also envied them painfully. He had always thought it unjust that village girls got to be properly educated, while boys must apprentice early, and were lucky if they were taught to read and write at home, as he had been. He often peered over his sisters' shoulders while they were studying, until they complained and their mother shooed him away.

By the time Patience and Rosamonde had left for the schola, trailing promises of good behavior they would keep only if absolutely necessary, Robert had revised his opinion of the day. *Chestnut pancakes, browned perfectly at the edges . . . pomegranate syrup . . . fresh milk . . .* there might be something said for living after all. Wolfing down his third cake, he asked, with his mouth full, "Who's the *engagé?*" He never referred to the people who hired him as *customers*, that being a term favored by those in trade, the people who sold things, rather than renting out their skills. In all honesty, he didn't actually care, but it mattered a great deal to his mother. She was intensely aware that her late husband's work, now Robert's work by inheritance, assigned them to the lowest rung of a steep and unforgiving social ladder.

"Medwyn and Norvyn, behind the granary." Odelette turned then, frowning as she saw Adelise on his shoulder. "Does she have to hear this?"

"Go help the others with the beds, Adelise," Robert said gently. The dragonlet flicked out her tongue and spread her minuscule wings, their inner vanes flushed purple as thunder-clouds, then glided to the floor and scuttled up the stairs to Robert's bedroom. The four of them always did his bed first, no matter how often he tried to get them to alter their routine. Sometimes they even tried to make the bed with him still in it.

When he was sure the little dragon was out of earshot, Robert turned back to his mother. "Medwyn and Norvyn? That's going to be nasty. Another caud of *Serpens flamma vegrandis*, I'll lay odds—it'd serve them right, not letting me sweep for eggs the last time. Five, what, six seasons in a row, is it? You think they'd learn."

"They didn't like your father. They like you. Maybe you can convince them."

"Not much chance of that so long as they both keep the books. They're too busy cheating each other to know a bargain, once nothing's blistering their ankles. Ah well," he sighed as he slid his seat back, "more food on the table, and new scrolls for the twins. There are worse livings."

But later, after he'd left the house to gather up Ostvald and the day's tools, he had to confess to himself that he really couldn't think of any.

TWO

The Great Hall of Bellemontagne was full of princes.

It wasn't that difficult to fill the Great Hall with princes, because it wasn't that big of a Great Hall. People had generally been smaller when it was first built, a good four centuries before; and besides, the Castle of Bellemontagne, while it had undoubtedly seen better days, couldn't remember them. The fireplace, open on both sides, was so remarkably constructed that it could roast an ox without throwing the least bit of heat to those huddling as close as they dared. The roof—easily high enough for a cathedral, if considerably narrower, and not nearly so gracefully curved—had over the years been home to thousands of transient birds and half again as many bats, as the cracked and begrimed portraits of royal ancestors along the walls bore mute testimony. Every sort of nameless vermin squeaked and creaked and rustled along the walls, or else inside them; and the princes crowded closely together on their seats, for comfort and reassurance as well as body heat. Somebody was heard to growl, "Stop kicking!" but for the most part the gathering was a quiet one, with most conversations going on under fiercely hissed breaths. Each prince had his own axe to grind, sometimes literally, and everyone else's ox to gore.

"No, you cannot borrow my hauberk—get your own! What do you need a hauberk for, anyway?"

"Battle? You're going to tell her you were in a battle? You've never been in any damned battle!"

"You might as well go on home—you're way too short for her. I despise—I mean, she *despises short men."*

Princes, as a rule, are not raised to be paragons of patience. Stuffed four to the bench and desperately uncertain of their pecking order, they did not show well. Indeed, most had started to wilt within minutes of their arrival, and some, having been waiting there for days, despaired of ever making themselves presentable again. The most depressed of the lot positively drooped; there was simply no other word for it.

"Who's that chap? The tall one, with the cheekbones—I don't care for the look of him, not at all. . . ."

"You slept in the servants' quarters last night? They gave me the pantry, practically to myself—"

"But I had a bed! All right, a bench . . ."

Good manners inevitably decay under siege, especially when an aggressor wakes to the fact that the walls being breached are his own. Even an eldest son can take umbrage then, doubting the value of royal purpose and the preordained blessings of his fate.

"I don't know how they get to call this a kingdom. We've got backcountry baronies bigger than this place—"

"We've got bigger backyards—"

"So does the Princess, if she's anything like the one I was courting in Malbrouck last week . . . oh. Oh my!"

"Oh MY*!"*

The Princess Cerise had just swept into the hall, deigning at last to grant this month's batch of princes the gift of her presence. She was accompanied only by the castle's chamberlain, a small, portly man who always looked more put-upon than he felt, and knew how to use that to his advantage. He carried with him a block of stretched parchment and a charcoal stylus.

The waiting princes came to their feet as one creature, smiling eagerly in Cerise's direction while hurriedly straightening each ribbon, button, medallion, decoration, ornament, epaulet, and feather in sight. One tried to snug up his father's best formal oyster-pearl garters from where they'd slipped, without being noticed, but he was too late; and another clearly didn't realize that his capotain no longer covered his bald spot.

None of them spoke. The rules of polite behavior in this circumstance were absolute, and only the Princess could break the silence, however long it might go on. But inside their heads, in diverse languages, the princes hummed like a plucked lute with variations of a single thought: *Goed/God/Gott/Mon Dieu/Good heavens, she's bloody breathtaking!* Unfortunately for them, she knew it well, and considered it more trouble than it was worth.

Cerise seated herself in the Great Hall's one comfortable chair, which was on a dais elevated just high enough to let her see all her suitors clearly. The chamberlain took post, standing, at her side, parchment and stylus at the ready.

After a perfectly calculated pause, to let the moment sink in, Cerise spoke. Her voice was low and warm, clear, and—she had been well-coached—not too amused as she sang out, "Good morning, gentlemen. I do hope everyone's taken a number?"

Everyone had, but even so there was a good deal of muttering and trampling on feet as they sorted things out. Cerise waited patiently until order had been more or less restored, and the princes lined up for review. First was the young man with the cheekbones, second son of King Denisov of Landoak.

His name was Lucan. He was tall, handsome, sincere, broad-shouldered, slim-waisted, well turned out, and possessed of precisely the brains of a rutabaga; sadly, his cheekbones were the sharpest thing about him. Not two questions into his interview—the easy starter questions that Cerise always used to begin these sessions, like "Have you a horse? And "Oh, what's its name?"—he had gone all sideways and tongue-tied on her. Which was no more than she had expected, but she heard him out courteously just the same, before smiling sadly and banishing him to the rear of the assembly with a polished wave of her hand. In desperation he finally found his voice, crying out, "Princess, I have slain the manticore of the Gharial Mountains, all to do honor to your name. It is being stuffed and mounted at present, but if you wait, I will have it shipped directly—"

The Great Hall filled with derisive catcalls. "Oooh, you liar!" "You never did!" "Stuffed manticores, twelvepence the bunch!" "What did you do—bore it to death?" Prince Lucan exited in shame and confusion, and was never seen in Bellemontagne again.

The chamberlain, vaguely nodding as the Prince's only farewell, put stylus to parchment and crossed off his name.

And so it went, one by one by one. Cerise endured the monthly audience as graciously as always, never giving way to the impulse to let this or that wooer know what she actually thought of single-handed triumphs over a dozen mysteriously trained assassins—or a pack of wolves—or a hundred armed mercenary troops; and the same for their reports of laden treasure vaults and vast landholdings, or juggling tricks, or attempts to demonstrate prowess on the dance floor (which, being based on turns unfamiliar to the court's musicians, were typically disasters from the first or second step). No. She managed the levee with practiced proficiency, smiling until her enchanting mouth hurt, silently reciting her favorite poems to herself by way of distraction . . . right up to the moment when her mother and father entered the room.

The chamberlain stiffened.

"*Attendez!* Their Royal Majesties Antoine and Hélène, King and Queen of Bellemontagne!"

King Antoine was a striking, commanding figure, with a full head of storm-gray hair and features that might have been carved from a weathered cliffside. His wife the Queen, on the other hand, was thin and pallid, and of a meek appearance that suggested she had never enjoyed a full meal in her life, nor a good night's sleep, nor a single day free from every sort of abuse. Not even the résumés of Cerise's suitors could have been further from the truth: Queen Hélène ate like an alligator, slept like a drunken coachman, and personally handled any abusing likely to be perpetrated within the walls of the castle, and the outbuildings as well. She did have nice eyes, though.

"Well, well," Cerise's father boomed jovially. "How goes the fox hunt, daughter? Start one up yet?"

"That young man on the left," the Queen said. "The one in stripes and slashes. I know him. He's the nephew of the Countess of Dortenverrucht. Call on him next, Cerise. By report, he knows any number of interesting songs."

"Mother, please, they've all got numbers." Cerise looked to the chamberlain for help, but he glanced away, knowing far better than to get involved. "Father"—in a lower tone—"I'm handling things perfectly well. I always do." Her unspoken *Can't you get her out of here?* was answered by a slight twitch of the King's thick gray eyebrows. *You know your mother—what do you expect me to do?* The Princess sighed and nodded just as slightly.

At that, she would most likely have gotten through the remainder of the morning without a hitch—there were only a few candidates left to consider—but for the Queen's further interruption while she was interviewing a shy, awkward, but likable young prince from a kingdom whose name even he had difficulty pronouncing. The Prince was telling her earnestly about his favorite book, and Cerise was listening with genuine interest, when her mother's sharp voice shattered the moment: "Cerise. Darling. Exactly what is the point of bothering with all this childish drivel? Finish with him, and get on to the Countess's nephew, for goodness' sake."

Cerise rose from the chair, her shoulders thrust back like wings. Her beautiful face was flushed with angry embarrassment, but her voice had turned cold and taut and expressionless. She looked down at the remaining suitors and said, "I'm sorry, but this audience is at an end." Then she stalked off the dais and out of the Great Hall without once glancing at her parents. A door slammed a moment later, and the dusty portrait of her oldest ancestor fell off the wall.

Cerise never looked back. She rushed from the castle and straight across the Royal Lawns (rather bare, thanks to a long struggle with dropfiddle), past the Royal Croquet Grounds (King Antoine had a passion for competitive sports, of a sort), past the Royal Gazebo, the Royal Grotto, and the Royal Folly; and so on into the Royal Woods, which stopped being Royal at a certain tangly place that the Princess knew well. It was miles from the castle, and well-shielded from view. There she sank down, amid the rustle of her several elaborate skirts, by a quiet, clear-running stream, and leaned back against a sycamore tree whose worn and battered trunk had never in its life refused to receive her. Cerise patted it gently, saying only, "Hello."

She sat quite still for some while; then looked quickly around her and began to dig with her hands in the soft earth behind a nearby boulder, humming very softly to herself. A few minutes' work uncovered an oilskin-wrapped bundle, inside of which were a flat block of hard wax, a pointed stylus, and a manuscript written on a roll of dingy vellum. Cerise held the manuscript up to the light, clearly trying to locate a certain passage; having succeeded, she began to recite the words to herself, moving her lips silently. When she came to a word or a phrase she could not comprehend—and there were many of those—she copied it down on the wax block. Often she would copy it over and over, each time staring as hard at the letters as though she had never seen them before. She bit her lips, now and again mumbling a very un-princess-like word. Once she even threw the stylus away into the long grass by the river, but she was on her feet immediately, scrabbling frantically to find it again. And no matter how angry or frustrated she became, she never stopped working. The Princess Cerise was going to teach herself to read if it was the last thing she ever did.

That silly boy with his wonderful book, she thought sadly. *He has no idea how lucky he is*.

THREE

Crown Prince Reginald, sole heir to the Kingdom of Corvinia, rode into the Royal Woods of Bellemontagne singing a joyous, manly chorus with a lot of *tirra-lirras* and *fa-la-las* in it. Prince Reginald disliked the song, and manly choruses in general; but he knew that if he were not to sing, his valet, riding close behind him, would start singing himself, or find some other way to remind Reginald that knights-errant—worse, princes-errant—*always* sang joyous choruses while in quest of adventure. Speaking personally, Reginald desired adventure about as much as he desired a third nostril, and he knew that the valet, who was called Mortmain, was aware of this. Unfortunately, he also knew that Mortmain was under strict and specific orders from Reginald's father, King Krije, to observe every aspect of Reginald's behavior on their travels, and report it all faithfully when they returned. So he sang—for the record, as it were. The Prince and Mortmain were as friendly as their relative positions allowed, but one of them could be whipped for his failure, and the other couldn't; though King Krije had more than once been heard to growl that he wished it were the other way around.

"What in God's name is the matter with him?" the King would bellow at anyone who met his son. "Looks like a man—rides like a man—struts around like a man—but there's nothing *in* there! Just a warm smile with a body wrapped round it. And I'm supposed to leave my kingdom to that? My kingdom, which I waded through blood to win, left to an idiot who faints if he cuts himself shaving? I swear I don't understand how anyone so tall can't fill my shoes."

The King suspected a curse was involved, and had some reason to think so. But he had never shared the details with Mortmain, and the valet—one of the very few people who sympathized at all with the terrible old man—was forbidden by position from asking.

Prince Reginald, for his part, was simply glad to be away from his father's loud disappointment. That was the one good thing about unspecified questing: getting out of the house. At least away from home he could indulge himself a little, even under Mortmain's eye; and these outlying kingdoms were always so absolutely thrilled to host the Crown Prince of so large and powerful a country, they practically turned cartwheels for him at a blink. It was most gratifying. And it made Mortmain frown, which was more gratifying still.

When he first started out, the Prince had considered places to go, thought, *Alphabetical or by proximity?*, and settled on a whim-driven mix of the two, modified as needed to avoid encountering any serious challenge or knightly obligation. As a result he was undoubtedly the sole royal personage not bound for Castle Bellemontagne in quest of the hand of the Princess Cerise. In fact, he had no notion of her existence, and might well have given the entire kingdom a wide berth if he had. Reginald liked women, certainly, but not to the point of disrupting a perfectly tranquil life—or what could be a perfectly tranquil life if his father and Mortmain would only leave him alone with it.

Still, even with all the bloody singing, the day was a pretty one, and the sun was warm. He wondered what the ale and usquebaugh were like at Castle Bellemontagne.

When the path through the Royal Woods briefly widened, Mortmain urged his horse up beside his master's to murmur deferentially, "Lord, our mounts need watering. If I might suggest—"

"Heavens, yes, Mortmain, suggest away, by all means."

"I can hear a stream, Highness—not all that distant, to judge by the sound. We would only have to turn off the path a little way—"

Reginald cocked his handsome head. "Right . . . right, I can hear it myself. Well, then, absolutely, let's divert to it." His usual enchanting smile appeared a bit twisted. "Divert—there's a good military word. My father would like it."

Once off the path, the undergrowth slowed them considerably, punishing their faces and entangling the horses' legs. But they pushed on until they reached the stream and dismounted to let the horses drink. Mortmain stayed with them, while Reginald, noticing wildflowers growing in profusion all along the bank, gradually wandered off upstream, plucking them with the cheerfulness of a child. "Just gathering a bunch for this local Queen," he explained over his shoulder to the valet. "Good to be ready. Women like flowers."

So it was that Cerise, grimly immersed in her struggle with the difference between "aweful" and "awful" and "offal," never heard Reginald's approach until he missed his footing and wet his boots in the stream up to the calf. The sudden splash, and the prince's yelp of annoyance, sent her springing to her feet with her back pressed against the old sycamore. She relaxed somewhat on realizing that he was plainly a gentleman, more on noticing the bunch of wildflowers in his hand; and altogether too much once she got a good look at him. In fact, she reacted to Reginald as most men reacted to their first sight of her. Her knees turned predictably shaky; she flushed and paled by turns, and her heart began pounding hard enough to echo along all her bones. Certain that this beautiful stranger must be royalty, wet boots or no, she faltered her way through a curtsy, whispering, "Majesty . . ."

To her surprise, the young man looked mildly chagrined at the word. "No, that's my father. I'm just the Crown Prince. Reginald of Corvinia, pleased to make your acquaintance. And you are?"

"Oh, I'm . . . I'm . . ." Cerise was unmoored; the familiar word *Corvinia* chimed in her heart like a bell, and for the first time in her life, she felt inferior. The ironic novelty of this moment was lost on her; the confusion, meanwhile, was all too real. She was startled to realize that she simply could not speak her name, not to this stranger whose casual riding clothes were more sumptuous than the very best in her wardrobe, not when just looking at him left her shy and humble as a servant girl. She stammered again. "I . . . I live here. Near here, I mean. Not really here, you see, but—"

"Ah. Yes." The beautiful young man scratched his head.

"Look, maybe you can tell me—would there be any kind of shortcut to the castle? Because we—my man and I, that is—we've been in the saddle all day, and I don't mind telling you, it's a bit wearing on a fellow. You do understand, girl?"

"Oh yes, sir, I do indeed, sir," Cerise assured him, relieved to speak of anything but herself. She gave him very precise directions, which he repeated carefully several times. "Got no head for these things, maps and plans and such," he told her. "In one ear, out the other, you know?" To Cerise, used to princely braggadocio, such modesty—she assumed it to be modesty—was overwhelming.

He watched in mild curiosity as she gathered up the waxen block, the stylus, and the manuscript from which she had been copying, and wrapped them up again. "Doing a bit of scribbling in the peaceful al fresco, hey? Charming, absolutely." He beamed upon her, and had it not been for the support of the sycamore, she would have fallen down.

"The flowers," she managed to say, trying to change the subject. "Your flowers . . . they're pretty. Very, very pretty. Very."

"What?" Reginald looked down at the blooms in his hand as though he had completely forgotten about them, which to some extent he had. "Oh, these. Here, m'dear, you take them." He thrust them at her. "Meant them for the Queen, but they'll likely be all wilted, time we get there, so you might as well have them." Another smile. Cerise felt such of her bones as had not already melted start to follow the rest. "You be good now, girl, hey?"

"Good. Yes. Yes, thank you. Good. Thank you." Cerise clutched both her bundle and Reginald's flowers to her breast, ducked her head in another clumsy curtsy, and hurried off into the woods. She dropped a daisy and stopped to pick it up; then bobbed again and bustled on.

The Prince looked after her with what for him counted like thoughtfulness. "What an odd girl," he said aloud. Mortmain called to him from downstream, and he turned to answer, "Right there, old chap!" But he did look over his shoulder once as he started back toward the horses and his valet.

The moment she judged herself out of the beautiful stranger's line of sight, Cerise put down the bundle and the flowers, lifted her skirts in both hands, and ran. She did not stop running until she had reached the castle, flown up the stairs, and burst into the Royal Privy Chamber.

She intended to shout, *Send them all home! I've found him, I've met him, his name's Reginald, he's on his way here!* Being totally winded, however, she tripped over the *s* in *send*, and all that followed was a hissing, strangled gurgle.

King Antoine, dozing peacefully on his second-best (but favorite) throne, wearing his third-best (but favorite) dressing gown, with both feet in a bucket of hot water, blinked awake and rumbled, "What?" Queen Hélène looked up from her tapestry loom to remark severely, "Dear, go straight back out and knock this time—and don't come in until you're rid of whatever you're chewing. I've told you before."

The Princess dutifully left the privy chamber and leaned, panting, against the doorframe. Inside the room she could hear her father repeating, "What? What happened?" She smoothed her dress and her hair, forcing herself to think only of cauliflower, broccoli, and her old etiquette mistress, all of which she loathed. When she was finally composed and breathing evenly, she knocked softly on the chamber door, entering at her mother's bidding.

Her parents waited quietly for her to begin, her father amused—he'd put the hot water away—her mother considerably less so.

Entirely unbidden, Cerise's mind abandoned vegetables. As if it were happening this very instant, she could see Reginald entering with her—arm in strong arm!—to be introduced to her parents as her betrothed. With that vision her banging, somersaulting heart immediately shoved her lungs off to one side, and she could barely summon breath enough to blurt out, "His name is Prince Reginald of Corvinia—*Crown* Prince Reginald—and he's the most magnificent man I've ever seen! He's coming here *today*, and I'll marry him tomorrow if he'll—"

She broke off with a shriek of horror, pointing toward the wall behind her father's throne. A tiny dragonlet lurked there, no bigger than the shoe the Princess stooped to hurl at it. The beast dodged into a barely noticeable crack in the plaster, stuck its green-and-black head out to hiss at her, and vanished.

"Oh, gods," Cerise moaned. "It's all got to be cleaned up—*all* of it, *everything*, and right *now*!"

The King and Queen stared at each other, for once similarly and simultaneously bewildered. The King ventured, "Child, Cerise, I can have the plasterer in tomorrow, if it's that important—"

"It has to be today! And it's *not* just the plaster, it's everything in this castle!"

She kicked off her other shoe and gripped her father's arms, pulling him off his throne and out of the room, all the way to the head of the extravagantly named Grand Stair. She didn't let go until she saw that both of her parents would follow on their own. "Look!" she said, pointing: the marble stair had clearly not been polished in some time and was showing a distinctly sticky accretion on the balustrade. Cerise swept down the stairs and on through the castle, waving vaguely at each offense to her senses, from the guano-splattered Great Hall to the many sins of the Royal Library, with its worn carpets and ancient shelves bowed hopelessly under the weight of dusty tomes, not to mention a few morose ravens. "Hopeless!" she kept keening. "Just hopeless, the lot! It's all got to be cleaned up, redone, renovated—all of it!"

"This afternoon?" the King asked reasonably. "The next fifteen minutes?"

"*I* am having a dress fitted," the Queen announced firmly. "And my palm read." Cerise—who, it must be said at this point, had never before displayed such behavior, even as a little girl—thumped herself down on the slightly warped library floor and started to wail in earnest. Her parents, after failing to persuade her to rise, sat beside her: pale terror and stone warrior for once united in purpose. The King said gently, "Cerise, sweetheart . . . Cerise, you know that's not possible. No matter *who's* coming to visit."

"It would take months," the Queen added. "For everything you're asking—years. And probably cost enough to—why, to buy another castle."

"Then let's do that!" Cerise wept. "Let's buy another castle right now, and just move in, all of us, bag and baggage." A sudden flash of hope checked her tears for a moment. "We could tell him we're in transition or . . . or something."

"But we like this one." King Antoine put his arm, a bit hesitantly, around his daughter's shoulders. "Of course it's a bit . . . perhaps a bit unsystematic, a bit disorderly even, no denying that—"

"But it's ours, darling." Queen Hélène's voice was surprisingly sympathetic. "We know it's a muddle and a clutter, but it's *our* clutter, do you see? We've lived here since long before you were born, and we'll still be here when you've married your prince and gone away to live with him in *his* castle. Now we'll tidy up here the best way we can—"

A raven cronked overhead, and all three of them ducked instinctively. The Princess Cerise attempted to wipe her eyes on a fold of her dress. "The walls," she said, her tone shaky but uncompromising. "The walls and the paintings in the Great Hall—they *have* to be cleaned."

"I'll have someone in first thing tomorrow," the King promised. "After all, it's not as though he'll just be popping by to say cheer-ho. I'm sure he'll stay on for a few days. And I know this isn't Corvinia, nothing like . . ." He stopped suddenly, focusing on the name for the first time. "Ah—you *did* say Corvinia, love? Yes? Well. We'll put on a good show, I promise you—"

At that moment two dragonlets—black and scarlet, the one chasing the other—jumped right over the royal family and scuttled to ground beneath the nearest bookcase. Both were larger than the one in the Privy Chamber, and the black almost failed to squeeze into sanctuary before Cerise could swat at it. She whirled back toward her parents, weeping hopelessly again. "Those! Those nasty little things, running around everywhere—they're *everywhere* in this place! You *have* to get rid of them, Father! If nothing else, *those*!"

"I'll have the chamberlain fetch the exterminator—" the King began.

"Now!" the Princess demanded. "Not tomorrow! Now!"

It was then they all heard the singing outside. Still not to the main gate yet, but getting closer—a rich, forceful baritone carried on the breeze. The words were yet indistinct, but the song had a manly-sounding chorus, with plenty of *tirra-lirras* in it.

"Oh no!" cried Cerise, running out of the room faster than the two dragons had whisked under the bookcase.

"Go find the exterminator yourself," Queen Hélène ordered her husband. "I'll entertain our guest. What's his name again?"

"Reginald," King Antoine said quietly. "Old Krije's boy."

The Queen, who had already started for the castle door, stood very still for just a moment before she went on.

FOUR

The fading daylight matched Robert's mood. He tried not to walk as though his feet were stones, and his heart an anchor, but they were, and both his friends knew it, though they said nothing. This was always Robert's way after a day spent trapping dragons: something they accepted with love and concern, if no actual understanding. To Ostvald Grandin, Robert's occasional assistant, the only sensible response was to pass by these aftereffects as he passed by most things that would otherwise trouble him: a useful habit in a young man whose sole gifts from Nature were a certain slow serenity of thought and the muscles of a dray horse. "I may be lumpy as a sack of doorknobs," he often said, "but at least I'm useful. That'll do me." Now he put his strength to work pushing the heavy cart that held their day's catch, focusing his attention not on his friend, but on the muted hissing and spitting he could hear inside the skin-covered metal cages, and on keeping the cart's wheels out of ruts.

Elfrieda Falke, by contrast, worried horribly about Robert at these moments but had long ago learned to veil her concerns behind a smile. She bounced along brightly, a little bit of a girl with raven-black eyes and hair, so light-footed by nature that she seemed always to be dancing, even when she was walking soberly into church. If the captive dragonlets bothered her—and they did—she was determined to give no sign.

The three had shared a round at Jarold's tavern, after Robert and Ostvald had finished clearing Medwyn and Norvyn's shop and barn, this time with a full and doubly profitable sweep for eggs: for once the two merchants' wounds (and wounded dignity) had overmatched their penury. Now Robert was turning off for home at the crossroads, which also served as the burial ground for local suicides, while Ostvald and Elfrieda went on together toward their own families' dwellings.

Elfrieda gave Robert a quick, shy hug and a kiss on the cheek, which he barely seemed to notice. "You'll come tomorrow, then?" she asked him.

"Of course. After I'm done at the market. And after I've bathed for an hour. A shandy fair's not much fun for anyone if you can't smell the gaff for the muckfumes. Ostvald, can you help with the cart in the morning?"

"Wish I could, but I'm hodding for Yager till three past and more. They're finally set to raise the south wall of the granary, so they've laid on extra masons. I'll be climbing up and down the scaffold all day."

"Trade you."

"No chance." The cart rocked hard for a moment, as something banged inside the covered metal cages with an angry shriek, and a trickle of smoke leaked out through gaps in the dragoncord stitching. "That's the white, I bet. God's eyes, Robert, when you went after that one . . ." Ostvald shook his great shoulders. "It breathing fire straight at you and all, and those poison teeth . . . well, *I* couldn't have done it. Not ever."

"Don't make it bigger than it was," Robert said. "Not outside the tavern, anyway. *Vegrandis* aren't poisonous until they're three years old. This lot was fresh-hatched. Ill-tempered as they come, no doubt of that, but any biting they do would be work for the barber, not a priest. You could have handled it if it had gotten past me."

"I push the cart, and carry the tools, and glad of the coinage. That'll do me."

Elfrieda said teasingly, "Ostvald doesn't like things that bite. That's why you'll never see him alone with Alphonsine Yager, no matter how much she tries to lure him into the bushes. He *knows* she's got teeth."

Ostvald looked at Elfrieda unhappily but made no answer. Robert felt himself smiling a little, and was grateful for it. "Till tomorrow, then," he said, taking over for Ostvald behind the cart. With a grunt he swung it around to face the straight path homeward, then set his shoulder in place for a starting shove. He wasn't as strong as his stout friend, but he'd pushed this cart for six years as his father's apprentice, and another three years on his own; its creaking weight and his shoulder were comfortable old acquaintances.

Elfrieda walked on with Ostvald, chattering happily, while he grew even more silent, because most of her talk was of Robert: of his wit, his kindness, his care for his family; of his skill and fearlessness in dealing with dragons. Ostvald's responses were largely monosyllabic, sometimes no more than a wistful grunt, as he stared at Elfrieda's curly black hair bouncing on her shoulders. He was still smarting after her mention of Alphonsine, wondering what Elfrieda knew that he did not, and wishing he was as good with words as he was with bricks, mortar, and the general movement from *here* to *there* of extremely heavy objects.

They were within sight of Ostvald's ramshackle house—Elfrieda lived some way farther on—when they saw King Antoine and four obvious princes approaching on horseback. The encounter itself was almost as surprising as the five riders' appearance: to a man they looked weary and more than slightly bedraggled. The hem of the King's robe was heavy with mud, and the princes' boots and the horses' legs striped with it, up to the hocks in both cases.

Ostvald and Elfrieda stopped where they stood and bowed respectfully. They knew perfectly well that the King himself never insisted on such courtesies, but they couldn't be sure about the princes.

The King bowed back and winced, immediately regretting the obligations of civility. The muscles in his back and neck were knotted as tangled fishing line. Hours before, he had ridden forth from the castle in a state of considerable tension, and nothing had happened since to improve things. There was, to begin with, the matter of the princes in his company, an assortment about whom he held decidedly mixed feelings, and not merely as prospective sons-in-law. Their determination to thrust themselves into any task at hand that might charm the Princess Cerise, no matter how small, did not impress him. He had always loved his private expeditions away from the castle, because they gave him time for the long, slow thoughts that were necessary for him to make up his mind about anything, and he had hoped that this ride would allow him to reflect on the hidden implications of Reginald's visit. But considered thinking was well-nigh impossible in the princes' fractious company. To King Antoine their vanity and insistent self-concern seemed the stuff of yappy, ill-bred puppies, and showed far less character than he considered suitable in a proper mate for his daughter.

Then of course there was the dratted dragon-exterminator himself, who appeared to have mastered the knack of invisibility. No one the King had encountered since setting forth had seen the man, but all had offered some earnest, if futile, suggestion, each lead sending the august assembly down a muddier path than the last.

"Your pardon, my good people," King Antoine addressed Ostvald and Elfrieda, with grace but no real hope. "Would you happen to know where we may find the dragon-exterminator Thrax? Been looking for hours, you know. I knew his father, Elpidus, but just now I can't think of the boy's name—Horatius, is it? Justinian?"

"It's Robert, sir," Elfrieda replied eagerly. "And he's not a boy anymore. He's eighteen, and nearly as tall as his father was, with blond hair down to his shoulders, except he mostly keeps it tied back. You can't mistake him. You can find him on his way home now, I suspect. We just left him a few moments ago."

The King brightened. "My dear, I can't possibly tell you how grateful I am for your assistance. Ah . . . you're sure?"

"Oh yes, milord." Elfrieda turned and pointed back the way she and Ostvald had come. "Follow this lane to the crossroads, then turn south along the knoll path and head straight on about a quarter mile. It'll be the third house you come to. It's well back from the road, so you might miss it, but if you *do* miss it, you'll know right away when you get to the fourth house. Because of the big dogs."

"*Big* dogs," Ostvald said, eyeing the princes.

The King and the four princes looked long at each other. The King said finally, "Well, you fellows can go back to the castle if you want, but I can't. Not without the dragon chap."

"We might as well continue with you," answered one of the princes.

"Yes," said the second prince in line. "Perhaps we shall get bitten by the big dogs and die horribly."

"Which would be better than lingering on hopelessly, like moths fluttering about your daughter's bright flame," added the third. "Much, much better."

The rearmost prince said simply, "I am afraid to think about talking to the Princess tomorrow. I will come."

"Well, then," King Antoine said, more convinced than ever that there had been a general decline in princes since he had been one. "There we are." He waved courteously to Ostvald and Elfrieda, and nodded as far as his poor neck could manage. "A delight to meet you both, I'm sure. And my royal thanks for your helpfulness."

Elfrieda and Ostvald stood to one side, silent together, and watched the searchers ride by. When they were out of view, Elfrieda said worriedly, "I hope they don't miss Robert's house. It's getting dark."

"Shouldn't have told them where he lives," Ostvald grumbled. "Don't tell kings nothing—that's what I say. Tell 'em nothing, you can't go wrong."

Elfrieda gave Ostvald the look he always dreaded: a blend of scornful impatience flavored with tolerance. "What are you talking about? Dragon-exterminator to the King—do you know what that would mean for him? For his family, with six mouths to feed, and two of them hungry as Hannibal's elephants?" She gripped his shoulders and shook him playfully. "And what could it be for you, did you ever think of that? The two of you—in and out of the castle, practically like royalty yourselves!"

Ostvald was slow to answer her, because he liked the feeling of her hands on his shoulders. It muddled his thoughts. "All I know, a king's looking for you, it's never a good sign."

"Oh, *you!*" Elfrieda said in exasperation. "Some other time I'm going to explain a few things to you, Master Grandin. But not tonight—I have to run, there's stitching to do, and it's my turn to milk in the morning. Come to the fair when you finish work. I'll see you then." She scampered off, turning to call back, "Unless I'm very lucky!"

She hurried on with a wave and a smile, to indicate it was meant as a joke, never guessing how much Ostvald mournfully agreed with her.

Queen Hélène was in the parlor—or, anyway, the homely private chamber that she always referred to as the parlor—when her equerry ushered in the tall, staggeringly handsome young Prince, and the smaller man who trailed behind him at a respectful distance. Similar types had been nineteen to the dozen around Castle Bellemontagne since Cerise achieved a marriageable age, but even so, the Queen would never have mistaken Reginald for any of them. He was simply . . . *more so*, in every inch of him, the original champion beside whom all others were copies of greater and lesser skill. Despite herself, she could feel a rush of sympathy for her daughter's passionate tears.

"Reginald! Dear old Krije's son! I should have known you anywhere—you're the very image of your father!" It was a lie, of course, on at least three different levels, but that was two less than she'd been prepared for. "I beg your forgiveness and welcome you as I would welcome him." She rose and crossed the bare stone floor to embrace the young man, then held him off to study his perfectly cut features. "And here you are, come courting my Cerise! She will be even more thrilled than I am, I promise you."

"Um," said Crown Prince Reginald of Corvinia. "Well. Yes. I mean—the fact is that I'm rather erranting, don't you know. That's it, just . . . wandering with my squire here"—one of Mortmain's eyebrows flickered the least trifle—"looking for adventure. Adventure, that's the word. *Adventure*. Yes."

"And what greater adventure than that of the heart?" the Queen said warmly. "Now, Cerise usually interviews her princes only once a month—I mean, the child has to have a *bit* of a life, at least, what with all her other responsibilities. I don't know *what* we'll do without her, once some gallant has at last gained her hand." She sighed deeply and fondly, then continued, saying, "So ordinarily you'd just have to keep wandering and adventuring until her next audience—but, as it happens, today's session was unavoidably interrupted, so it's being carried over to tomorrow morning, and I'm certain she will be much more than happy to include you in her schedule. I'll see to it myself."

She squeezed Prince Reginald's hand between both of hers. "Now you must tell me, how *is* that grand old bear of a father of yours?"

Reginald shot a frantic glance at Mortmain, who moved forward as smoothly as though he were on tracks, or small wheels. "Well, Your Royal Majesty, if I may venture to speak—"

Then the door to the parlor opened, and the Princess Cerise walked in.

She had changed her dress, redone her hair and her makeup, and was smiling in shy embarrassment at the Queen, saying, "Mother, I'm sorry, I'm all right now," when she saw Reginald. To her credit she did not squeal or faint, nor did she begin weeping again, and with some effort she managed to keep from breaking out in hysterical giggles. She merely said, "*Eek*," in a very small voice, and stared, and sat down—in a chair, fortunately, not that she would have noticed.

Smiling in delight, Queen Hélène said, "Darling, I know you've already met, but may I informally present Crown Prince Reginald of Corvinia?"

"Yes," the Princess said in the same small voice. "You may."

Again Reginald looked desperately at Mortmain, who could only shake his head. Never having met Princess Cerise, Reginald was currently undergoing his own version of the seismic tremors that affected any man upon seeing her for the first time, overlaid with a heavy dollop of simple but heartfelt calculation. If thoughts could be made audible, his would have sounded like the sudden thunking snap of a ballista.

The Prince blinked a good deal; then suddenly brightened, remembering the odd young girl scribbling by the stream. "Oh," he said. "*Oh*. Yes, of course, we're already acquainted—practically old schoolmates or something, absolutely." He bowed over Cerise's hand, lifted from her lap almost by force. "Charmed, charmed." When he stepped back to Mortmain he was still smiling, but out of the side of his mouth he muttered, "Never *said* she was a princess. How's a fellow to know, if they don't say?"

Cerise did not hear him. Cerise was aware of nothing, in fact, but the rejoicing of the blood in her veins and the throbbing of her skin itself, as it turned white and pink and white again. She gazed at Reginald very nearly as blankly as he stared at her, until the moment she finally realized that her mother, somewhere far away, was speaking.

"Cerise, why don't you take your friend for a tour of the castle grounds? I know it won't be what you're used to, dear Reginald, but perhaps you'll find it has its own quaint appeal." She paused and frowned. "Cerise? *Cerise?*"

"*Mais oui*, Mother," Cerise answered. She rose unsteadily from the chair, as Reginald—prodded only slightly by Mortmain—offered his arm.

Queen Hélène sighed as she watched the two of them leave the room, the beautiful Prince explaining earnestly, "Actually, I'm just wandering, you know. Needed to get away for a bit—see something of the world, have an adventure or two. That sort of thing. Serious business, adventuring." If her daughter made any reply, the Queen did not hear it: but the glow in the girl's eyes and cheeks was easily enough observed, and this time they had nothing to do with tears.

"Young people," she said wistfully to Mortmain. "Young people."

"Yes, Your Royal Majesty," replied Mortmain, making leave to follow his charge and lord. "The eternal wonder, to be sure."

◆ ◆ ◆ ◆

At Robert's house, his mother and sisters—despite the hour, the boys were not yet home from the fields—exclaimed over the white dragon he had brought inside from the cages. Jaws tightly noosed, wings and hind legs strapped, still angry from the forced journey in the cart, the *vegrandis* crouched and bristled on the kitchen table. Adelise stood on the tabletop as well, just out of claw reach, inspecting it belligerently, her neck frill fully erect, while Lux hissed an out-and-out challenge before flapping to a perch on the cook fire's mantel stone. Reynald, on the other hand, was fascinated by the newcomer. He tried to match tails with it, a game that nearly got him gouged for his trouble. Robert whisked him out of harm's way, placing him on a chair for safekeeping, next to Fernand, who had given one disinterested glance at the proceedings and then gone back to sleep.

Rosamonde asked, "What are you going to name it?"

"I don't know her name yet. *Stop* it, Adelise," Robert said as the green dragonlet snapped once at the newcomer. "I mean that!"

"Can I name it?" Patience pleaded. "I never get to name *anything*, and it's not fair."

"I've told you, I don't choose their names," Robert said patiently. "Dragons tell you what they like, if you wait." He shot a quick glance toward the mantel stone. "And no trouble from you either, Lux!" The gray, whose hind legs had been bunched in preparation to swoop, subsided with a crackling grumble.

"How do they tell you?" asked Patience. "They can't talk. All they ever do is make noises."

"It's not words. They just do. You have to wait really hard, until you feel the name. It takes practice." Robert gripped Adelise gently behind the frill and set her nose-to-nose with the larger stranger. She hissed savagely, wide-stretched jaws crowded with teeth no less sharp for their minuscule size, but did not attack. The white dragon responded by lashing her neck violently from side to side, and digging her foreclaws into the wood, the only threat displays she could currently manage. Robert caught one of her horns between two fingers and his thumb, holding her head steady now as well, then bent close to say—not loudly, but as clearly and precisely as he could—"Adelise, this is a friend. She is going to live here with all of us, from now on, and you will be her friend too—you and Lux and Reynald and Fernand. As for you, my nameless one, in this house you will be warm and welcome so long as you behave yourself, which I know you can. And don't either one of you pretend that you don't understand me, because I'm almost as smart as a dragon, and I know better."

He released them both. The *vegrandis* blinked her odd-colored eyes, one blue and one gold, and tilted her head quizzically. Adelise hissed again, but half-heartedly. Her neck frill sank slowly back to its normal flattened shape.

Odelette, who had been looking on with tolerant forbearance, now demanded, "Gaius Aurelius, if you would be so kind as to get your dragons off the table, friends or no, we could perhaps get dinner *on* it." She made a quick sweeping gesture with both hands.

"Go see if the chickens are all settled for the night," Robert told Adelise and Lux. From table and mantel stone the two dragonlets leaped to the floor, letting their dainty wings slow their fall. As they went out the door, taking care to nudge it closed behind them, Robert called out, "And remember, no snacking!"

The new dragon stared at Robert in amazement, looking quite as if she had suddenly grown an extra wing, or spit ice instead of fire, and was doubting the rules of creation. "They're very happy here," Robert said, picking his catch up as gently as an infant. "And so will you be, I hope. No fire indoors except to light the oven, no biting, keep your claws to yourself, do your business in the dirtbox in the barn: those are the basic rules. The rest we'll work out as we go. Agreed?"

The white dragon gave no evident response, but after a moment Robert nodded in satisfaction. One by one he unsnapped the creature's restraints, then carried her over to his sisters. She shook all over for a moment and stretched out both wings before finally settling down in Rosamonde's arms—though she kept on looking at Robert.

"You can bed this one down, if you like," Robert said to the twins. "Just make sure there's water where she can reach it. *Vegrandis* need a lot of water, this age."

The door opened with a shove, and Caralos and Hector stumbled in from outside. Both had plainly been running: they were flushed and rumpled, and spoke with equally disheveled breath.

"The King's coming!"

"Heading straight here!"

"Couldn't be nowhere else, they—"

"Four others—"

"Four dukes or something—"

"Just the five, like. No soldiers, no trumpeters . . ."

Odelette instantly took over the crisis. "*Quick*, everybody, grab a dragon! Take them to the cellar, the barn, anywhere—just get them out of here!"

"No!" Robert countermanded her. "I'll handle them." He had already scooped up Fernand and Reynald—both chittered in surprise, especially Fernand, woken without warning—and was turning to reach for the startled, panicky white. "Go on, get dinner on, set the table, act surprised. Stall as long as you can, and when that stops working, then call for me!" With that he ran from the kitchen with his three wriggling burdens, ducking low as he scrambled across the yard for the barn, calling softly for Lux and Adelise.

When King Antoine knocked on the door, all the family but Robert were seated for dinner, passing a steaming tureen of Odelette's three-mushroom soup around the table. Odelette rose to answer.

"Your Majesty!" she cried out on sight of him, feigning surprise. "You honor our dwelling, lord. Command us as you choose." With that she sank into the grand curtsy of a proper court lady, just as if she practiced the move daily—which indeed she often had, when no one was looking. In homespun it should have looked silly, but sincerity has a way of trumping circumstance, and where royalty was concerned, Odelette Thrax had always been a true devotee. King Antoine was instantly and thoroughly charmed.

"My dear woman, please rise. You are far too gracious to intruders. We needn't stand on ceremony, not when I come to your home without any warning. Please."

Glancing past the King as she rose slowly to her feet, stretching out the moment, Odelette saw the four princes waiting behind him in the yard. They sat firmly in their saddles, making no move to dismount, and were clearly unhappy to be there. Light from the doorway played across their mud-spattered finery and coats of arms. The rich caparisons on two of the horses were ripped and dragging on the ground, as were the pearl-decorated left-side leggings of the sourest-looking prince.

"My lord, such *guests*—we cannot possibly do honor to these noble gentlemen in your company."

"Just tell me you don't have any dogs, madam," said the prince with the damaged leggings.

The King spoke before she could reply. "Am I fortunate enough to have at last arrived at the home of the dragon-exterminator—ah—Flavius, is it? Augustus?"

"You speak of Gaius Aurelius Constantine Heliogabalus Thrax," Odelette answered him proudly. "My son." She moved to one side of the doorway and gestured the King in.

"Your son, yes—yes, of course, Elpidus's boy, that would be him. Ah—*he* . . . It's been so long." King Antoine wandered toward the dining table, sniffing the air in decided distraction. "My goodness, that soup does smell superb. You have chanterelles in there, do you not?"

"And morels, sire, fresh from the woods this morning. If you would deign . . ."

"Alas, dear lady, we must be off as we came. But perhaps you could—"

"Say no more, Majesty." Odelette whirled to her children, snapping her fingers. "Rosamonde, find the copper-bottomed pot with the handles. Patience, you fill it full for the King. Stir your lazy stumps, girls. Don't stand there gaping and dawdling! Hurry!"

The girls shot from the room, racing each other for the pantry. Behind them they heard King Antoine continue. "Mrs. Thrax, along with your excellent soup, we must also take your son—in his professional capacity only, I hasten to assure you. Is he at hand?"

"He is indeed, Your Majesty. And he will be thrilled to serve you in any capacity at all." Odelette had been expecting this from the moment she saw the crown at her door and took measure of the King's face and manner; but she kept her voice well under control. "If you will pardon me for just a moment? He is in the barn, putting away his tools. I will bring him to you." The King nodded, still eyeing the soup tureen, and Odelette left the kitchen almost as swiftly as her daughters had done. She paused only once on her way, in order to address a heartfelt prayer to Vardis, consisting mostly of the words *yes* and *thank you*. Vardis actually preferred Her gratitude danced around a suitable sacrifice, but that would have to wait until later. Odelette blew a quick kiss to the heavens and hurried to find her son.

She found him kneeling well back in the barn, deep in shadow, coaxing a reluctant Adelise into an old wooden tool chest with a cunningly hidden set of airholes. The other dragonlets already waited inside—even the white, to whom Adelise still took quiet but clear exception.

"The King has need of you," Odelette said.

Robert didn't look up from gently stroking Adelise's throat sac with one hand, while he tried to tip her front dewclaws over the chest's rim with the other. "Had to be that, didn't it? Last clearing Father and I did at the castle was four years ago. But why's he coming *now*? And why on his own? He always sent messengers before."

"What matter? He's here and he needs you."

"It doesn't make sense."

"Kings don't have to." She reached down and stroked her son's hair. "I'll finish here. You go on in."

"No promises, Mother. You weren't ever there. It's been a bad enough day already, without having to deal with that lot."

"There's only good in this, Gaius," Odelette said, sounding his name tenderly.

"As you say." Face carefully expressionless, betraying nothing at all and thus betraying everything, Robert rose and turned toward the door. He walked out of the barn like a man expecting to be hanged, head held high for the noose.

Odelette looked down at Adelise and smiled. "Go on, climb in. We both know you were just holding back to get some extra attention." The little green dragonlet looked offended for a moment, but yielded nevertheless. Seconds later all five of the creatures were curled up together like scaly balls of twine, beginning to drowse. Regarding them, Odelette thought—not for the first time—that they were very pretty, for all the trouble they caused. They weren't the ones she'd seen when she was young, and still saw in her dreams . . . but her son loved them, and she loved her son. That was reason enough to keep them safe.

When she got back to the kitchen, Robert was saying to King Antoine, courteously but firmly, "Sire, I have already worked a long, full day—as has my assistant, whom we would surely have to rouse from his bed by now—and to speak truly, it would be far wiser for us to wait until morning—"

"I couldn't agree with you more, Mr. Thrax," the King responded, equally earnest. "But I've no more choice in this matter than—ah—well, than you have. My daughter, the Princess Cerise, has, as you might say, *spoken*, and her mother agrees with her, and . . . well, there we are, you see. Castle Bellemontagne is to be dragon-free as soon as possible, in order to impress Prince Reginald of Corvinia, who is already in residence. Terribly sorry for the imposition and inconvenience, but there we are." He coughed and looked down at his feet like a small boy.

"I understand," Robert said. "Very well, Your Majesty, I accept the contract." He went to his mother and embraced her. "I'll send someone to tell you how we're getting on, and when I'll be home."

Odelette's eyes were shining with pride. "I only wish your father could have been here to share this moment. *His* son, summoned by the King himself to clear the castle of dragons—and all for the sake of a princess's happiness. Go on, then, my boy—my little Gaius Aurelius—go to your destiny." She kissed him on both cheeks and stood back: a general sending her troops into battle. King Antoine looked on, beaming.

"You have no shame," Robert said to her under his breath.

FIVE

It was, without question, an oddity, and it set local tongues to wagging for days. Those villagers fortunate enough to see the late-night procession pass by were delighted to spread a story that required neither embellishment nor exaggeration to be splendidly strange; while those who didn't see it with their own eyes soon believed that they had, and said so firmly, adding layers and twists to the tale. In the end almost no one remembered it the way it really happened, except for six of the seven who made up the formation; and four of those would have much preferred to forget.

Leading the way, at a pace as slow as an apology, was King Antoine, his attention focused primarily on not spilling anything from the cooking pot he carried. This was made trickier by the jounce and roll of his horse's back as the animal carefully found its footing in the moonlit dark, and the fact that the King couldn't resist lifting the pot's lid from time to time in order to sniff deeply of its contents. Just behind him, in a line, rode the four princes. Each of these worthies was deeply preoccupied: first, by personal embarrassment at the task the King had assigned; second, by a profound sense of the wrongness of the world in general (there are some things princes simply *shouldn't have to do*—ask any prince, he'll tell you); and finally, by the determination to get even with their prospective father-in-law at the earliest opportunity, should that relationship ever become real instead of frustratingly potential. As it was, with every step the King's imposition grew more galling.

Prince #1 had been told to carry Robert behind him on his horse, even though Robert had declared a preference for walking, and such close proximity to a social inferior chafed the prince. Even so, he felt himself luckier than Prince #2, who now carried Ostvald—Ostvald, who had cost them another hour, this night, to be wakened and dressed, then negotiated with; then bought free (in an even lengthier negotiation) from his coming day's obligations to the builder Yager, only to top it all off by falling cheerfully asleep while riding, his head and chest pressed heavily forward against his suffering companion.

Meanwhile Prince #3 quietly cursed something he normally took pride in, the bloodline of his Percheron, since the dark brown warhorse's size and strength had made it the obvious choice to tow Robert's rattletrap tool cart. From the prince's point of view there could be no greater insult, and he hoped the Percheron would forgive him.

And Prince #4, the one with the torn leggings, had been given the worst task of all: to follow at the end of the line, doing nothing. It made him stand out all the more, somehow, implying that he wasn't good enough to be used, even badly, by the King. He had started this day the eldest son of a noble family, a young man with glittering prospects and all the self-absorption of his breed. He was ending it a rich fool in need of tailoring, and the feeling unsettled him. It was only the last tiny shred of his self-respect that kept him from pelting homeward on the spot.

On reaching Castle Bellemontagne, the party was met, late though the hour, by the Queen and the castle's chamberlain. Both looked rather cross, though only the Queen really meant it. She loved her husband—more deeply than she would ever allow herself to say out loud—but he did *dawdle* so. How could a simple errand have taken so long? She eyed the iron pot in his hands with suspicion.

"Milady wife," the King said gently, looking down at her.

"Milord husband."

"I have brought the exterminator and his tools."

"And?"

"Well. Had to go through all kinds of bother on the way, so I brought us some soup. You'll like it."

"Right now I'm thinking that my mother was right about you. For your sake, that pot had better hold something fit for our Lord and every one of His angels." The Queen's frown grew deeper, but her eyes gave her away, as she knew they must. Antoine had always understood what part of her face to pay attention to as she spoke. It was half the reason she'd chosen him, all those summers ago.

"And our new guests?" he asked.

"Abed like sensible people, unless Cerise has dragged Reginald off for another private conversation. However . . ." Now Hélène's eyes grew as tense as the rest of her features, and Antoine realized that she truly was worried. But about what?

The Queen stepped close and lowered her voice, speaking just to him. "Make of this what you will, and I hope not too much, but his man insisted on the two of them sleeping in the stables. Said it was Krije's decree. Tried to lay it all to the discipline of the noble quest, and smiled brightly enough as he spoke, but I wonder . . ."

Antoine leaned close as he could, handing his wife the pot as cover for his action. "We will discuss that inside," he whispered. Then he turned to the chamberlain, and in a normal voice said, "Please see the exterminator and his fellow to their task. The Queen and I must retire." Finally he sat up straight, twisting stiffly in his saddle until he could see all the princes. "As for you, gentlemen, I am well gratified by your support this day. Good night and good morrow . . . and if any of you should feel like joining the Crown Prince of Corvinia in his choice of accommodations, by all means, please do! There's nothing like the smell of hay and horse dung to make a man; my own father swore on it."

He dismounted then, and the princes dismounted smartly in turn, cold, blank smiles on their faces. Put their horses to rest in the stables? Assuredly; but that was the end of the matter. Better a warm scullery cabinet or broom closet than a drafty barn, no matter whose daughter you were seeking to wed.

Robert slid clumsily backward to the ground and rushed to catch Ostvald. Without benefit of royalty to lean on, his friend, still asleep, was slipping farther sidewise by the second.

"It's going to take bloody *forever* to clean out a place this size."

Robert grunted without answering, and joined Ostvald in

pushing the cart deeper into the expanse of the Great Hall. When they got to the center, where shadows pooled and danced just beyond the reach of the room's scattering of torches, they stopped and stood back from their burden, looking up. To Ostvald the view was overwhelming. He felt lost and insignificant under the looming, bird-spattered pillars. High above, the aviary ceiling erupted in warning cries and cackles at the approach of strangers; while with each step he and Robert took, the gaps in the ancient carpets under their feet seemed to spread like puddles. On these rugs, the normal clatter of the cart's wheels was hushed, and Ostvald was surprised to discover that the lack of this familiar irritation disturbed him most of all.

"I started coming along to help when I was nine," Robert said softly. A faint echo shaded his words. "Elpidus would cover the place from top to bottom in a single day, four times a year—once every season, give or take."

Ostvald sneezed. "Wasn't enough."

Robert stood still, listening. "They're in the walls," he said. "The walls and the air shafts. Been no one in since Elpidus died, or I'd have heard, and that gave the cauds a chance to burrow. There'll be fifteen or sixteen species here now. *Vegrandis*, *skashins*, *misher-tails* for sure. *Snap-so*'s and *thivettes*. Hundreds of dragons just in this hall, gods rot it—maybe a thousand or more in the whole castle. All dust and bellows work, and we'll be at it the week." He drew a single deep breath in through his nose and held it for a moment. "Smell that? They've even got *tichornes*."

"The blue ones with the green teeth?"

"No, those are *vechts*. Think *skashins* but bigger, six claws instead of four, three times the teeth, and fire that water won't extinguish. You have to cut the flame off from air with something thick and powdery, like flour. We'll need to get some from the kitchens."

Ostvald shook his head. "Next time you come to my door after sunset, I'm going to make my brother tell you I'm dead of plague."

"Next time I'll send the King in to catch it from you."

The two young men spent hours examining and marking the Great Hall. Much of the time they were on their knees. Every gap, every hole, every crack and crevice in the floor and walls had to be uncovered or identified, examined for claw marks, both faint and obvious, and tested for scaleflakes or other residue of a dragon's passing. Every gap, hole, crack, and crevice had to be probed with the stiffly bendable metal pokers of Robert's trade, which allowed him to measure and trace the tunnel's inner angles; then they had to be tracked even further by a trick of tapped soundings—a wide, flat hammer covered with cured doeskin to thud the wall, and two cupped ears pressed against it, alternating high and low, to puzzle out the meaning of the sound. It was noisy work, and the dragonlets in the walls had given up on sleeping. A few even skittered forth to see what was going on. These brief sightings made Robert raise his estimates. Some of the curious were species he had never seen outside the importer's cages at Dragon Market, presumably carried here, unwittingly, by visiting trade caravans and dignitaries from neighboring kingdoms.

Eventually Robert felt that he had a reasonable grasp of the main passages and most likely escape routes. It was never possible to reach a complete understanding, of course, and in a job as big as this there would inevitably be some repetition and backtracking, as dragons retreated into burrows yet to be discovered, or made their way back to old haunts despite fear of the poison that had driven them out. But the first step was now obvious. Moving quickly—it was always good to leave the tedium of marking behind—Robert and Ostvald blocked off certain exit points with gravel and glue from the buckets in the cart, then pegged smooth, carefully chosen river stones into place to strengthen the seals. Other crevices they left open but barred with intricately wrought constructs of folding metal that clamped down across the irregular edges of the hole. The idea was always to herd, if possible: the fewer dead dragons left in a wall at the end of a job, the sooner a space became livable again. That made the right combination of barred and blocked holes essential—part of the art of the work—as these choices determined what air currents the panicked dragonlets would taste and follow in their hurry to get away.

"We don't have cages enough for this, you know." Ostvald looked directly at Robert. "It's trap and kill, not trap and catch."

"We've got enough to start. I'll tell the chamberlain to bring in more. Not like they can't afford the hire."

"You know what I'm saying, Robert. This many dragons. This big a job. This much mucking *poison*. We're not going to be pushing the cart off to Dragon Market at the end of this, making a few deals to sweeten the pot and buy another round at Jarold's. We're going to have to bury the whole bloody lot off in the woods someplace, or shove the carcasses into the caves back of the cliffside. You've never done one like this, Robert. I bet your da never did, either."

"Maybe not, but he would have loved it. I never will."

Robert shook his head. "Enough of that. There's a princess waiting, or so I'm told, and we've enough troubles without her turning cranky. Let's lock down the traps and get on with it."

It took fifteen minutes to unfold the six metal cages to their largest extent, then strap them down solidly into position, their entry portals braced snug and tight against the dragons' most likely exit points. When that was done, it was finally time for Robert and Ostvald to change clothes. Ostvald, relegated to support in the task to come, had it relatively easy: a suit made from supple leathers backed with dragonskin strips, a fireproof dragonskin smock, a thick hood to pull over his face if needed, and gloves just heavy enough to be a compromise between protection and flexibility. His role was to back Robert up, quickly bringing him the proper tools from the cart as they were called for. Anything that made him slower than he already was would be bad, and unless things went horribly wrong—for which there were other measures—Ostvald would never need any greater protection.

Robert's working costume was more formidable. He was dressed head to toe in three thick layers of dragonskin, cut to cover everything, including even his face, except for a grill of thin slits over his mouth and both eyes. Under the suit he wore soft cloth padding, to help soften the impact that could get through the dragonskin layers in a fight, even if teeth and claws and fire couldn't; and extra layers of cotton-and-dragonskin strips wrapped around knees and ankles and elbows, neck and groin—the weak places any larger dragon would instinctively strike in close quarters. As for his metal-studded gloves, a hard blow with just one could make a wild boar reconsider charging, but so far he'd never had to use them that way.

It was Elpidus's suit, and it didn't quite fit, but Robert hated it too much to have it changed. In some strange way it seemed to him that if it ever felt comfortable, he would *become* Elpidus, and lose all hope of any other life than this.

"Ready?" Ostvald asked.

"Ready. Put the big bludgeon and the snatcher by that cage. *That* one, there." He pointed at the one to the south. "I've got a feeling. Then bring me the bellows and a bottle of *drachengift*. And be careful. We're both tired, I know, but I'd much rather not go to sleep permanently, thank you."

When Ostvald returned to Robert, he was carrying a patched old bellows with brass handles that had been in the Thrax family for five generations, a thick green bottle with a wax seal on one end, and a heavy cloth bag lined with parchment and oiled leather. Under Robert's watchful supervision, Ostvald gently cut away the wax on the bottle. Then he poured the bottle's contents, an evil-smelling powder, into a special pinholed chamber built into the front of the bellows. When the bottle was empty, he put it inside the cloth bag, cinched the bag tight shut, and closed and locked the port on the bellows. Done at last, he stepped away, a tingle of relief licking at his shoulders. Loading the bellows was the one part of the job he truly hated. *Drachengift* became deadly poisonous on exposure to air, but its efficacy fell off sharply after only ten or fifteen minutes, and was entirely gone in a few hours. There was no way for Robert to make the pour while suited, no way to use the *drachengift* safely when not, and too much time wasted in pouring first and dressing second: so it had to be Ostvald.

Now Robert stepped forward, his face somber but set beneath his mask. He fitted the tip of the bellows into the small hole he'd deliberately left in the first sealed gap and pumped the bellows several times. Then he moved to another hole to repeat the process, and so on across the wall, listening carefully as he went. Choosing the right holes to poison was also part of the exterminator's art, and Elpidus had taught him well.

By the time Robert had covered one section of one wall, he and Ostvald could hear a range of sounds coming from behind the stone cladding: chittering squeaks and grunts, scrabbling claws, the rushing tumble of small armored bodies scrambling to escape the *drachengift* even as their own growing agitation spread it farther. The noise built in one place, then another. As it did, Robert moved stiffly with it, choosing his bellows points with care, like a surgeon seeking to tease a great gallstone loose from his patient's body.

The first dragonlet came stumbling free of the deadly wall, straight into the cage that Robert had indicated to Ostvald. It was a bright purple *camai*, a youngling with all three vestigial wings still intact. A moment later its caudlings came scrabbling after it, and the trickle became a tide. Soon every cage in the room was filling up with frightened dragons, white and blue, black and golden, green and red, packed so tightly they could barely cry out, even if so many hadn't been suffering from the first paralytic symptoms of their poisoning. A few could still manage to breathe fire, but their exhalations were short and weak—more spark than flame, and no real threat to anyone.

The work went slowly and arduously, and it seemed to Ostvald—who was not introspective—that his friend was somehow poisoning himself, as well as the creatures they had been hired to destroy. At one point Ostvald saw Robert lift his dragonskin mask and wipe the sweat from his eyes: in the sputtering light of the tallow-coated torches along the walls, Robert's face looked increasingly gray and bleak, gaunted as though with illness. Ostvald suggested more than once that he stop to rest, so they could go outside and breathe in the cold, clear night air, but each time Robert bluntly dismissed the notion. "I want it done. So many of them . . . *too* many of them. I want it *done*."

Neither the bludgeon nor the snatcher—Robert's own invention for snaring dragons without hurting them—ever came into use. The dragons they had driven out were sick and dying, too weak now to break free or wriggle loose. But still Robert found himself reaching out as he passed the cages, placing gloved hands on the glittering bodies crushed up against the bars. Several of the dragons died as he watched. He stroked each one softly, whispering, "I'm sorry . . . I'm sorry . . ."

There were never tears in his eyes. But after a while, mask or no, Ostvald could not bear to look into them.

SIX

Occupied as they were with clearing out the cages in preparation for a second round with the bellows, neither Robert nor Ostvald noticed the stranger watching them until he was well into the Great Hall. Only when he cleared his throat did they turn and see him: fortyish, middle-sized, neatly dressed, darker than light, with nothing at all memorable about him except his own eyes, yellow-brown and attentive to everything. He bobbed his head in a manner that managed to sidestep servility, saying, "Your pardon, gentlemen—I intrude upon you. My name is Mortmain."

"We aren't 'gentlemen.'" Robert's voice was tight and toneless. "For now we're servants, just like you, only you smell better. And we're working."

"I am perhaps a bit more than a servant." Mortmain's own voice had a peculiarly distinctive quality about it, being at once husky and rather high, with an actor's perfect diction—all the result of years of trying to make himself heard over, under, or through King Krije's roaring. He asked, "These are dragons? I had been given to understand that dragons were somewhat . . . larger? We do not have them anymore where I come from."

"Oh, there are larger ones." Robert was inspecting a pinpoint leak in the old bellows and wishing the man would go away. "Some very much larger."

Mortmain reached curiously to pick up one of the dead dragons, but Robert banged the bellows down almost on the reaching hand, sending a small puff of dust into the air. Not knowing that the danger from this batch of *drachengift* was well past, Mortmain quickly covered his mouth and nose.

"Don't touch them," Robert said.

Mortmain took a step backward before the quiet voice.

"They're dragons," the young exterminator continued. "Vermin. *Ungeziefer*." He and Ostvald had changed back into regular clothes to deal with the corpses; there was no mask now to mute his tone or hide his anger. "Everybody hates them, as they should. And most everyone looks down on me and my profession, also as they should, because I do the dirty work they won't touch—killing, poisoning, trapping the poor bloody things to sell at Dragon Market. You've never been to Dragon Market, Mortmain. They skin them there—some dealers do it while they're still alive, because the skin and meat stay fresher that way, and don't get so hard. What I'm doing here is a bit kinder, I think, but I could be wrong. Hard to say, you know?"

Ostvald put a wary hand on Robert's shoulder, to no avail: Robert couldn't have stopped now even if he'd wanted to, which he didn't. "Yes, there are larger ones, friend Mortmain, and there is one largest of all. Perhaps he will come to visit Dragon Market one day. I would like to see that."

Mortmain was still backing away, but so smoothly and gracefully that it was hardly noticeable. "Of course," he responded. "Absolutely, I quite understand your point of view—enlightened, really, admirable. Your pardon once again, but I came in search of my lord the Crown Prince Reginald of Corvinia. I am his—ah—counselor, as well as his valet, and as the day begins there are matters we must speak of. If by some chance you should encounter him during your labors . . ." And with that he was gone, still backward.

"Toady," Ostvald commented absently. "Worse than kings, you ask me."

But Robert wasn't listening. Dulled by work, lack of sleep, and his troubled emotions, he hadn't really been paying attention to what the stranger had said. Now the most startling part registered. He stared after the vanished Mortmain, whispering, "A valet . . . *a prince's valet* . . ."

Ostvald could barely hear him. Then Robert said, plainly, "He's a real valet. From Corvinia."

"Yes," Ostvald said. "Got that. Don't much care." He shook his head wearily, thinking about how big the castle was and dreading the next several days. Not for the first time, he wished that dragon-exterminators had a guild, like hod carriers. "What did you mean about there being a really big dragon somewhere, bigger than all the others?" he asked. "Is that true?"

Robert did not answer him immediately; he seemed still to be lost in visions. Finally he said, "It's supposed to be the oldest of the Kings, sleeping in a cave for a thousand years, but I don't know. I'd like it to be true."

"*I* wouldn't." Ostvald felt his stomach shrivel at the thought. "Not if it's going to wake up while I'm around."

"Ah, it's just talk, for all I'd have it otherwise. The Kings are gone. You and I will never see them."

They worked on well into the morning, Robert driving himself as ruthlessly as he did Ostvald, until both of them were dazed and giddy and had no choice at last but to rest, even with two high walls of the Grand Hall yet to go. Neither of them had strength enough to speak: they sat back against a pillar, eyes closed, taking what warmth they could from the sunlight limping through the stained-glass windows.

They were both nodding off, despite themselves, when the Princess Cerise walked into the Great Hall.

She was accompanied by someone who could only have been the Crown Prince everyone had been talking about. He was almost grotesquely handsome, if such a thing could be: tall and golden-haired, with dazzlingly blue eyes, the bones of his jaw, cheek, and brow as sharp as swords and yet gentle as well, as if softened from inside by the warmth of an early summer sky. It was a heroic face, a champion's face—a dragonslayer's face—and Robert hated it on sight.

Nevertheless, he and Ostvald scrambled to their feet and bowed deeply to the newcomers. The dragonslayer type bowed elegantly back, in complete disdain for his own station, which made Robert hate him more.

The Princess Cerise said, in genuine alarm, "But you are utterly exhausted, you poor men! Have you worked all night on my account? Oh, I am so sorry—I never, never meant you to go without rest! Please, will you tell me your names? It is so hard to apologize properly when you don't know whom you are speaking to."

"Ostvald Grandin, begging your pardon, please."

Cerise looked at Robert. "And you, young man?"

"We are already acquainted, Princess. I am Robert Thrax, son of Elpidus Thrax, the former exterminator. I was my father's apprentice for six years, and in that position helped him here many times. My own memory of our first meeting is a vivid one."

Cerise looked puzzled, then abruptly not. Her eyes widened. "Oh. Oh my. The boy who broke into my bedchamber! That was *you*?"

Now it was Prince Reginald who looked puzzled. He blinked at them both.

"In my defense," Robert replied, "let it be noted that I was holding on to the tail of a breeding *thivette* at the time. It dragged me down two hallways, through your door, and nearly out the window before my foot caught on your nightstand. It got away—"

"And you broke everything on the table—"

"Not by choice."

"And I called you horrible names—"

"Yes."

"And it was quite the funniest thing I'd ever seen. I told my father about it that evening and we laughed and laughed." She smiled fondly at the thought.

"Really. When I told my father about it, he beat me. Said I should have known to reach for the *thivette*'s neck instead of its tail, and just twist." Robert turned to Prince Reginald, who still looked somewhat puzzled. "The Princess and I were both nine."

"Wait," Cerise said. "You can't be the dragon-boy. He had some sort of Latin name. I remember now because it was so old-fashioned, and I used to tease him by making rhymes with it."

"'Aurelius smelly-us,' 'Heliogabalus bother-and-babble-us,'

'fool of a boy' . . . Yes. I remember. These days I prefer plain Robert."

An uncomfortable pause settled into the space between them. In truth it was brief, but all such instants feel like forever. Cerise retreated from it, taking refuge in the ready shielding supplied by her birth.

"Well," she said, "I must say, how charming to meet you again, and I *am* so grateful that you have come to my family's aid. Will you be done soon?"

Robert was too tired to offer reassurance. "No. Four days? A week? Perhaps more. I cannot truly say, Princess. The castle is infested, as you must know."

"Indeed I do," Cerise replied, returning to herself and the problems of the moment. "Infested by other things than dragons—infested by age, by carelessness, by habit and routine and . . ." She turned an imploringly apologetic face to her companion. "This is our Great Hall, Reginald. I am so embarrassed to be bringing you here now, when it should have been properly restored so long ago."

"No need, no need, my dear," the Prince replied placidly. "My father's just the same as yours, won't change a thing around the old homestead." He had a deep, rolling, *round* sort of voice, just as he should have had. It irked Robert all the more. But even so he noticed that while the Princess held tightly to Reginald's arm, gazing up at him like a starving cat at an empty food dish, her guest appeared somehow less enraptured—benignly affectionate, perhaps, but not hungry in quite the same way.

Robert asked, "Did your valet find you, lord?"

"Who, old Mortmain?" Prince Reginald smiled down at the Princess and patted her hand. "Yes, yes, he caught up with us.

Finally got him to understand that wherever he finds Cerise, he'll find me. Simple as that, really. While I am in Bellemontagne, I am at her service."

The Princess blushed—all the way down, Robert could not help imagining, to the tips of her toes. She said simply, "I will see that you are brought refreshment—but please, the Great Hall *must* be free of dragons by afternoon, for Prince Reginald's presentation at court. You may take your leave then, and return tomorrow to continue with the rest of the castle."

Robert and Ostvald heard her saying to the Prince as they turned away, "I do so hope you won't mind our country simplicity—I know it won't be anything like the grandeur you're used to in Corvinia." Prince Reginald winked back at them over his shoulder.

"I don't know what all the fuss is about," Ostvald announced, once they were gone. "Been hearing 'the Princess Cerise this' and 'the Princess Cerise that' for years, but ask me, Elfrieda's *much* prettier." Robert would have answered, but something appeared to be wrong with his throat.

Eventually servants appeared with a late breakfast, no doubt sent by order of Cerise, after which they labored on past noon. Their biggest task now was one of disposal: it took twelve trips with the cart to carry all the corpses off to temporary storage in the castle's deepest keep, and by the time they were done the pile of bodies there stood taller than their heads.

Robert and Ostvald could hear trumpeters warming up outside as they returned to the Grand Hall to collect Robert's equipment and remove the last traces of their presence. Barely able to stand straight, they loaded things back onto the wagon and swept up the last of the now-harmless *drachengift*. Ostvald watched Robert out of the corner of one eye, observing—without always interpreting them—the emotions that pursued each other across his friend's face. The grief and guilt were easy enough to read, Ostvald having his own human associations with these; but they were succeeded by a look that he had never seen before on his friend's face or anyone else's. It was anger—that, yes, certainly—but a kind of rage that seemed actually to alter the features themselves into something that Ostvald barely recognized as a face. This shadowy metamorphosis lasted only a moment; then Ostvald couldn't see it anymore, just the face familiar to him since childhood, albeit weary to the bone. Robert grunted, "Let's go, then."

Ostvald hung back. "Do you think we could watch the—what she said—the presentation? I'd like to tell Elfrieda about it, account of she's never been to court. Just for a little bit?"

Robert sighed. He wanted nothing more in the world than to be out of the Great Hall, out of Castle Bellemontagne altogether, away from everything to do with the death of dragons. But Ostvald so rarely asked him for anything other than a day off or a second mug of ale that Robert could not find it in his heart to deny him. He said, "Very well. For a little."

They found room at the back of the hall to stand and lean against a pillar, watching as the trumpeters and drummers marched in, the other musicians took their places in the gallery, and the aisles began to fill with people in full court dress, splendid enough to keep Ostvald's eyes round and his jaw slack wherever he stared. Adding to the crowd were the assorted princes, none of whom wanted to be there any more than Robert did, but all of whom felt they had better be, knowing full well that the level of competition had just risen drastically. They all wore their best royal and semi-royal regalia and glanced anxiously around for a sight of their new rival.

Then a dramatic flourish of the trumpets announced the entrance of King Antoine and Queen Hélène, both clad in their grandest style. The King welcomed everyone—very nearly name by name—to this reception for Prince Reginald of Corvinia. Ostvald kept exclaiming, "Elfrieda would *love* this!" and muttered wistfully that he couldn't possibly memorize all this magnificence for her. But Robert had been up for most of two days without any real rest, and nothing here really mattered to him. Ostvald could tell him about it later. He closed his eyes and sighed, letting go.

He had almost fallen asleep on his feet when the trumpets flared again, the drums went off in a hysterical eruption of celebration, and the Princess entered the Great Hall on Prince Reginald's arm. They looked so perfect a couple as to make the notion of perfection meaningless. Robert was profoundly annoyed to feel a twitch in his heart at the sight of Cerise, and an absurd surge of jealousy over the way she gazed up at her companion. "Enough," he growled. "Enough, let's go."

But Ostvald remained mesmerized by the spectacle and wouldn't be budged. There was nothing for Robert to do but wait, with no possibility of closing his eyes again.

Now the Princess Cerise spoke, in the warm, gentle tones that affected his insides altogether too much, saying, "Father, Mother, I present to you Reginald Richard Pierre Laurent Krije, Crown Prince of Corvinia, Archduke of Bornitz, Hereditary Sovereign-in-Waiting of Southeastern Selmira." The trumpets went mad with joy, and the princes looked at each other in horror. This was as bad as it could possibly be.

King Antoine rose, extending his hand to Prince Reginald as the latter bowed deeply, dropping to one knee to do so.

I'd never learn to do that in a thousand years, Robert thought.

The King spoke out clearly, saying, "Good my lord, you do honor to our land and our people, and we receive you as is your due." Cerise looked slightly annoyed, and Robert, who felt himself distantly understanding her in wordless ways he didn't want to think about, could see her point. He'd seen warmer greetings between brothers sparring over the family will.

King Antoine continued, "Reginald of Corvinia, son of King Krije, who overthrew the dread wizard Dahr ere you were ever born . . . Krije, scourge of evildoers and—ah—doers even thinking about being evil . . . Krije, master of land and sea, and most of his neighbors—" Queen Hélène clutched a handful of his robe, but the beaming King was not to be diverted. "Krije, terror of the mighty, trampler of the triumphant, destroyer of the—well, of the really rather feeble, actually—" The Queen was hauling now like a fisherman trying to boat a grampus, almost yanking him off his feet. The King went on valiantly: "Krije, never in his life desirous of another's territory, but only for what joined his own—"

At this point he did finally lose his balance against the Queen's grim tugging, and fell onto his throne with a last determined cry of "Reginald, son of Krije, we bid you welcome to Bellemontagne!"

Under the thundering music, Robert heard Prince Reginald's deep, mellow voice as he returned the royal greeting, first pressing the King's extended hand between both of his own, and then taking Queen Hélène's hand to kiss it in dutiful humility. He turned away, after a moment's formal conversation, to pay his respects to other court dignitaries, with Princess Cerise still holding his arm, and Robert said to Ostvald, "Now. We're leaving now."

Pushing and guiding the cart out the door, they passed Mortmain, who stepped aside, bowing graciously, to let them by. Robert paused, feeling himself full of questions to ask the man. But the moment was all wrong, even though there might never be another. He bent his shoulder again to the task his father had left him.

That night, Cerise went to her parents' chambers to speak her mind on the twinned subjects of personal public humiliation and the normal treatment of honorable guests. Both the King and Queen did their best to soothe her indignation, but neither seemed to be putting the right feeling into their reassurances, and she left for bed more upset than before.

When the echo of her footsteps had faded down the hall, Queen Hélène said, "That went rather well, I think." She smiled in deep satisfaction. "If he's here for her and not saying so, a suspicious father is simply one more obstacle in the quest. If he's here to scout for Krije, to seek out our weak points before invading, let him try—now he'll know we are onto him, and he'll be lucky to find five waking minutes to himself without Cerise trying to make up for your horrible behavior. That means the only person we really need to keep an eye on is the other one, the valet—if that's what he really is. Mortmain."

"I don't like using Cerise this way, dear. I truly don't."

"She plays her part, as must we all. And it *was* your idea. Don't worry—when the time comes, one way or another I'm sure I will be the one to explain it to her."

seven

The dead dragonlets from Castle Bellemontagne did not, after all, wind up rotting in some damp cliffside cavern or hastily dug forest pit. Either of Ostvald's predictions might have come true in the normal course of events, given King Antoine's relaxed approach to decision-making; but his purse-minded wife regarded business affairs—and the world itself—from an entirely different angle. Resigned to living with dragons up to a point, Queen Hélène saw no reason to pay for their deaths and then let the carcasses go to waste—not when the one person who could guarantee a handsome profit was already on hire. And so Robert found himself heading off to Dragon Market in no fashion that he could ever have predicted or imagined.

"You shouldn't expect too much," he said, shaking his head. "I'm not the haggler my father was, and not at all frightening. I won't be able to bully anyone into more than a fair price."

"Hmmph," said the chamberlain. He was seated on the

opposite side of the horse cart in which they were riding, his face dressed in its usual professional thundercloud. "I used to hire and pay Elpidus Thrax, young man. If this were *his* task, do you know what he'd have done? Swaggered through the arch like an Argonaut home from the sea, that's what, then downed enough ale, mead, and mulled wine to float him straight back. And in between the drinking and the back patting and the spitting contests, he'd have been robbed blind in every deal he made. Not a bad man, your da, as men go, for all his failings. But he wasn't bright outside his measure. And this"—he gestured back behind them—"*this* would have been outside the maddest fancy he ever drank to."

Robert turned, not wanting to look again but unable to stop himself.

Trundling along behind the large horse-drawn cart in which he and the chamberlain rode were twenty-eight more just like it, each driven by a carter in royal livery, each marked with the royal colors, and collectively bearing an extraordinary number of dead dragons. By the Queen's order the creatures had already been sorted and organized by species, sex, color, and such other distinguishing characteristics as might facilitate their more rapid sale, then divided among the carts for greater efficiency. It had taken Robert two days to guide the castle's servants through the task of identification, deep in the keep's cold cellar, light glittering off dragonskin as if the bodies had been dusted with bits of brass and crushed diamond. The final tally was frighteningly exact: seven thousand two hundred and ninety-eight dragonlets of twenty-one different species, including two thousand two hundred and thirty males, two thousand nine hundred and forty-five females, thirteen hundred and eighty-three belonging to hermaphroditic varieties, and seven hundred and forty still too young to be accurately sexed. The largest dragonlet was five and three-quarters hands long; the smallest not even half a hand from snout to tail tip.

Robert could only guess at how many corpses still remained within the walls.

Briefly he had considered refusing to participate, telling himself that the broad language regarding disposal in his verbal agreement with King Antoine could not be stretched to cover delivering a year's normal kill to Dragon Market in a single day. But he knew it wasn't so. Nor could he abandon his due share of the sale, knowing the state of the Thrax home and the needs of his mother, brothers, and sisters.

In the end, what did it matter? Dead was dead, and guilt grew no sourer with quantity, merely deeper. His life was as father and fate had willed: it had rules he could never violate, no matter how much he might dream of such impossibilities.

They passed under the curved rib-bone arch marking the entrance to Dragon Market and entered into chaos. Some of the noise and commotion was the natural cacophony of the market itself—the squalling and hissing of captive dragons, the shouting of vendors, the squealing and laughter of children at play with this or that toy, crying out for this or that confection—but the greater part was of their own making, as cart after royal cart came rocking and swaying into view. Their arrival was spark to dry tinder, and it set the market gossips ablaze. As word spread, sellers and customers alike abandoned their haggling, crowding close to see the miracle. Cries and questions flapped in every direction. *It's Robert! That's right, Elpidus's boy! Swog me if you can guess what he's brought in . . . no, no, I didn't believe it either, but one of the cartwheels clipped the toe of my boot, so it's no illusion!* The clot of goggle-eyed wonderers grew thick as old milk, making it difficult for even the stern-faced chamberlain to bring the carts into some kind of practical order within the open space at the market's entry.

Robert stood up on the lead cart's seat, where everyone could see him, and gestured for silence. It was not at all quick in coming, but after a time it finally did.

"Good my friends and neighbors, you know me well!" he shouted as loudly as he could. "And as some have already heard, I've been at hunt this past nine days in the King's own untended preserves!"

"Well, you surely haven't been at Jarold's," someone called back. "I figured your mum wasn't letting you out of the barn!"

A ragged burst of laughter and catcalls swirled through the crowd. Robert feigned shock, then let free a smile. "I'll see you at Jarold's tonight, Guillaume—and I know you'll be there, for I'll be buying. The castle's loss in tenantry is my gain. The castle's loss is *all* our gain, as you can plainly see. Albrecht Schenck, are you here? I've got a dozen *surikaks* for you, perfect for tanning, not a mark on them. And you, Bernard Ullie Gabrie, scoundrel of scoundrels—I've got *tichornes*, God bless me, you know you were begging for some to appear from thin air last time we spoke! I've got something here for everyone, and a promise from the King that half the coin I get out of you will be freely given to the Queen's good charities throughout the kingdom. So tell me, you great gaping jackanapeses, what say you? *Is there anyone here today who came to buy a dragon?*"

◆ ◆ ◆ ◆

In earlier days Dragon Market had been a mobile affair, casting anchor with the seasons, never settling for long near any one town. The reasons for this were a mix of the superstitious and the practical: never recorded, but simply understood. Needs, however, may change, and when they do, beliefs have a way of being bent or reimagined. To Dragon Market, there came in time a winter when the sheer volume of ongoing commerce was too costly to interrupt. Simple as that—barely a tinker's finger snap, really—the traveling life turned stationary. Evidence of the abrupt transition could still be seen in the market's wandering layout and haphazard construction; in ungainly booths that had once been sleek wagons; in walls and signs and fittings built by accretion and loud compromise rather than design. Dragon Market had grown roots but was imperfectly fitted for such permanence, twisting and turning on itself like a cat unable to settle on the right absurd posture in which to sleep.

Robert knew every hateful, noisy, stench-filled inch of the place. He never stayed longer than he had to, not since his father had died and he gained choice in the matter. With the King's sale complete—at last, after many hours—all that remained was to finish his normal obligatory rounds, after which he would be free for home or Jarold's, whichever offered the swiftest relief.

As he walked the market's crimped and curving path, he tried to ignore the furtive glances cast his way, and the whispers, focusing his attention instead on the unusually heavy wallet laced down inside his shirt. It was not a good day—no day at Dragon Market was ever a good day, as far as Robert was concerned—but he prayed there might yet be something he could do to turn the thorns of his conscience.

The sky now warned of rain, but even so the market was still alive with merchants and buyers, not only of dragon hides and teeth and organs (the liver and the tail meat of certain species were considered special delicacies, while the dried-and-ground heart of a *snap-so* was reputed by some to be an aphrodisiac), and all things that might possibly be made from them, but also with vendors selling ale and hot soup and candy dragon claws. Robert briefly watched an old woman energetically bargaining with a dealer over the price of a tail, not yet removed, while a young woman with three small children climbing her skirts tried to outbid her, and the poor dragon itself looked on with eyes like topaz fire. One vendor was offering snares and traps for half price, but finding few takers. Robert could have told him as much; no professional trapper would have bought workmanship this shoddy, and most ordinary people wanted nothing at all to do with the job. Risk a bite or a burn or worse? No thank you, please, and call for Robert Thrax or one of his fraternity. Let them face the danger and live with the scorn.

He studied the drying hides and the live captives alike, noticing when a catch of a rare variety was brought in. He tested the edges of skinning knives, complimenting their makers. And after a time he came to a stand more gaudily ribboned than any other in the market.

Dagobert Swane's specialty was imports. He took pride in the breadth of his sources, and in blithely offering creatures such as no other merchant had ever seen. Sports of birth, distant oddities, startling and improbable hybrids—all these and more were his stock in trade, and he reveled in both the notoriety they brought him and the prices he was able to command.

Today the centerpiece of Swane's display was a large floor cage containing a matched pair of *Serpens avramis karchee*, reputed to have come all the way from Egypt or Kalmuks or some place in Afrique called Monomotapa—only Dagobert knew for certain, and he changed his public story on the hour. The *karchee* were like nothing else in the market: all rainbows from one angle, shimmering like the sky after a storm; and a deep blue-green from another, as though they were wrapped, head to tail tip, in the sea. Half again as big as the largest house-dragons of Castle Bellemontagne, they had been huddled together in a far, cramped corner of the cage, hissing fiercely at inquisitive viewers; but when they saw Robert peering in, they came slowly forward, gazing intently at him out of pure white, seemingly pupil-less eyes. Robert knelt and put his hands flat against the wire mesh, letting the *karchee* smell him.

Seeing him there, Dagobert called out a greeting. "Pretty little things, aren't they, Robert? First we've had in ages."

"You had one six years ago, and three the year before that. I remember. They were all bigger than these, though."

"Not a bit of it. *You* were smaller, that's all, so they *looked* bigger. But it's true I mean to grow these a bit yet before selling, and not just 'cause I like to wipe Bosset's face in the mud. A *true pair*, Robert—do you know what they'll go for, once they tip the scale at twenty?"

Robert stood up. "More than you deserve to get. As usual."

The merchant laughed amiably. "Someday you'll cut your lips with that tongue, boy. There's no room for shame in this business. I can't afford it. Nor can you, with all those mouths to feed." He eyed Robert shrewdly, scratching his head and knuckling his chin. "You want to buy those two?"

"Why would *I* be buying? That's not my trade."

"I know you just sold a bunch of dead ones, that's what I

know. I know that you're suddenly fat on one side of your belly, and I doubt it's from eating the left half of your last meal." Dagobert made a show of considering; then his small eyes suddenly brightened. "Could be a man with resources might want to expand his options, is what I'm thinking. Go into a more respectable line of business, and needing special stock to start. Skins like these would do it. Or maybe looking to partner, hmm? Thing is, Robert, you're as easy to read as Elpidus was. You want those two, or leastwise you don't want *me* to have them, I can see that plain enough. Tell you what, tell you what—*really* special rate. They'll get me thirty silver apiece in six months, but there's at least fifteen in food and care between now and then, plus the headache of repeating this conversation the next time you come round, all hungry like. So give me thirty-six today and they're yours. Or twenty-nine, and you put in a good word for me with your mother." Robert stared at him, but Dagobert only grinned back, hooking his thumbs in his belt. "Handsome woman, that one, and I'm not the only man here who thinks so. A good word, nothing more—I'll do the rest. Can't say fairer than that, can I?"

Robert opened his mouth to answer, but at that point noticed the valet Mortmain standing in view behind the merchant, discreetly back and to one side. Mortmain smiled upon catching Robert's attention, clearly mouthed the words, *When you're done*, and then wandered unhurriedly down the row toward a display of clothing and armament.

Without even looking at Dagobert, Robert told him, "I'll be by later," and hurried after Prince Reginald's man.

When he caught up, he found the valet fingering a simple dragonskin shirt and listening diffidently as its seller assured him of its many virtues, which at latest count included protection against fleas, lice, crossbow bolts, and anything short of a battle-axe wielded by a giant. It was a brilliant pitch, and Robert hated to interrupt it, but he had good reason.

"I wouldn't recommend buying," he broke in. "This is house-dragon stuff, *Serpens domus borenza* at best, and not *feuerdrach* for a minute. It won't turn anything sharper than a serving spoon."

The vendor darkened. "God rot you, Robert Thrax—"

Mortmain lifted an eyebrow. "As you appear to know this young gentleman, proprietor, I assume that what he says is true. Just as I had already assumed everything you were saying was not . . . though you did say it prettily, I must admit. And I do like the stitching. So in the interest of not marring this wonderful day, I will pay you a fifth of what you were asking, which is twice what the shirt is worth. How is that?"

That was apparently fine, and the transaction was quickly completed.

"A piece of advice, sir," Mortmain concluded, "to increase the value of our exchange. The next time you hear a Corvinian accent, pray remember that as bargainers go, my people consider me quite a dullard." He turned toward Robert, his eyes seeming somehow to belong in a different face. "And now, Master Thrax—if you'd walk with me?"

"Yes, I came here looking for you, and yes, I will tell you why. But first, another question." The valet picked up the dagger he had been examining and turned it this way and that in the afternoon light. "Would you say that this inlay is real dragon bone? And if so, what species?"

"*Serpens flamma uxbeck*. Shaved thin like that, you can see the silver threading in the bone. And before you ask me about the next one down in the bin, and the one under that, they're fakes. Most of what's here is fake. Hannes could afford better, but likes his margins where they are."

"Lord, I swear to you, on the golden heads of my three little children—" The short stallholder was in full hawker cry, literally dancing with anxiety to make the sale.

"You don't *have* any children, Hannes—none who know your name, anyway."

"Yah, but he didn't know that, did he? Jesu!" Shrugging, Hannes turned from Robert and rounded on Mortmain, all pretense dropped. "See here, do you want it or not?"

"No. But I'll have one of the counterfeits, if you please."

Hannes and Robert both stared, but the valet insisted. He spent several minutes picking through the contents of the bin, perfecting his selection, before finally announcing himself well-pleased.

They walked on. Mortmain moved through the crowd with an unstudied grace that fascinated and eluded Robert, and kept his silence until they were near the market's fringe. Once there he turned his back on everything, facing the dark green quiet of the forest. His gaze hardened.

"I have three more questions for you, sir. Or one, depending. Can you be discreet?"

Robert thought of the dragonlets he kept at home, secret from all save his own family, and nodded.

"Yes." Mortmain had clearly reached a decision. "All right then—what is the largest dragon you've killed?"

"Largest or most dangerous? They aren't the same thing."

"Both, if you please."

Answering accurately meant weighing memories that Robert normally tried to avoid, but curiosity had firm hold of him. "Most dangerous would be a pregnant *mistdrake*. No bigger than your fist, but *mistdrakes* are live-birthers, one drachling to the decade, and the mothers have a little trick of spitting poison. Nasty stuff. A couple of drops will kill a horse, and the fumes alone can raddle the lungs till you spit blood when you breathe."

"And you killed one."

"Done five, so far."

"Five!"

"Worth too much to walk away from. There are people here who brew up powerful medicines from the glands. As for size, since you were asking, at least once every season a hungry *rakai* wanders in from the mountains, and I have to deal with it before too many sheep or goats are taken. Mostly that's trapping work, but last year I had to kill one that was at least two of you long. Spear job." He paused. "Why do you want to know?"

Mortmain lifted a bemused eyebrow. "Because I have need of certain . . . services . . . and you seemed a likely candidate for the job. You know dragons, you keep your own counsel, and you clearly want something I can provide, though what it might be beyond money—which you now have plenty of—I can't begin to guess. Piercing that mystery was, in fact, the point of my third question. You may consider it asked."

"I don't need anything."

"Nonsense. I've seen you watching me at the castle. The Princess Cerise doesn't distract you from your work. My master doesn't. But *I* do. And I would know why before we speak a moment further."

Robert's mouth tightened. "There's nothing to say."

Mortmain looked at him, measuring the moment. At last he sighed. "Indeed, dragonslayer, there is nothing. I apologize for wasting your time."

He turned in perfect dismissal and walked away.

"I'm not a dragonslayer!" Robert shouted. "I just kill the damn things! What do you *want* from me?"

Mortmain stopped but did not turn.

"More truth," he said, his voice as certain as carved stone. "What were you going to do with those sparkling dragons you were about to buy?"

"I—" Robert's voice faltered before he could say, *I wasn't going to buy them*, because he realized, with frightening certainty, that the valet was right—another minute standing before that cage and he would have. Family responsibilities or no, he truly would have done it. The understanding gutted him.

At last he said, "Why the fake knife, and not the real one?"

Mortmain turned at that, the look on his face a mix of admiration and surprise. "We're to trade, then, are we, like all the good, honest merchants of this market? Your truth for mine, unhindered?"

Robert felt increasingly unmoored, as though the world had just changed around him, but not knowing how or why. "I . . . I don't know. Are *you* discreet?"

"My honest answer: as needed. Now your turn. *Did* you want them for their skins? Was it business, or was it something else?"

"I wanted to set them free." Robert looked down at his rough, open palms as if he might find an explanation lurking in the calluses. "Somewhere safe. Though God knows where that might be."

"Well," Mortmain mused. He began to walk back toward Robert. "Well, that's really interesting. A fellow who slays—all right, then, *exterminates*—dragons for a living, wanting to rescue other dragons from slaughter. A puzzling sort of dedication, wouldn't you say?"

"I don't want to be an exterminator," Robert blurted. "And I don't want to be a rescuer, either, if it comes to that."

"Really. What *do* you want, Master Thrax?"

"To be like you."

Mortmain gaped at him in true and total astonishment. "Like me? A valet?"

"A valet to a great prince!" Robert hesitated, now abashed by his own eagerness. "All right, it wouldn't have to be such a great prince. It could be anyone, really, as long as their path led far away from here. To be free of this place and my father's work. To never again be 'Elpidus's boy,' but just my own man, doing decent and honorable service appropriate to my station. I've dreamed of it all my life."

Mortmain was still taken aback. "You make it sound romantic. But a valet's life isn't one that most people would consider romantic. I don't myself. It's harder work than you might imagine. Especially in my particular circumstances."

Robert frowned, his words emerging in puzzled bursts. "I don't see why. Prince Reginald is . . . well, he's *perfect*, isn't he? I mean, just look at him."

"It is an old wonder to me," Mortmain mused aloud, "that the false and the genuine so often tend to live hand in hand—as with that dagger I purchased, for instance. You wonder why I chose the fraudulent over the real? Because of precisely this puzzling divide. The haft is not in the least what it pretends, being more beautiful than the reality it imitates; while the blade is as honest and moral and straightforward as any blade could possibly be. Are the two, together, a truth unspoken or a lie concealed? Without the lure of that charming handle, would anyone have picked up the dagger at all? And without the truehearted blade, would anyone hold it for more than a moment? I ponder such matters. I do indeed. As I must, given my responsibilities."

"But he *looks* like a prince. The way they should look, I mean. Exactly."

Mortmain's thin mouth twitched at one corner. "You are aware that the Crown Prince and I make our beds in the stable. What you are certainly not aware of, but must understand in order to serve my needs, is that this accommodation was neither his choice nor King Antoine's command. *I* ordered it."

It was Robert's turn to be astonished, and Mortmain drew rueful satisfaction from the play of emotions he observed passing across the young man's face. "He will continue to sleep there," Mortmain continued, "and he will cook his own meals with the grooms, as they do, for as long as I say. Just as he will decorate the Princess Cerise's arm and trouble her observant parents for as long as I say. As I told you in the castle, I am something a bit more than a servant. Just a bit, mind you. I am under orders from King Krije to turn his son into something at least *resembling* the hero he appears to be. As you will see when you know him better, it's rather a job."

"When I know him better?" Robert was beginning to feel light-headed. "And how should that ever happen?"

"Because—assuming we can settle on terms, which I no longer doubt—you are going to help him find and kill a very large dragon."

EIGHT

It was a day of considerable frustrations, odd as a Mazarin-cut diamond and just as unyielding: the sort of day where yellow sunlight is an insult, green grass a complaint, and gossamer white clouds a magnificent, endless irritation . . . or so it felt, at least, to the two people at the center of everyone's concealed ploys and machinations (including, admittedly, their own). It was rather as though their lives were being written by dueling playwrights—and not terribly good ones, either, scribblers who ought to have known better than to ply their trade outside the provinces.

Consider the Princess Cerise—her pink tongue-tip poking out of the right-hand corner of her mouth, as it often did when she was concentrating on her writing—utterly alone on so beautiful a morning, sitting in the shelter of her private forest nook and unsure, for the first time in her life, if she was cut out for the royalty business.

Nothing was *working*.

Oh, things had gone well enough for the first breathless week or so, that much she had to admit. Prince Reginald was positively celestial, a moon, a comet, a star, and she had floated in his company as if carried aloft, gazing dreamily down at all Bellemontagne, so far below her.

Except for that one jarring moment with the exterminator, the breeze of their passage above the everyday world had been as sweet as the secret language of a lily . . . but oh that moment, and oh how it now tormented her. The Prince had been a perfect gentleman, of course: perfection was the essence of his nature. Yet looking back on the incident, she felt certain she had revealed something false within herself, a foolish childhood moment in which *noblesse* fell rather short of *oblige*. Though he had never said so—that would have been imperfect, and therefore impossible—she was certain this knowledge marred her in his sight.

How else to explain his careful distance? For two wonderful years, princes of every stripe and variety had come begging for so much as a nod from Cerise, let alone the gift of a perfumed favor, or the dizzying pleasure of her direct glance; and she had turned them all away. Now she stared deeply into the cobalt wonder of Reginald's eyes, ready to pack her trunks and move in, just left of the twinkle, but found no entry there. She casually stroked his splendid forearms—not *too* often—by way of emphasis within certain turns of conversation, yet his voice never caught or quavered even the tiniest bit. She leaned her head against his shoulder as they stood together on the castle's parapet, caught up in a particularly rapturous sunset, hoping the beauty of the moment might convey what she could not, only to have him smile and announce, "Pretty colors, those, don't you think?"

To her fiercely straining senses, he might have been made

of Venetian glass. She had withdrawn then, her cool "good evening" accepted with the same bland pleasantness as her morning-blossom "hello."

That night she caught herself considering a modification to the necklines of all her best dresses, something midway between *petite annonce* and lowering a drawbridge. The enormity of her self-abandonment made her gasp; pink-cheeked and shaken, she promptly sent orders instructing her seamstress to stay home for three days, a ward against further temptation.

But in fact that precaution had proven unnecessary. From the very next morning, which was foul and rainy as her mood, straight through to dawn on this horribly perfect one, she had seen Prince Reginald hardly at all. Day after day, no matter how early she rose, the Prince and his valet were abroad earlier—off on some mysterious business that no one could politely ask after, and that they silently yet graciously refused to acknowledge on their ever-later returns. This was the subject of much gossip and speculation around the castle, a great deal of which Cerise knew included her. The only thing anyone understood for certain was that *whatever* the Crown Prince was up to, he always came back from it with dirt and tufts of grass marring his clothes, which Mortmain then stayed up half the night washing.

Cerise felt abandoned, adrift, ignored . . . and angry. This last was only a spark, as yet, and not yoked to any purpose. But still: anger. It was not an emotion she had ever needed to grow used to.

Fat lot of good being royal, she thought bitterly, *if you can't get your dream prince's attention even when he's standing right next to you*.

Cerise considered the block of parchment in her lap with

every bit of her usual concentration, but with a good deal more resentment than joy. The first half dozen or so sheets, written days earlier, were filled with carefully scribed names. She had begun with *Princess Cerise of Corvinia*, but that was too easy, and quickly became boring. After that she had alternated between *Mrs. Crown Prince Reginald* (which somehow didn't look right) and *Cerise, Princess of Bellemontagne, Countess of Corvinia* (which looked better, but was too long and cramped her fingers). Then came two entire pages of plain *Countess of Corvinia*, notable for ever more elaborate capital Cs; a single doubtful, rather tremulous *Queen Cerise*; and finally—this morning's production—an avalanche of increasingly ragged cursive that began *What's wrong with me?*, veered briefly into *What's wrong with him!*, and after a variety of fruitless explorations concluded *I shall become a holy sister and devote my life to caring for lepers. Do we have any?*

The last sheet in the block held only two words, the last still incomplete.

Father?

No.

And there it was, thuddingly unavoidable. She knew only one person who might possibly help her.

Cerise sighed, looking up through sycamore tangles at the infuriatingly tranquil sky. A day can lie in so *many* ways, she realized; for though the sun was shining, she now saw mother-shaped thunderclouds in every direction.

At that moment Prince Reginald was looking at the sky as well, but from a supine position. A supine position in the mud, to be absolutely exact, and still attempting to find the wind that had been driven out of him when empty air had so suddenly replaced his horse. He lay still and wheezed, and watched the little white clouds going around and around.

Mortmain smiled and called out, "Very good, my lord! That swing came *much* closer."

"A . . . bit . . . *overbalanced*, though . . ." Reginald gasped. "Wouldn't . . . you say?"

"By inches. Next time move your hands back on the hilt, and don't lean forward."

"Bloody hard . . . not to." Reginald was finally moving to sit up. "Bloody blade carries you with it." He shook his head, wiped the sweat-tangled hair from his eyes, then wiped again with his other hand to remove the mud he'd just streaked there. "I wish I could use my sidesword. I *like* my sidesword. Get in, get under, make the thrust, get out—that's what we should do."

Mortmain frowned. "According to Master Thrax, who has good reason to know, a *Doppelhänder* is the only blade sufficient to the task. Anything smaller and you risk becoming your *rakai*'s high tea"—he had taken to using that phrase these last several days, *your rakai*, as if the beast were already penned and waiting—"an outcome I confess I do not favor explaining to your father." After a moment's thought, he added, "Or you could use a spear. He said a spear was safer."

The Prince was now standing on both feet, though not at full height, as he leaned to one side and rubbed his lower back ruefully. "Never. Not with witnesses. Spears are for Sunday afternoon boar hunts. I'll just have to get the hang of this, no matter how long it takes." He looked down the open green of the clearing, to where his horse patiently waited at today's charging point, then back at the dozen ragged straw bales that hung from tree limbs, as targets, at differing heights. One in particular had proven today's devilment; he'd unseated himself three times attempting it.

"Did I really come close?"

"Yes. But even with an addled dragon, close is worse than missing altogether. Come. Let's try again."

Reginald picked up the huge sword—it took both hands and a sharp *huff* to lift it—and the two men walked back toward the Prince's horse, who looked on as if privately amused.

"Tell me again that this plan will work, Mortmain. Tell me I'm not falling off my horse a dozen times a day for no reason."

"My lord, I have thought for years that a deity of some sort watches devotedly over your fortunes." He did not add that he suspected it of being the same deity assigned to protecting drunkards and stray dogs. "You could not have wished for a more fortuitous turn of events."

"I certainly could have! I could have wished for a life where I had never heard the word 'dragon' and didn't have princesses trailing after me every waking moment—"

"Astonishingly beautiful princesses," Mortmain could not help interjecting.

"—and where I didn't have my father bellowing at me night and day about growing up, facing my responsibilities, learning to be a *man*! Sending me off with you in hopes that that I'll fight things and kill people, just the way *he* does—to sleep and eat and scratch fleabites with the people he wants me to rule." The prince's face twisted as harshly as it could, which wasn't much; fine bones will out. "I don't want the blasted crown—I don't want anything *he* wants! Is that so very much to ask?"

"It is for the Prince of Corvinia," Mortmain said gently. "Permission to speak freely, lord?"

Prince Reginald grunted and kept walking.

"Good fortune has brought you the exterminator, and all his knowledge and skills. With his help we will find and prepare a proper dragon. Kill it, and you will go home as much a hero as your father could demand. Marry the Princess in the bargain and you will also bring him, without bloodshed, a country he would be delighted to take under—ah—his well-known firmly benevolent supervision. A single dragon, a single princess—that is all you must endure, and I guarantee that you will never have to sleep in discomfort again, or fight with anybody, or put up with anything it does not please you to put up with."

Reginald was silent the rest of the way, and while he reclaimed his horse and mounted. But as he fumbled for a moment with the reins and the *Doppelhänder* and his saddle, trying to find the right combination of grip and balance, he finally muttered, "Did you see him, the exterminator, Mortmain, that first day? He handled this monster like a twig. I was certain it would be easy." He took a deep, resigned breath, already apprehensive about the outcome of this new charge. "The fellow is stronger than he looks."

"I think Master Thrax is a good many more things than he appears to be, my lord. Now. Again."

NINE

The announcement, when finally made, went off like a charm. But it took careful preparation.

In the first step of the dance (distinctly a minuet, rather than a gavotte or a pavane), Mortmain casually mentioned to the castle's chamberlain that the Crown Prince had given thought to consulting the King and Queen on a minor point of no great urgency, but was uncertain as to local custom; what did the chamberlain think best—to wait one month or two before making a formal request for an audience? The chamberlain replied obliquely, stating that such procedural traditions as Bellemontagne favored were more in the nature of potato patches than lofty oaks, try as he might to make them otherwise . . . but that even so, King Antoine and Queen Hélène were too busy with issues of state to be concerned with something the Crown Prince considered minor. Both men retired from the exchange delighted: in any profession, encountering true skill is a rarity.

On the next day—meeting by apparent accident in the very same place, at the very same time—Mortmain allowed that in terms of reflecting his master's thoughts he had been tragically in error; that in fact the matter in question was only minor from certain angles, and quite intractable without benefit of their highnesses' wisdom, experience, and most gracious understanding, which the Crown Prince hoped they might be willing to share at their earliest convenience. Mortmain further hoped that the King and Queen would comprehend that delicate issues of a personal nature were involved, suggesting the need for privacy. The chamberlain patiently listened to this volley, but made no show of being moved. Instead he expressed sincere and heartfelt concern for the Crown Prince's health, state of mind, and general well-being—which, him being a royal guest, was obviously of grave concern to the entire nation—followed by the regretful observation that while things might be different in urbane Corvinia, the peasant gossips in Bellemontagne made confidentiality next to impossible. Why, speaking to the King and Queen in private was nearly as good as shouting from a church tower, most days. Perhaps the Prince should consider taking his problem, whatever it might be, to a wise woman or a priest?

As they parted company this time, the chamberlain couldn't help but giggle; while Mortmain, smiling slyly, thought to himself, *We really must play chess.*

On the third day both men knew better than to stroll by that corner again, or speak together at all. A seed, once planted, must ripen, and no one ever managed a minuet by getting ahead of the beat.

On the fourth day they nodded to one another.

On the fifth day they smiled and formally, if invisibly, changed places. The chamberlain politely inquired as to Mortmain's health, asked him if the castle's ostlers were properly seeing to the Crown Prince's modest needs in the stables, commiserated over the Spartan difficulties of life in service, then mentioned that Tuesday next all of Bellemontagne would be celebrating the Feast of Saint Amalberga—not Saint Amalberga of Munsterbilzen, he hastened to add, but Amalberga of Maubeuge, the one *not* generally pictured as standing on top of King Charles Martel. Fortunately for the valet and his master, the chamberlain said, one of the features of the event was a ceremony in which the King and the Queen would be available for a *public* audience, should the Crown Prince still be desirous of conversation. After which there would be cake, he added, showing real pleasure for the first time in Mortmain's experience.

In terms of the hidden conversation they had been having these past five days, this gambit was so balanced, so wonderfully delivered, so absolutely exquisite in the way it landed the quoit while upping the stakes, that good manners compelled Mortmain to let the chamberlain preen for a moment. Then he ruefully (and falsely) admitted that the Crown Prince *never* celebrated the feast of *any* saint, on grounds that such gaiety was inappropriate. To honor a martyr took suffering, not celebration: at these times the Prince preferred standing for hours in the middle of a freezing river, or hurling himself off low walls onto a pile of stones. It depended on the season.

Mortmain took his leave, whistling cheerfully down the hall. The chamberlain looked after, thinking, *Sod me, but there goes a master. Tomorrow the first formal letter will be peeking out of his coat pocket. I must think of the best way not to accept it.* Then he rushed to tell the King and Queen the good news. For it was as inevitable as dawn now, to anyone familiar with the proper running of a kingdom: Prince Reginald meant to propose.

And by the day before the Feast of Saint Amalberga—the Amalberga who was the mother of Saints Emembertus, Gudila, and Reinalda, not the Amalberga who miraculously cured Charlemagne even after he broke her arm—everyone in Bellemontagne knew it. Which was precisely the result Mortmain had sought.

Upended. That was the word: Cerise felt upended. Also uprooted, in an uproar, put upon, barely upright, and caught utterly in upheaval. Her emotions splashed through the treasured words in her head the same way she had splashed through puddles as a child, with the same gleefully muddy results. If her tablet and stylus were with her, she could try to contain her feelings within a parchment cage; perhaps then this roaring vertigo might pass. But she didn't dare bring her writing tools into the castle, and she couldn't possibly slip out this afternoon or even tonight, to try and scritch away her nervousness by lantern light. Not with everything that had to be readied for the feast, and all the castle staff busy straight through moonset and sunrise at their tasks. There was nothing for her to do but sit in her room as quietly as she could, the very portrait of grace and serenity, while her unanchored mind hammered at the walls.

Her mother had been insufferable for days, of course. No doubts there, no trembling uncertainties, no panicky midnight questions. Her earlier advice and guidance had been proven correct—*which was only sensible, really, don't you see?*—and now she dismissed her daughter's concerns.

Yes, dear. We've all gone through this. Just before my own formal betrothal I was an absolute wreck, as you are now—and as your own daughter shall someday be, if you are blessed with one. There's just something upsetting about getting what we want. I suggest knitting.

It hadn't helped.

Cerise thought, *I am frightened*, and in the wake of that admission felt strangely calm, the way an invalid finds relief at the flattened peak of a fever. She couldn't remember ever feeling frightened before: not even when she'd first gone to her mother, weeks before, seeking help.

That had been self-doubt and frustration and anger, not fear.

On that sun-blessed morning she had found her mother and father together in the Royal Gardens, directing some servants in a fervent campaign against a colony of particularly entrenched aphids. Based on the King's evident agitation, she might have assumed the insects were wearing armor and had stormed the castle, swinging battering rams, to take his *Rosa damascena* hostage.

"We can't talk now, my dear," the King had said to her. "Busy. Quite."

"I only need to speak with Mother. Please, it's important."

That had gotten his attention. Little seizes a royal mind like being set to one side. "If this is about the warrior-bunny," he'd said, frowning, "there is nothing to talk about."

"You're not being fair. You don't even know him!"

"I know he's King Krije's son, and that's more than enough for me. I've no ill will toward the boy, Cerise, no hard feelings at all, but his sire is a murderous old monster, and I don't trust *his* intentions one bit! Do you hear me?"

"She hears you," Queen Hélène spoke from behind him. "So do I. So does half the castle. Go away, Antoine, you're upsetting our daughter." When he hesitated, the Queen stamped her foot. "Go *on*—go pass an edict or bother the cook, but go *now*. And *you*," she said to the gardeners, "you keep working. I will be watching."

The King left, briefly annoyed at his wife's dismissal but delighted not to participate in what he'd always thought of as "that sort" of conversation. While he loved his daughter dearly, he was also keenly aware of the spheres of his capability. "Some of us are born to ride and rule," he said to the chamberlain, "to lead men and—and, yes, pass edicts. Others are born to take tea and counsel young lovers. I think it's fairly obvious which sort *I* am." The chamberlain, who had his own opinion regarding his monarch's destiny, had not become chamberlain by expressing it.

Queen Hélène passed Cerise a fragile lacy handkerchief and, taking her left elbow in hand, began to steer her gently toward the Royal Gardens' prettiest arbor. "There—blow your nose, and don't even think of crying."

"I'm *not* crying." The suggestion annoyed Cerise, in part because she knew how close she was and hated that her mother could sense it.

"I didn't say you were," the Queen answered with surprising mildness. "Now blow your nose." She stroked Cerise's hair, waiting patiently while the Princess did so. Finally she said, "Darling, your father is not your problem. I'll deal with your father. The problem is the Crown Prince, yes? Tell me I'm wrong."

Princess Cerise sniffled. "Mother, I know he *likes* me. We've walked everywhere there is to walk in this castle, and in the woods, and I've held his arm while he told me all his adventures, and all about life at King Krije's court, and what ladies are wearing there. And he's recited poetry to me, hours and hours of it—he knows lots of poetry—and we've ridden together, and he has been just as sweet and . . . and *chivalrous* as he could be—"

"But no further than that," said Queen Hélène. "That's where it ends."

Cerise nodded miserably. "And now I hardly see him at all. He's off each day with his valet, doing something he won't talk about."

"I wouldn't worry about that." Her mother took some internal measure Cerise could only guess at, then continued. "Well. To the heart of things. Let me tell you what I know. Your Reginald cannot be entirely direct with you, my dear, because he is a man, and men believe themselves to be all straight lines and right angles—an illusion you will find it important to allow them, though in fact they are as hopelessly snarled as a ball of yarn after a cat gets through playing with it. Part of their charm, my own mother always said, and I have lived to think her wise. Furthermore, your Reginald is a prince, which adds its own annoying tangles to the concatenation."

"I've known lots of princes now, Mother. And if I'd given a sign, any one of them would have proposed on the spot. Just not *him*."

"Don't interrupt, Cerise. Reginald isn't just any prince, he's a Crown Prince. More to the point, he is Crown Prince *of Corvinia*. You must remember, dear, Reginald's going to be king after Krije dies, if the dreadful man ever actually does. And he's going to rule over a much larger, much wealthier, much more important land than our little Bellemontagne. While I believe you worthy of him, and—unlike your father—see great opportunity for benefit in such an arrangement, if carefully made, it is not something to be committed to on impulse. Consider the matter from a higher vantage point, as it deserves. Compared to Corvinia, we are a backwater, a bump in the road. And naturally Reginald has no idea whether you're capable of being the sort of companion he will need when he ascends the throne. So he spends time with you, and studies you, and then goes off to hold counsel with a man who is obviously here with him at King Krije's specific direction, no doubt the vicious old raptor's designated eyes and ears. And this consideration is only as it should be. Here, in your home, you are still a beautiful child, your potential untested; there, you would have as great a responsibility as he. Greater, if you ask me."

"Mother, I know I could be what he needs!" Princess Cerise cried out, passionately clasping her hands at her breast. "I just know I could."

"Could you? He will rule the land, but you will have to rule the castle—which is twice the task, believe me, for a country largely governs itself. Castles don't. You will have to be a royal hostess, managing more noble guests in a week than your father and I see in a year's time. You will be overseeing kitchens bigger than our Great Hall—you will supervise servants who outnumber our local population—you will be hounded endlessly, morning and night, by maddening hordes of people begging you to intercede with your husband on their behalf. And on top of that, Reginald will be expecting you to be his partner, his trusted adviser"—she paused for a significant moment—"his playmate, his lover, the mother of his children . . . all that, at all times, at a moment's notice. Are you prepared for such a life, my Cerise? My little girl?"

"Yes, Mother," the Princess answered quietly. "Yes, I am sure I am. But how can I convince him now, when I don't even see him? How can I make him realize who I really am?"

Queen Hélène studied her daughter for a long moment, and then reached out to take her into her arms. "We will simply have to show the Prince that he cannot live without you. Good works, charity, taking soup to ailing servants, that sort of thing. Don't worry about it anymore, dear—he'll come around. I had to do the same with your father. You just have to make them understand. They never do on their own."

Thus counseled, if not terribly comforted, Cerise had returned to waiting for her prince of choice to make up his mind. She filled her hours with every action that her mother prescribed, plus a few good ones she conceived for herself, and she even stopped watching from the main battlement to see what time Prince Reginald returned from whatever he was doing. After a week she started taking her meals alone in her rooms, so she would not accidentally have to speak with the Prince in company.

But none of that had made her feel any better. To her own surprise and her mother's unreserved irritation, each generous act of giving, each moment of self-abnegation and sacrifice, actually made her feel worse. This wasn't what she wanted at all. She wanted *him*, and she wanted him *now*. Let other princesses play these ridiculous games. Behind the mask of her features, she was screaming to take Reginald by his elegant silk sleeves and shout, *Don't you know I'm* yours? until he simply had to say *Since before I was born, yes*.

Which is why she was particularly shocked to discover, on the day that the chamberlain entered with written proof of

Prince Reginald's intentions, that the elegantly turned-out letter in his hands did not make her feel any better, either.

Patience and Rosamonde stared up into the vast, dark green reaches of the old oak. There was no visible sign of the five dragonlets, though the sisters could hear scrabbling claws and flapping wings at play somewhere out of sight in the tree's upper branches.

"They won't come down," Patience complained to Robert. He was stretched out on the ground on the other side of the tree trunk, hands laced over his eyes, trying to nap.

"I wouldn't come down either, if I knew the two of you didn't have any treats for me."

"Told you so," Rosamonde hissed at Patience.

"How could *they* know, all the way up there?"

Robert laughed gently and sat up. "They know. So open those fists, grab your skirts, and go bring me as many hazelnuts as you can gather. Do that and we'll play some roast and catch."

He rose to his feet as the two girls ran off, shouting and laughing at each other, then he stretched with all the rapturous luxury of Reynald or Fernand at their most self-indulgent. Last night his mother Odelette hadn't been able to talk about anything but the marriage rumors, and this morning he'd overheard Elfrieda tell Ostvald that she was making a new dress for the feast, to honor the Princess and Prince at the evening's festivities. Which meant that the Royal Ceremony before the feast really was going to be it, and about time, too. After that, just one more task for that crafty valet of the Princeling's, and Robert's new life could finally begin.

He grinned a crooked grin and rubbed his neck, working a cramped muscle there. Then he whistled for the dragonlets to come down and join him. Tomorrow . . . tomorrow was going to be a wonderful day.

The greatest philosopher in Corvinia's history, Bernard of Trèves—who was not actually from Corvinia, but passed through it once on his way from Avignon to Prague, and left a deep impression on the general populace—wrote in his *De Facetia Divina* that nothing on Earth was what it seemed. It therefore followed, he continued, that to value substance over appearance was to mock God's obvious preference for His world. As with many of Bernard's observations, no one could say whether he was serious or joking, which in some ways underscored the point. Crown Prince Reginald grew up surrounded by such quotes and listened better than anyone knew. His own personal interpretation of Bernard's maxim had become both a defense against his father and the guiding rule of his life: *When in doubt, smile*.

But he wasn't smiling now, in any part of him. Not with every voice in the Great Hall stilled, and every eye focused solely on him, as he stepped forward in order to kneel before the King and Queen.

He knew the sharp prodding of Mortmain's stare best of all, having endured years of it. If he had to, he thought, he could point straight at the man without even looking—wouldn't that surprise him!—then shout, *This was his idea! He wrote the letters, he even wrote my speech! I just wanted to ride away in the middle of the night, but he wouldn't let me!*

Instead Crown Prince Reginald bowed to King Antoine and

Queen Hélène with all the gravity that came with his storied ancestry, and settled to one knee in a descent as sure and graceful as a sunset. The dark cloth of his best jerkin and cape fell around him like evening clouds over the sea.

He lowered his eyes, grateful that he could do the beginning part without having to look at anyone. *Get through this, that's all.*

"Majesty—ah—Majesties. For all your kind and gracious forbearance, it can hardly have escaped your notice that I am but an uncouth, unlettered prince from a poor kingdom, so far below your beautiful Bellemontagne in the world's esteem as to be all but invisible."

It was a good start. Patently false, of course, and everyone present knew it, but they felt complimented all the same.

"That one such as I should dare lift his eyes to the vision of feminine grace that is your daughter, Her Highness the Princess Cerise—it is not to be tolerated, and strikes even this vulgar crowned peasant as absurdity piled on grotesquerie. Truly, I can hardly believe that these are my own words as I speak, or that this is my own voice, and I feel I must make petition for your pardon before speaking any further. Your daughter is of marriageable age, as am I, and we are both unbetrothed—"

He paused, and in the echoing space that opened, he could hear a brief, sharp intake of breath from everyone in the room, the Princess's own perhaps an instant ahead of all the others.

He raised his head, his blue eyes moving slowly from the Princess to the Queen, then finally to the King. Their gazes locked, and Reginald waited for what seemed an eternity before King Antoine lowered his chin in a nod so subtle that only Reginald could see it.

Thus cued, the Prince continued.

"But I am not here this afternoon to sue for her hand."

For three heartbeats the Great Hall was lost in pandemonium, much of it stemming from the rejoicing whoops of the last remaining visitor princes, who had spent the day glumly packing for a humiliating homeward journey. Then King Antoine lifted his hand sharply, gesturing for silence.

"We would hear what our guest has to say, and we would hear it without interruption. Be silent!" When all voices were finally stilled, he continued. "You tell us now, Prince Reginald, that you have *not* come here to wed our daughter, Princess Cerise. Yet we were given to understand otherwise. You will explain yourself, or face our displeasure."

Here's the tricky part now. Mustn't get it wrong. What did he say to say? Ah, yes . . .

"Your Majesty, I did not come to your country seeking treasure of any kind, least of all such living treasure as your daughter, the most beautiful flower of this extraordinary kingdom. Indeed, I did not come here of my own will at all, though I now bless the stars that charted my path. But he may not wed who is not at liberty to do so . . . and I will not be free until I have satisfied the obligations set upon me by my father, King Krije, monarch of Corvinia."

"Then you do wish to marry the Princess?"

"With all my heart. But I cannot."

By now, most of those watching understood that the Prince's confession was no surprise to the royal family, but rather some kind of prearranged ritual, and wonderful theater to boot. They barely breathed, hanging on every word and gesture of the display, thrilled to the marrow—even the rejected princes—to be there.

"And if you were free? If the obligation that binds you were removed?"

"Then I would come to you as the beggar that I am and make offering—my life and my future lands, my circlet and my future crown, everything that I own and am, and all that I may yet be, for your daughter's hand. But between now and that day there is a shadow, for it is the custom of my people and the command of my father that I prove myself worthy of my heritage. Before I may be a suitor—before I may be anything else—I must be no crown prince, but a simple knight-errant in search of a mission, a quest, a great deed that awaits the doing."

His voice rang out now, filling the Great Hall like some brass-and-iron bell. "For all that I am his only son, he will not rest satisfied that our humble realm can safely be left in my hands until I have accomplished something of valor and value, something to show my father I have attained the stature of a true king. This is my task, before any other." He lowered his voice and head together, humbly. "You are Bellemontagne made flesh, and set in place by God to guide and protect it. In all this land is there nothing for me to do, no hero's task to achieve, no great wrong to right, that will both meet my obligation and prove my worthiness for your daughter?

"Pray speak, Your Highness. Direct me. For I am your sword and your shield, your arrow and your bow. Use me and free me—or send me on my way, to live forever in the empty darkness that would be life without your daughter."

Afterward, everyone who had been there agreed it was quite the best betrothal they had ever seen.

TEN

It was to be something involving a dragon, of course; that part had been prearranged in accordance with Mortmain's suggestions. What else could Bellemontagne seriously offer a wandering prince in need of a Herculean labor? Lacking Nemean lions, hydras, golden-horned stags, wild boars of heroic size, Augean stables, Stymphalian birds, Cretan bulls, man-eating mares (so much as one, let alone four), girdle-wearing Amazons, monstrous cows, golden apples, and three-headed watchdogs from hell . . . well, absent any of these classic obstacles, a decently sized man-killer *rakai*—or two or three, they were common enough in the southern mountain passes—would simply have to do. And none but Mortmain, Reginald, and Robert would ever have to know the truth of the journey.

Thus, as preparations moved apace, it appeared that everyone was finally going to get what they wanted. Even King Antoine was feeling pleased with the way things had turned out.

Though he still harbored concerns about King Krije's intentions, better a wedding than a war—and the young man really had been quite admirable in his presentation. The fact that all the other princes still lurking about the property disliked him immensely was just something of a bonus, like a proper Tokaji wine after a superb meal.

As for the Princess Cerise, seeing and hearing Prince Reginald speak his heart had lifted the tides of her spirit to their former level. She was not only thrilled by the notion of her practically intended setting off to slay a dragon or two: she was determined to organize the entire expedition. Her mother approved enthusiastically, saying, "Let him see how useful you can be, and what a help you *would* be to a king—a young king at the beginning of his reign. This is certainly not the time to allow him any second thoughts. And don't forget to take the gentian-blue court dress, whatever else you pack. Men are helpless against gentian blue, every one of them. My grandmother taught me that."

As it happened, Cerise did not pack the gentian blue, thinking (correctly) that it did not flatter her eyes. But in Robert's estimation, there was very little else she left behind.

From the start—right from that afternoon at the Dragon Market, when he had laid out the basics of the idea in response to Mortmain's carefully phrased questions and proposals—Robert had assumed that the expedition would be small in total number and lightly equipped: just himself, the two Corvinians, a guide, a surgeon—because you never really knew—and two cart drivers. Now, however, he discovered that there would be a flotilla of servants, cooks, court officials, and men-at-arms accompanying them, in addition to several of the Princess's ladies-in-waiting, two doctors, a priest for the blessing of Prince Reginald's weaponry and sword arm, and even King Antoine's personal jester, on special loan for the event.

"On top of all that," Robert told his family, "we're stuck with half a dozen useless sightseeing princes tagging along. They're all hoping to see Prince Reginald fail, and they want to be right there to impress the Princess if he does. Worse than that, two or three will probably sneak off to try and bag a *rakai* on their own. And there's not a thing I can do about it. They're princes; they wouldn't listen to me even if I could make them sit still for the lecture. I'm sorry, Mother, I know how you feel, but royalty doesn't wear that well when you get close."

"I don't care," Patience declared. "I wish *I* could go!" Her sister Rosamonde chimed in, "I want to see a big dragon too! Everybody else is going, why can't we?"

Robert's quiet voice silenced both girls. "*Rakais* aren't like our Adelise, our Lux, our Reynald. They aren't charming, and they aren't friendly at all. And while it's likely that a *rakai* will take a cow or a goat over a little girl, were the two standing side by side, they'd choose the little girl if she was one step closer. They like to eat people, Rosamonde. Very much."

"Is the Princess coming along?" That was Caralos, the older of Robert's two brothers, who had always shared more than a touch of Odelette's veneration for the nobility. One morning Princess Cerise's entourage had ridden past a field he was working, and he had been addled for a week. Robert smiled at him, wryly but with affection.

"She's in charge, more or less. But don't worry, no dragon's going to get her"—this to Patience and Rosamonde, recognizing the anxious looks on the two girls' faces—"because Prince

Reginald won't let them. He's the dragonslayer, and he's very brave, and very strong. So you needn't worry about the Princess."

In fact, however, Robert *did* worry about Princess Cerise, more than he was willing to admit to himself . . . which was probably for the best, since what he did accept was already much too unnerving. He worried about Prince Reginald too. Rather, he worried about the Prince's being worried, which Reginald could hide effectively from everyone else, perhaps, but not from Robert, not after so many training sessions. There was the thing that happened in his eyes whenever he actually said the word *dragon*, for example, not to mention the way he quizzed Robert about the sizes, habits, diets, and even the social customs of the various types and species, especially the sort he was about to hunt. Although the questions themselves remained offhand and unconcerned—"I mean, it would help if I knew a *few* things about the beggars before I start whacking at them. Useful things, best places to whack, and so forth. Don't you think?"—he gave extraordinary attention to Robert's answers, as if listening with his entire skin rather than his ears, even as he strained to make it appear that he didn't care at all.

More than once it occurred to Robert that he didn't understand the rules of being a prince. But he was determined to watch and learn, so that Mortmain would have no excuse to reconsider their bargain.

His own role in the expedition was officially a minor one, at least until they reached the mountains; but his professional expertise was much in demand during the planning and packing. Several times a day, messengers with questions from the Princess would find him wherever he was working, and he was on standing commission to come round the castle each evening to inspect and approve the day's preparations. Despite himself, he was beginning to enjoy these visits—for while there was never anything important to do, they made him feel like his new life in service had already begun.

And then there was the Princess Cerise.

More and more, the Princess was a confusion to Robert. Unlike Prince Reginald, or the King and Queen, who wore their royalty from the bones on out, to Robert's eye the Princess seemed too constantly busy to bother being aware of her position. She was everywhere: forever reorganizing the line of march, checking supplies against manifests, going over recipes with the cooks, making sure that tents were weatherproofed, even taking it upon herself to make certain that all armor and armaments were in the best possible condition, down to the type and amount of polish to be employed. Prince Reginald's quest may indeed have been the official reason for the party, but there was no question whose party it was. There was something in this commitment that Robert recognized and respected—an entirely new feeling for him where anything royal was concerned. It was one thing to want to work for them, if it got him where he wished to go. But this was perilously close to thinking of one of them as a *person*, just like himself or his friends or his family, and that would never do.

King Antoine and Queen Hélène saw the expedition off, the King in stoic sniffles, the Queen waving her scarf emphatically, blowing kisses to her daughter and Prince Reginald alike. To Robert—what with the musicians striking up all together, King Antoine's jester tumbling in the lead, dogs and children scampering and yelping in the parade's wake—the whole affair seemed much more like a wedding procession or a grand festival pageant than anything to do with fire and blood and dragons. Princess Cerise rode proudly ahead, stirrup to stirrup with Prince Reginald, who kept looking over his shoulder toward Mortmain and Robert riding with the servants and supplies, barely visible through the dust clouds raised by the leaders. Mortmain smiled and waved, in a tidy manner, encouraging his master; but Robert shrank back further, trusting to the dust to shelter him from Odelette's loving gaze. *She's out there somewhere*, he thought, *thrilled to see her gallant son in such company. But if she knew what I was really doing here, or what I was buying with the deed, would she be so proud and happy? Not likely*.

Within a few hours, after most of the assorted hangers-on had fallen away, things began to look almost disciplined. The Princess Cerise, a fine rider, set a pace that was steady, but not unduly grueling; the supply wagons held close together at the rear; and all in between bore up handsomely, even singing spirited catches and come-all-ye's from time to time. Robert did his best to shake off his sour mood but could not bring himself to join in with the general gaiety: his knowledge of what lay ahead rendered it shallow and absurd.

Mortmain was still riding next to him. He turned in his saddle to face the valet and said, "This crowd is going to make matters more difficult."

"Not at all, Master Thrax. A minor complication, no more, easily finessed."

"So *you* say."

"And so it shall be. Indeed, I see more than one way to turn it to our favor. Meanwhile, I suggest you sing along with everyone else, as the Prince is doing. Quite egalitarian, that's one thing about him."

Robert made a face. "Easy to sing in the sun, early on the first day's ride. Let's see how this merry band sounds when we're nearer the mountains."

And so indeed they did see. On the second day all novelty had paled for the procession, and random bursts of song and merriment were replaced with the quieter pleasures of tasting the air, enjoying the sunshine, and gossiping about anyone currently out of earshot. They passed through three villages before nightfall: each march-past bringing with it an echo of the previous day's festive sentiments, which by the third promenade was beginning to feel rather forced. On the next day the weather turned cold and overcast, and the horses grew fractious, fighting saddle, bridle, and burden as they had not done since they were bruised and unruly colts. The only village they encountered, early into the first foothills, had been dourly suspicious, not friendly, its inhabitants as narrow and stony as the few arable strips of land they farmed. The jester had worked overtime to jolly them along, but no one had smiled except for one small boy, who was promptly whisked inside by his mother before he could laugh.

And on the morning of the fourth day, before anyone was awake to face the thin drizzle that had begun while they all slept, *Robert dreamed . . .*

This was not The Dream, but a dark mirror of it. He stood in a clearing filled with white bones and black ash, screaming defiance at something he could not see. But his voice was not his voice, and when he reached out to seize the man who opposed him—it was a man, somehow he knew it was a man—he saw that his arms were not arms at all, but vast ebon wings.

The dream faded as he dressed, leaving behind nothing but the twinned certainties that something was wrong, and that he was not equipped to face it.

Prince Reginald was waiting outside Robert's tent, boots soaked, mist drops glistening in the tangle of his hair. Somehow even that dishevelment contrived to look elegant on him, as if he were growing his own net of jewels.

The Prince was nervous and unhappy. "It took me five minutes to calm my horse enough to saddle him," he complained, "and after that it was everything I could do to get him over the next ridge. Is this it? Are they close?"

Robert sniffed at the wet air.

"Nothing has changed since we made camp last night. This is old scent, freshened by the rain, that's all. You can rest easy, Prince Reginald. We're a day or more yet from where *rakais* are usually found, this time of the year. Still . . ."

"Still *what*?" The Prince's voice squeaked on the question, ever so slightly, surprising both of them.

Robert answered in the flat, knowing voice that he used with his most nervous clients. "Dragons are animals like us, Prince, and no more individually predictable than we are. But each species has its own patterns of behavior, within whose bounds they commonly stay. This scent is stronger than I'd expect, even allowing for the rain. It means there have been *rakais* here—more than one—later in the season than usual. I can only assume that something ahead has disturbed their normal patterns. It would be wise to proceed with caution."

"How I let Mortmain talk me into this . . ." Prince Reginald set his mouth firmly. "Very well, then. Caution it is. From this point on, you will ride with me in the front."

◆ ◆ ◆ ◆

The company gained height that day, moving from the lower to the upper foothills, but mud slowed their forward progress. They stopped again for the night having made only half the distance intended, and grateful for even that much. The village planned as their final stop before reaching the old forests of the central range would have to wait until the following morning.

Nothing startling had happened—unless the priest losing one of his best boots to a sucking mud pit qualified—but a growing tension possessed them all nonetheless, and the conversation around the evening's campfires rang with false laughter and more than a few harshly spoken words.

At least the rain had stopped.

Robert chose to keep to himself, having found the day more difficult than expected. He had felt out of place and out of sorts the entire time he spent in Reginald's and Cerise's company, and answered their occasional questions as tersely as possible. Flashes of his dream had stayed with him throughout the ride, flickering in his awareness like a smoke scent on the breeze, and all along the muddy road he saw odd and troubling bits of evidence that made no proper sense.

Now he rolled over, lying awake in his blanket, thinking furiously. A little way from him, Mortmain slept deeply and placidly; but when Robert closed his own eyes, he saw great angled green ones, crystal-cut eyes large as both his fists, with green fires behind them that rose up until they swallowed the sky.

When he could see nothing else, even with his eyes open, he wrapped his father's old cloak—redolent of dragons, like this night itself—around his shoulders, and walked through the silent camp, pacing the perimeter. He roused drowsy sentinels, checked his sword and spear where they were stowed, and spent an hour talking softly under the stars to the increasingly nervous horses. Then he strayed a little way into the darkness and lay down to press his cheek hard against a patch of moist but solid earth that had been sheltered from the worst of the rain by overhanging stones. He cast his other senses away from him, focusing on his ears alone, and listened as intently as though to a woman's heartbeat.

The Princess Cerise very nearly tripped over him.

"What are you doing?" she demanded, springing back. "Who are you?" She recognized Robert when he stood up, and quickly sheathed the dirk that had leaped into her hand. "Oh, it's you. Why aren't you sleeping?"

"For the same reason you're not, Your Highness," Robert answered her. "Trying to keep this parade safe, for as long as I can."

The Princess tossed her head indignantly. "But that is *my* task. And Prince Reginald's."

"It's everyone's job, but not everyone is doing it." As they studied each other in silence, a long, resonant snore came from the tent where Prince Reginald slept. The Princess said, somewhat defensively, "He has had a very long, hard day."

Robert did not reply.

"Well, he did," Cerise said. "And he'll need to be rested tomorrow." She paused. "You were listening for dragons, weren't you?"

"You can feel the big ones sometimes, walking on the earth. If they're big enough and close enough."

"And these? Answer me." It was somewhere between a command and a plea.

Robert looked away, searching the empty night. Even from this relatively low vantage you could see a great distance, once your eyes had adjusted to the starlight. "I don't hear anything," he said quietly. "Not a blessed thing. I wish I did."

"But that's . . . that's a good thing, isn't it? Not to hear them?" She already knew it must not be, and Robert knew she knew. He did not reply, and they looked steadily at each other without speaking, until the Princess finally said, "Tell me why it's bad. Please."

She had a right to know, and he debated his response only briefly. He said, "This is their country; with a scent this strong, *rakai* should be as thick on the ground as pignuts. I *should* be able to hear their movements. Yet except for the scent, all the signs are months old—no fresh tracks or droppings, no unweathered scorch marks or claw marks on the trees . . . it worries me. I don't mean to frighten you—"

"You are," she said. Her voice was surprisingly even, if her eyes were anxious. "Could something have driven them away? Or . . . or . . . ?"

She did not finish. Robert said, "*Rakai* aren't like the little dragonlets I forced out of your castle walls, Princess. I've never met anything that could drive a *rakai* away . . . and that's not what happened here. Only one explanation satisfies both scent and silence: the *rakai* we seek are dead. Every one, dead for months. Whatever killed them soaked the ground for miles with their blood, and left nothing else behind."

"Oh," said Princess Cerise softly. She lowered her head, and actually scuffed one dainty boot-toe on the ground, like an abashed child. Then she raised her face to his, tossing her hair back, and looked straight into Robert's eyes. "Well," she said, her voice steady and calm as she answered. "Whatever they are or aren't, they've never met *us*, either. What do you think we should do?"

"That's for you and Prince Reginald to decide. You're the leaders." There was no mockery in Robert's voice; merely Elpidus Thrax's old caution about nobility, recited sternly to his prentice son: *do your job, tell them what they want to hear, and get out*. But Princess Cerise took his tone as derisory, and her own voice turned cold and royal.

"So we are. And I asked for your opinion."

"Then," Robert said, "I would send everyone home—*now*, this minute, wake them all—everyone except Prince Reginald and me. And Mortmain, I suppose. That's what I'd do, since you ask."

The Princess stared. "And you and he . . . you imagine that the two of you could slay this unknown danger by yourselves?"

"I don't know. But if not, then at worst only three people would die, instead of almost a hundred. If you start getting this whole carnival pointed toward home right away." He was standing close enough to see her expression go from defiant to stricken, and back again. On an impulse to make her laugh, he added, "Don't forget, we'd have Mortmain with us. He wouldn't *dare* let anything happen to Prince Reginald."

Princess Cerise did not laugh. She simply said, "No."

Anger enfolded Robert, enveloping him in sudden flame, as it never had done in his life. "That's very foolish of you, Your Highness." The anger blazed higher, frightening him, but he plunged on. "No, that's more than foolish—it's stupid. *Stupid!*"

The royalty of Bellemontagne was, by tradition, far less autocratic than many of its neighbors—Corvinia prominent among them. Even so, Princess Cerise would have been well within her historic rights to order Robert arrested and imprisoned for addressing her as he had. But she said only, "Lower your voice. People are sleeping."

Robert opened his mouth to continue berating her decision, but she silenced him, surprisingly, by laying a finger on his lips. She said, "I will follow your advice, on one condition. Everyone else will turn around and go directly home, back to the castle, as you suggest. But I will stay here with Prince Reginald and you—and Mortmain, I suppose"—she smiled slightly, mimicking him—"and face this horror with you. If that is what it comes to." There was only a slight quaver in her voice on the last words. "Are we agreed, then?"

She took her hand away, and Robert burst out, "No, we certainly are not! How could you fight anything that could slaughter a *rakai*?"

"The same way you or anyone else would—with a sword and a lance." The Princess drew herself up proudly. "I have been taking lessons since I was six years old."

Robert could hear himself screaming inside, as in the dream, but he knew that letting it out would do no good. He took a deep breath instead. "I understand that you don't want to leave Prince Reginald to face danger without you. But if you're here, he'll be so distracted that at some point he'll take his eye off whatever this is, just for an instant, to make sure you're safe. It will happen, Princess, we both know that. And maybe he'll be lucky when he does, and maybe he won't be. But it *will* happen."

There was a moment—only seconds, perhaps—when Robert's gray eyes and Cerise's dark, dark ones sought each other's depths and, strangers still, they understood each other beyond words. Then, as though it had been scheduled and rehearsed, Prince Reginald turned in his sleep behind them and uttered a soft whimper. It was a curiously forlorn and vulnerable sound. Robert knew he had lost even before the Princess said, simply and shortly, "No. I stay." Then she walked away abruptly, vanishing into the blackness that still burned green, so very green, all around him.

ELEVEN

After breakfast (which the traveling kitchen staff deemed "not our best work" and spent nearly as much time apologizing for as serving), Robert privately shared his reservations with Mortmain, holding back only what he remembered of his dream and the fact that he had shouted at the Princess. On the subject of their very probable deaths, he wasn't vague at all.

The valet listened carefully but in the end was undeterred.

"Just as well she refused you," he said, his normally bland expression clouded. "Had you succeeded at turning this company around, my master would have used protecting the Princess as an excuse to return with them. That would have been—" He shuddered and did not finish the sentence. "I can hide a great deal from King Krije, in my reports, but I couldn't have hidden that. And between King Krije and a hundred mysterious dragon-killers, I'll take the mystery danger, thank you very much."

"I'm not making this up, Mortmain."

"Of course you aren't. But it could actually turn out better this way, don't you see? There's no reason our plan shouldn't work just as well against this . . . this *whatever-it-is*, as it would have against a *rakai*, assuming that concoction of yours is as effective as you promised. And if the Prince brings home the head of something truly new and unusual, something fierce beyond measure when unpoisoned, well—just think how much greater the acclaim! Show some faith in yourself, Master Thrax. I assure you that you have mine."

Robert made a sound somewhere between a sour grunt and a snort and wandered off to help see to the saddling of every horse and mule in the Princess's train. It had amazed him to learn that royalty and the servants of royalty knew so little about making a pack or a saddle actually *stay* on an animal's back over rough terrain. Five, ten, a dozen times a day, for this and other reasons he would find himself thinking wearily, *Oh, Mother, if you ever knew the truth*. But Odelette would arrange not to know, no matter what he told her. It was a quality of hers that he was gradually coming to admire, and even envy.

The weather got no better, and the road grew worse as it wound up and up into the mountain passes. There had been more rain, diminished now to a heavy mist, and mud splattered the gay trappings of man and mount alike. Creepers got tangled in the wheels of the provision wagons, and the massive roots that veined the pathway frequently forced the drivers to jump down—if they were not walking already, to lighten the load—and gang up to lift the wagons over the obstruction. The great dark-gray boulders intruding on either hand made it necessary to ride, first three abreast, then two; and by the time the pass widened and the procession emerged into a comparatively level and less precarious area, the line was laboring in slow single file, with many of the horsemen afoot—including, Robert noticed from his position just behind her, Princess Cerise. Prince Reginald offered several times to take her up before him, but she shook her head and kept walking, so by and by he got down from his own horse and walked beside her. Robert also noticed that she smiled and accepted the Prince's arm.

It was late in the afternoon when they rounded a sharp bend in the road and saw the village spread out ahead of them. Rather, they came to what most likely *had* been a village—they very nearly had to take the fact on faith. All the buildings seemed to have been torn apart, literally board by board, brick by brick, shingle and slate by shingle and slate. Not so much as a chimney or a baker's oven was left standing; anything that grew had been crushed flat. Here the road itself was seared and split, and there was nothing at all recognizable that had not been burned black, nor was there a living soul to be seen.

The entire expedition stood in silence as complete as the silence of the ruin. Then, as the immediate shock receded, and the impossible scene did not change, at least a dozen of the company dropped to their knees and began to pray in muffled whispers.

The Princess Cerise's voice sounded almost unhumanly clear—if a bit shaky—in the cold air. "Did dragons do this?" And suddenly everyone was looking at Robert.

He nodded without answering.

Prince Reginald said in a thick voice, "Must have been really *big* dragons . . . ?" Mortmain spoke not a word but moved close to his master, as though to prop him up if it became necessary. Robert still did not speak but began to walk ahead very slowly, gazing down intensely at the blasted, trampled ground. The Princess came after without questioning his precedence, and the company fell into silent order behind her. Robert never looked back.

He guided them through the scattered and tangled debris, raising a warning hand when the horses had to step over one of the all-too-fresh humps that no one wanted to look at closely, some of them dreadfully small. It was like picking their way through a nightmare, and soon enough even the quiet praying stopped.

When they reached the blackened fields on the far side of the devastated village, darker still for lying under the shadow of the mist-curtained mountains, he paused, turning to catch the Princess Cerise's eye. He nodded toward three ash heaps, rain-sodden now, but distinctly—even pointedly, by contrast with the mass of shapeless others—quite recognizable as having once been human. They appeared simply now like a small tattered pile of children's abandoned toys, outgrown and casually, thoughtlessly tossed aside. One of them—Cerise imagined that she must be the oldest, though she would never ever be sure—had her toothless mouth open in a silent withered wail.

Robert's own voice, when he spoke at last, sounded as hoarse as though he had not spoken aloud for a very long time. "These would have seen them first. And tried to warn . . ." He did not finish.

Prince Reginald spoke one word: "*Rakai?*"

"No, Your Highness." Robert shook his head. "Excuse me." Ignoring the Prince and everyone else in the party, he unstrapped an iron-tipped spear from the set hanging on the side of the lead wagon, then walked forward by himself, crossing the field toward the forest. He moved slowly, staring intently at the ground, stopping from time to time for no reason that anyone watching could discern. No one followed.

"We will go no farther today," Princess Cerise announced. "Nightfall is only a few hours away, and the forest will not offer us a better place to make camp." She began briskly directing the setting up of the tents and the traveling kitchen. Her face was without color, and her eyes altogether too large, but her tone was steady, and her orders were obeyed. Yet when she had a moment alone with Prince Reginald, she clung to his arm as though he were a raft, and she a castaway drifting far from shore. "I wish we had not taken this road," she told him. "By the Savior, I wish we had not taken it."

The Prince's own dearest wish was to be anywhere at all but where he was standing. Yet he found that he could not take a step: somehow his feet knew that if they moved even an inch, they might carry him pell-mell downslope and away, not stopping until these mountains were a faint gray bump on the horizon. As much to comfort himself as Cerise, he took shelter behind the surface self-assurance that was his mask, his habit, his principal stock in trade. "When we find the creatures that did this, we will deal with them."

"The people who lived here must have tried," the Princess answered sharply. "I hope we do better than they. Thrax—the dragon-boy—he doesn't think we will. You can tell."

"Ah . . . yes." Prince Reginald could indeed tell that from Robert's manner, and it alarmed him a good bit more than he had already been, which he had not thought possible. He wanted very much to get Robert alone for some sort of reassurance—and perhaps a fast lesson in dealing with the sort of dragon that wiped out entire villages—but he was royal and therefore was assumed to know these things from birth. *Gods*, he thought, *why was I born a prince? What bloody good has it ever done me?* His father's stern and unforgiving face rose in his memory, and for the very first time it seemed to him that there might actually be an answer to his own self-condemning questions. In such a moment as this, what indeed would King Krije do? Certainly not sit down in the mud like a Songhai baboon.

"We'll just have to prove Master Thrax wrong," he said, feigning a conviction he did not feel. "And in that proof do honor to your country. I suggest we begin by arming the company as best we can, down to the last pastry cook's apprentice, and then organize a watch. Fear cannot breed where there is action."

These were the right words, and he and the Princess set to with a will, but Cerise did not feel comforted. She felt guilty and alarmed. They were here now, all of them, because of her own stubborn decision, and she found herself urgently desirous of a way to take it back. The dragon-boy obviously knew nothing of correct comportment in the presence of a lady, let alone a princess, but he knew *dragons*, and looking around, she knew she had been wrong to place her pride above his knowledge. After the tasks at hand were complete, that failure would require correction. And if she were seen to be depending too firmly on the guidance of a peasant . . . well, so be it. There would be time to tend to appearances when this expedition was at an end, and the assembled company far away from this horrible place.

Each step carried Robert deeper into mystery. *Everything here is wrong*, he thought, unable to make sense of what he saw and smelled around him. His hands gripped the haft of his spear so tightly that his knuckles ached. For once he was glad of the weapon's ridiculous weight—the *Ostrya* ironwood, a hop hornbeam imported from the south, had cost Elpidus nearly a month's earnings, but there was nothing like it in Bellemontagne for merged strength and flexibility. Harder than oak, yet nearly supple as ash, strapped round with sintered iron in three places, and tipped with twin spikes ahead of a modified rondel. It was a device of many options, equally useful when thrust or spun or swung, any of which might be necessary depending on the dragon. Very practical.

He felt sick to his stomach, as he never had done. Tension coiled in all his muscles, a serpent to his soul. *Everything here is wrong,* he thought, prowling alone through the ruins of the devastated settlement, forced to face the limits of his understanding, as he had increasingly suspected he would be. Whatever dragons he was dealing with here, they were not any sort he had heard of, whether from his father or from anyone else.

Strangely, he found himself talking to Odelette in his mind. *Mother,* rakai *kill and eat, whether their victims are mountain goats or human beings—they breathe fire when they're roused or frightened, or sometimes during the mating season. But they don't destroy wantonly, they don't wipe out an entire village, not like this. I'm as ignorant, as far out of my depth as Reginald, the Princess, any of them. I don't know what I'm looking at, Mother, what I'm seeing. I* feel *something, yes—there's some part of me that knows something—but I don't know. . . .*

And why do I have this very odd sense that you *would?*

◆ ◆ ◆ ◆

By the time King Antoine's jester had long since tumbled home to Castle Bellemontagne, most of the court followers had stopped following, except for the six princes, who plodded on grimly, still determined to share in any romantic glory that might accrue to Prince Reginald. As for the musicians and the men-at-arms, they too were showing distinct signs of wear, but they marched ahead almost as briskly as ever, playing the Bellemontagne anthem, "Our Beautiful Bellemontagne," at least once an hour, as required by law. They were playing at sunset, also as required—King Antoine was *really* fond of that song—already entering the pleasant wood where the Princess had planned to make camp, when the first dragon struck.

The creature seemed to explode out of the ground before them, where it had been lying in wait in a deep trench scored across the shattered road. Vast and black, the green highlights on its scales glittering in the sunset, it reared over the terrified troupe with open jaws, from which issued no sound at all. Robert had covered his ears against the expected earthshaking bellow; but absolute silence from that blazing red gullet was more chilling than any roar would have been. The dragon spread great midnight wings, fanning them fiercely enough to blow the helmets off most of the men-at-arms, but it did not leap into the air to attack. Instead, it simply charged.

Robert had dealt with fire-breathers before—some of the common house-dragons could give you a painful singe when cornered, along with a mildly venomous nip. But diving for cover as a white-hot flame sizzled between his hair and his hat . . . this was terror, this was bowel and bladder and legs all turning to water together, this was abandoning all concern for any other person in the world. This was the moment when Gaius Aurelius

Constantine Heliogabalus Thrax, eighteen years old, realized that he really was going to die.

If the dragons—two others were converging from left and right—made no sound, the horses made up the lack. Screaming like the wind, they threw their riders and bolted, falling on the torn ground, scrambling to their feet and blundering in every direction, most often to fall again. The column panicked in the same way, some lying where they had fallen—stunned or worse—while others fled in such desperate madness that many headed directly toward the dragons. Robert saw the result of that. Ever afterward, for the rest of his life.

It was the horses that saved them. The dragons were plainly diverted and excited by the smells and cries of the frantic beasts, and more often than not passed over human targets in favor of horseflesh, roasted or raw. The scarlet dragon—the third was as greenish-black as the first—seemed to be laughing, the flames lapping out of its mouth like a playful dog's tongue. That one preferred humans, and took its time in the savoring.

Cautiously rising onto his knees, Robert looked dazedly around for the Princess Cerise, whom he had last seen only moments—ages—ago, still riding in the lead, her horse the first to run mad at sight of the dragons. He finally discovered her, sprawled unconscious in a black-blistered clump of weeds at the side of the road. Prince Reginald was nowhere to be seen. Robert crawled toward her, almost on his belly, praying not to attract the dragons' attention.

Everywhere around him, men staggered, wailing and crying, easy prey for white fire and red fangs. One of the men-at-arms fell directly in his path, burned almost transparent, his skin melted to his mail shirt. Robert crawled around him. Off to his left, a man-shaped cinder lay curled into a fetal position, recognizable as a musician only by the horn clutched in his two hands, as though he had brandished it against the dragon that killed him. Robert crawled on.

By the time he reached the Princess Cerise, she was trying to sit up. Robert pushed her back down unceremoniously and threw himself on top of her, shouting into her ear, "Keep low! Stay low and follow me!" An insane impulse to kiss her ear came over him, but he resisted it. "Follow me! Do as I do!"

He was starting to lead the Princess away on hands and knees, when she croaked out of her raw throat, "Reginald . . . where Reginald . . . ?"

The slight twinge—very slight, surely—somewhere south of Robert's lungs annoyed him, even in the midst of massacre. He said only, "We'll find him. Stay low and keep moving."

They found Prince Reginald and Mortmain together, as might have been expected. The Prince was berating his servant with as much energy as though his splendid mustache and half his hair hadn't been burned off his head. "One dragon! You promised—'guaranteed' was the word, I seem to remember. And what do I find myself facing? Three! Count them—*three* dragons, and every one of them breathing fire. Mortmain, the moment we are safely out and clear of this nightmare, you are dismissed from my service. With *no* reference!"

"Yes, sire," Mortmain replied meekly. "I don't blame you at all, sire, not at all, I certainly don't. But meanwhile—"

"Meanwhile, *down! Down!*" Robert's voice was a cracking hiss, and his arms somehow managed to encircle three backs and slam three people flat on their faces. "Don't look up—shut your eyes! The red one's coming straight for us! *Shut your eyes!*"

But he could not help keeping his own eyes open, as though some dreadful enchantment were compelling him to watch the scarlet horror stalking toward them over the charred forms of the men he had been riding and singing with for five days. The dragon, still displaying a curiously sportive air, paused now and then to nibble almost daintily at a body, or merely to toss one high in the air and catch it on its flaming tongue—or not, as it chose—on the way down. Robert turned his head and threw up in the splintery grass.

Then a thing happened.

It happened, not so much to him as *through* him and over him, and all around him. The anger that had terrified him when the Princess Cerise refused to go back home with the Castle Bellemontagne crew—*oh, gods, how many are left alive?*—caught him up again, embracing him more fiercely than before, itself consuming as dragonfire. He stood up, wiping his mouth on his sleeve, so that the scarlet dragon could see him, and felt the fury inside him calling out to it, challenging, commanding. There were no words, no more sound than the dragon itself made.

And there was suddenly no room for fear.

The scarlet dragon sat back on its haunches—which is a comfortable enough position for a small dragon, but not at all for a really large one—and cocked its head to one side. Somewhere very far away, Robert thought, *Oh, Adelise does that when she's trying to figure out where Patience is hiding from her.* He began walking toward the dragon.

Behind him, he heard the Princess call out, but he neither halted nor looked back. He felt his right arm come up of its own volition—he watched it with vague curiosity—and sweep in a half circle, pointing not only to the scarlet dragon but to the other pair, grazing among the bodies now like cows or deer. And if he remained silent still, the rage that roared up his arm echoed and pounded in his blood until he heard nothing else. The scarlet dragon took a step backward.

Robert had no idea, then or ever, what he wanted from the three dragons. He could never recall anything like a direct order; only an inchoate desire for them to *go away*, to go away and leave him and his companions with their dead. He would have said it in words, but there were no words left in the world just then, so he threw back his head and ran his own tongue out, to make them *know*. He tasted the bloody wind, and he tasted fire, and he licked the fiery wind, to make them *know*.

But what followed was nothing he could have imagined, even if there had been words to set around it. The two black dragons turned from their feeding, shook their heads sluggishly, as though they had just awakened from a long sleep, and began to breathe fire at each other. Wings flared out to their fullest, they charged together like warhorses, snapping viciously at necks and chests and bellies already seared to a crackling blackness that did not glitter at all in the last of the sunset. The scarlet dragon almost danced to the fight, ripping chunks of flesh by turns from the great bodies that could not be bothered to respond to its assault. And through all of this, adding to the sense of endless nightmare, there was still silence.

Robert came to himself then, suddenly as cold as though he were naked in the wind, watching the dragons tearing each other to pieces a long way off. He turned and stumbled back to the Princess, Mortmain, and Prince Reginald, falling down beside them, mouth agape, desperately thirsty. The Prince was first to recognize Robert's need and carefully dribble what water remained in his canteen between his lips. He was also the first to croak, dry-mouthed himself, "Saved us . . . you saved us. *Saved* us, the dragon-boy . . ."

"What happened?" Mortmain asked in bewilderment. "What did you do?"

Princess Cerise was on her feet, staring around her at the burned, trampled, blood-dark earth. She said very quietly, "I killed them."

Robert shook his head weakly, but did not speak. He thought he might never speak again.

"I killed them," the Princess repeated. "If I had listened." She turned to look at Robert, but he looked away, unable to bear the pain in her eyes. Prince Reginald put his arms awkwardly around her, but she stood stiffly, without responding. She said, "I cannot go home. How can I ever go home?"

Robert did face her then, and found his voice at last. He pointed beyond her, to the handful of men-at-arms, musicians, a few servants, one doctor and three princes: some on their feet, some struggling to rise, others twitching and whimpering where they lay. He said, "Because *they* have to. We will bury the others in the morning, but these must come home."

"I will dig graves," Prince Reginald said. "I am good for that, at least." He did not look comical half-bald, but sad and shamed.

The scarlet dragon and one of the black dragons were already dead; the third—red itself now, except for the wings—perched on their bodies for a triumphant moment, before toppling over on its side. Mortmain said, "Your father would have been proud today, my lord."

Prince Reginald said, "Another word about my father,

Mortmain. One word." He said nothing more, but he had never spoken in that tone before, and Mortmain moved slightly away from him.

But the Princess Cerise sat down on the ground and put her beautiful face in her hands.

TWELVE

It took them two days to bury their dead. They were too few, and the corpses too many, and not all of the survivors were in any condition to dig graves. The remaining doctor ministered to those as best he could, and the priest lived long enough to bless the wooden markers the Princess Cerise herself drove into the hard soil with bleeding hands. Prince Reginald wanted to do it but was silently refused. When it was done, they started home.

The Princess never once spoke during the return journey. She still rode at the head of the pitiably shrunken procession, but she kept her eyes on the ground, and her body slumped in the saddle, all pride and royal dignity gone out of it. Robert continued to ride at the rear of the party—though the distance between them was sorrowfully shorter than before—keeping constant watch to make certain that no vengeful dragons were following from that wood of slaughter. But even from behind, he always knew when the Princess was weeping again.

They avoided the last, dragon-ravaged village by silent consent, but whenever they passed through a town of any size, the inhabitants poured out to offer welcome. Word of the near annihilation of the company had somehow run before them, and shocked and decimated as they were, many of them—though not the Princess Cerise—managed a wrenching smile or a feeble wave. The throngs were usually composed primarily of women and children, the men being mostly at work in the fields. But Robert took particular notice in one village of a tall old man leaning on a knotty staff, who seemed to be staring angrily at Prince Reginald as he passed. It was a plainly personal anger, directed at one specific individual, and Robert recognized it—or thought he did—in every town or settlement farther on. He told himself that he must be mistaken, that there was no possible way for so old a man to be keeping pace with them, but the visions troubled him all the same.

It was only when they were nearing Bellemontagne that he thought to ask Mortmain, riding beside him, "I suppose this is a bad time to speak of my becoming a valet?"

"Actually, it would be the most logical time in the world," Mortmain responded. "In fact, I was about to bring it up myself."

"You were?" Robert had come to like Mortmain well enough over what now seemed a lifetime since their first meeting in the Great Hall, but trusting him was another matter.

Mortmain's first allegiance was to his own smooth, sallow skin; his second to King Krije by way of Prince Reginald. Robert suspected that he himself came rather further down the list of loyalties, but that no longer seemed to matter much. He said, "When should we begin my instruction?"

"Well," Mortmain said. "That depends, somewhat." Robert

looked at him. Mortmain continued, "You saved our lives. Prince Reginald was the first to acknowledge that. The very first, as I'm sure you remember."

Robert shrugged. "I suppose I did. I don't really know how it happened."

"Exactly. The dragons might simply have fallen on each other out of hunger, or stupidity, or . . . who knows why such creatures do what they do?" Mortmain lifted a finger, his eyes widening slightly, as though at a sudden new realization. "Or conceivably they were frightened to madness by the sight of a fearless, menacing hero such as Prince Reginald. That's possible, don't you think?"

Robert's expression did not change. He said, "I don't recall Prince Reginald being anywhere in sight until the Princess and I found him with you." He paused, holding Mortmain's gaze with his own, feeling very much older than he had only a week before. "We were all mad with terror when the dragons attacked, every one of us. I think the Prince ran straight to you for shelter, and no blame to him if he did. Tell me if I am wrong."

Mortmain opened his mouth to answer, but Robert never learned what he might have said. A dull, toneless voice on his left said, "You are not wrong," and he turned to see Prince Reginald beside him, riding one of the supply-wagon horses. His own had been literally burned out from under him with the first charge of the first dragon.

"I ran away," he said. "I threw away my weapons, and I ran blindly, trying to find Mortmain, weeping like a child who has bruised his knee. And now he is going to ask you to let me take the credit for destroying the dragons, so that I can go home to my father a hero. That was always the plan, didn't you know that? How else would I ever have dared to go anywhere *near* a dragon hunt?" He leaned toward Robert and gripped his arm with surprising force. "But don't you do it, don't you listen to him! I don't care what my father thinks of me—I know what *I* think, and that's bad enough. You're the one, you faced the fire and . . . and the screaming and the horses, and the . . . the awfulness—you're the one, nobody else." He jerked his head forward. "You're the one who should have been riding with the Princess from the beginning—and she knows it, too. Don't let Mortmain make me the hero, I don't want it! I don't want it!" He swung the lumbering horse away to the far side of the trudging line, dropping back to ride alone.

"He's upset," Mortmain said. "He's been under quite a strain." Neither he nor Robert spoke for a time after that.

"Very well," Robert said finally. "I agree to your plan. Prince Reginald can be the dragonslayer—tell any story you like to the King and Queen, I don't care. I'd forget all of it this minute, if I could. Give him the credit, as loudly and publicly as you wish, but while he is being celebrated, while the festivities are going on—and the mourning—and they should last for some while, you will be teaching me to be a prince's valet. Are we agreed?" His voice was very tired.

Mortmain nodded in some surprise. "We are. In the time we have together, I will instruct you in every aspect of the personal servant's art. And it is an art, I assure you."

"Every aspect," Robert repeated. "Once I merely dreamed of traveling with a prince or a duke, seeing other lands, other peoples, everything that isn't Bellemontagne, just as such a man would see it all. Now . . . now I want to learn, not just what you do, but what you are. How to flatter, how to praise, how to make someone do what you desire while he thinks it's his own idea—how you put your own words into his mouth, how you dress and school and advise and *shape* a great lord all as you choose, all to your will. Clearly, this is what a humble exterminator needs to know, if he is ever to rise in the world. Do you understand what I am seeking, Mortmain?"

"I understand," Mortmain said. "I will teach you."

Robert laughed softly and sadly. "Odelette—my mother—she always tells me that the goddess Vardis put the soul of a hero into me at my birth. But she doesn't know very much about heroes, and maybe Vardis doesn't either."

"Never laugh in the presence of your master." Mortmain's own voice had abruptly become clipped and severe. "They always think you might be laughing at them, underneath. And never say troubling things involving souls and goddesses. Your constant aim must be to keep them happy and simple, so you must constantly tell them simple, happy things." He smiled his dark, dry smile at Robert. "Here endeth the first lesson."

Home with his family, all crowded into the kitchen along with Ostvald and Elfrieda, Robert was lovingly compelled to relive the dragonquest and the slaughter in the pleasant wood over and over, as Rosamonde asked him to describe the three dragons again, so she could squeal and shiver deliciously, or Hector requested particulars about the Princess Cerise's behavior in the face of terrible danger. Ostvald wanted every detail concerning weapons and armament, as useless as they had all turned out to be; while Elfrieda simply looked on worshipfully. For her part, Odelette was only interested in how well he had eaten and slept on the journey, in the relationships he had formed with his noble companions, and in what he had felt when he began walking toward the dragons, alone and unarmed. When he described the moment to her, as best he could, she clapped her hands, very nearly dancing with rapture. "I *knew*! I *knew* the gods would answer my prayers!"

"Mother," Robert said firmly, "if your idea of a hero's soul is something inside that makes a person do something completely daft, completely suicidal, all the while wetting himself with fear and barely able to stand up—"

"Yes!" Odelette interrupted him. "That is *exactly* what I mean, but it's not what I'm talking about. You were afraid of the dragons, of course you were—we didn't raise any idiots, your father and I. But there was something *else*, too, something *else*. . . . Wasn't there?"

She stood close to him, looking intensely up into his face, as his brothers and sisters watched in puzzlement. Robert said, "I was . . . angry. They were killing everybody, burning them, devouring them. I was very angry."

"Yes," his mother whispered. "I thought so." Robert could barely hear her. She turned away for a moment, crossing and uncrossing her arms at the wrist three times in a gesture he had never before seen her make. When she turned back to him, she was smiling, but her face was pale and her eyes were glittering with tears. She said softly, "*Dragonheart*." Robert stared.

Odelette said, "Vardis did not merely give you a hero's soul. She gave you the heart of a dragon. I have heard about such things—my own mother used to tell me—but I thought . . . I thought it was just a story." She clasped her hands tightly in front of her. "*Dragonheart*."

Looking around him, Robert realized that his listeners had each unconsciously moved a step or two away—all but Elfrieda, whose eyes were shining like his mother's. It alarmed and irritated him at the same time, and he said, "No. *No*. I never believed that story about a hero's soul, and I don't believe this one for a minute. I'm *me*, and I've got *my* soul and *my* heart, along with my liver, my kidneys, my teeth, my flat feet—"

"Your poor father's feet," Odelette said fondly. "He did suffer so from those feet—"

"My feet. And my very own intense desire not to be a hero, not to be a dragonslayer—"

"Of course not! You couldn't be, not the way you feel for them." She pointed past him, and Robert noticed for the first time that the dragonlets—even the nameless white one—were in the kitchen, perched variously on chairbacks, shelves, and shoulders, plainly listening intently. Odelette said, "You talk to these little ones, and they hear you." Robert remembered Mortmain saying the same thing in Dragon Market. His mother went on, "You *felt* those big wicked ones—I told you, they couldn't be the Kings—and what they felt you turned against them, so that they turned against each other. Only someone who shared a dragon's heart, a dragon's very being, could have done that. Only a dragonmaster. Only my son."

In the silence Robert heard a murmured, reverent "*Yes*," and knew the voice for Elfrieda's. He shook his head to clear it, and his eyes met those of Adelise, her scaly neck stretched forward to its fullest extent, her sea-green eyes aglow with awareness. They held his as he struggled to answer Odelette. "I'm just me. I'm a human being who wants to be a prince's valet. That's all."

"A prince's valet?" Odelette laughed scornfully at what had

been her fondest dream a week before. "When Prince Reginald knows what you are, he'll beg to be *your* valet, I promise you—"

"No! You tell him nothing—you tell nobody *anything*!" Robert looked around at the others, all gaping in bewilderment. He said slowly, "I thought I understood dragons. I don't. I don't want to. I've seen them too close, and I don't want their hearts or their spirits, or anything of theirs, inside me. No more. Never." He patted his mother's hand absently and put her gently aside. "Now, if you'll all excuse me, I've got a lesson to go to. Ostvald, we have to be at the Gerhards' dairy tomorrow early—they've found a clutch of wyvern eggs near hatching, and the mother's footprints near the barn. Meet me at the crossroads at eight o'clock."

He walked out of the kitchen then, and out of the house, without looking back. Odelette called after him, "There is no choice for you, my son. You cannot return a goddess's gift," but Robert never turned. In the silence, his sister Patience began to cry. Several of the dragonlets went to her—Adelise even touched her face, to make the tears stop, but Patience continued to weep.

"They *want* to be told what to do. That's the most important thing to remember about them."

"Princes? Dukes? The great lords?"

"All of them. Deep down, they *know* they're fools—they *know* they don't know what they're doing when they order men into battle, when they make policies and draw up treaties, when they decide to marry this one, promote that one, throw the other one into a dungeon. They love to be told what to wear, what foods will make them fat, what dances are currently fashionable at what court—even when to go to bed, if you'll believe me. Discipline, system, consistency—there you have it all in a nutshell. And I think that will do very well for your second lesson."

They were in the stables, where Mortmain had been showing Robert how to fold cloth shirts and polish iron ones for Prince Reginald, as well as the tricks involved in cleaning muddy boots. The Prince himself was brooding in the hayloft overhead, where he had lately taken to spending most of his time, even though it made him sneeze. Robert said, "You speak of them as though they were children."

"And so they are—large children, yes, who can be dangerous, if not properly controlled. It's what they want, it's a great relief to them after a day of playing grown-up. No, you've left a spot, right *there*, over the instep. They do love their boots so, lords do." Mortmain put a neatly folded shirt carefully down on a feed barrel and turned to study Robert out of his strange yellow-brown eyes. "You're not ever going to be a valet, you know."

"Yes, I am." Surprised by the remark, Robert was indignant. "You can't say that, after just two lessons."

"I wouldn't have before certain recent events occurred. Then, you might actually have managed it, as badly as you wanted to transform your life. Now . . ." Mortmain shook his head. "Now you want something altogether else, and we both know it. It doesn't matter how many lessons I give you, it'll just be a skill. You won't be a valet—you'll be a man who knows how to be a valet. Useful, doubtless, but . . . different."

Robert met his eyes for a moment without replying, then

bowed his head. Mortmain said, "Look on the bright side, boy. Princesses hardly ever marry valets."

Robert's head came up so fast Mortmain actually heard the crackle of his vertebrae. "What are you talking about? Princess Cerise is going to marry Prince Reginald—everyone knows *that*!"

"Maybe not," Mortmain said. "Maybe not everybody."

They regarded each other in silence, though Mortmain's left eyebrow kept flicking quizzically. Robert said at last, "It's right. She *should* marry him. He's . . . well, he's a prince and a hero."

Mortmain's mouth twitched like his eyebrow. "He'd really rather not be a prince, just between ourselves. He's not good at it, and it only embarrasses him. As for his heroism, the King and Queen may swallow that, but the Princess knows . . . what she knows. And soon everyone else will—except perhaps you yourself." He chuckled, so dryly and softly that Robert barely heard the sound. "Perhaps you really are a hero, after all, born a favorite of the gods. You're certainly thick enough."

Robert did not bother to take the time to feel insulted. He said, suddenly and sharply, "The old man." Mortmain blinked. Robert said, "Coming home . . . the towns we passed through. You saw him—didn't you?"

The valet frowned thoughtfully. "An old man. The same old man, all the time?" Robert nodded. "I wasn't in the best possible shape to recognize anyone, you understand . . . but I do recall—*yes!* Yes, I . . . tall, was he? Long hair, a bit like yours, only white, yes. Leaning on a staff, didn't look happy—very odd. If I could travel from place to place as swiftly as he seems to, *I'd* be happy."

The strange eyes probed Robert's eyes more deeply than usual. "You think he's some sort of wizard, don't you?"

Robert shrugged and sighed. "I wouldn't know a real wizard

if I met one on the road. It's just that I started to wonder, seeing him everywhere, all the way back . . . maybe he had something to do with those dragons, some way." Mortmain looked utterly uncomprehending. Robert said, "The ones that attacked us—they weren't like any dragons I've ever heard of. My father taught me all the different kinds—he'd go over and over them with me, and he'd shout at me, or even whip me with his suspenders if I missed one species. He took his job very seriously, my father did."

Mortmain said, "*Suspenders?* How do you beat somebody with your suspenders?"

Robert went on. "I know dragons the way you know your alphabet, even the ones I've never seen in my life. They didn't fit any of my father's descriptions—they didn't match anything I've ever heard or read anywhere. Somebody . . ." He hesitated, never having put into spoken words what he needed to say aloud. "Somebody *bred* them."

THIRTEEN

ou don't have to wait with me," Ostvald said. "It's cold, you're shivering. You go on into town. I'll wait for Robert."

"He'll be here soon. I just wanted to say good morning, and see how he's . . . you know, doing." Elfrieda was indeed trembling with the early chill, her teeth chattering uncontrollably, and Ostvald wanted to wrap his heavy old leather coat around her shoulders, but he knew better. She looked around the crossroads—there were no other folk in sight, and only one fresh grave—and smiled, a little wistfully. "When you think of all the times we three have met here—since we were children. How long ago it all seems."

"We're all eighteen," Ostvald pointed out. "No, you're not even that—you're still seventeen. How long ago could anything be?"

"Oh, *you*," Elfrieda said, as she said to him so often. "You don't understand, you never do." She took a few impatient steps in the direction from which Robert would be coming. Ostvald turned away.

The hoofbeats coming from town startled them both, and they whirled to see Prince Reginald cantering toward them on a bay mare Ostvald knew from the castle stables. Reginald himself he hardly recognized at first: the splendid swaggerer had given way to a weary, sad-eyed man, disheveled in his dress and shockingly aged in his bearing. When he reined up to speak with them, they saw that his eyes were heavy and red-rimmed, as though he had not slept in days; when he spoke, his voice sagged like his shoulders. He said, "I have a message for your friend the dragon-boy. Will you carry it for me?"

Ostvald nodded silently—even despondent royalty made him uneasy—but Elfrieda answered eagerly, "Indeed, lord, that we will, on the instant you impart it." Her own reverence for crowned heads rivaled Odelette's; and besides, this was something involving Robert. She held out her hand for a scroll or a parchment.

"No, girl, there are only a few words to this. Tell him that I have gone to make a lie come true. Can you remember that?"

"Yes," Elfrieda whispered, overawed by his somber manner. The Prince clicked to his horse and started on, then turned back briefly to say, "You may tell the Princess Cerise the same, should you see her." He thumped his spurless bootheels into the horse's sides and was gone, leaving Ostvald and Elfrieda to gape after him: the one in bafflement, the other in speechless alarm.

The speechlessness lasted only until Robert appeared, a few moments later. She recounted the meeting and the message to him, her words stumbling over each other, while Ostvald shuffled from foot to foot, occasionally muttering, "We ought to get going, before those wyvern eggs hatch at the Gerhards'." Neither Robert nor Elfrieda heard him.

"I don't like this," Elfrieda was saying, as she had said it three times before. "I don't *like* this, Robert. Something bad's going to happen, isn't it?" She sounded like a frightened little girl.

Robert was standing by the cart, looking down one road and then down another, plainly caught between impossible choices. He looked at Ostvald, seemingly becoming aware of him for the first time since his arrival. "Ostvald, you're going to have to deal with the eggs by yourself. I'll be back as soon as I can."

Refusing an order of Robert's was as foreign to Ostvald as saying no to Elfrieda would have been. He said in a small voice, "How soon is that?"

"I don't know," Robert said. For the third time he asked Elfrieda, "He really said that? Like that? About making a lie come true?" She nodded miserably. Robert was looking around him with a distracted, unfocused air, speaking more to himself than to his friends. "I've got to borrow a horse. Who's got a horse?"

"Don't go," Elfrieda said. Ostvald, speaking louder, said simultaneously, "Walter's got a good one. Walter the brewer, not Walter at the tannery. Bought it at the fair last spring—it's a stallion, so it might give you some trouble, but it'll run all day."

Robert winced. "Walter hates me. I told Jarold he was using cheap hops and coloring his mash. He was, but still. He'll never let me borrow his horse."

Ostvald looked at his feet and mumbled, "I just said he had a horse. I didn't say you should *borrow* it."

Robert began to smile slowly. He thrust the cart's shafts into his old friend's hands. "Thank you, Ostvald. I won't be long, I promise."

He set off toward the village at a run, veering off toward the brewery while he was still in sight, but vanishing quickly beyond a clump of trees. Elfrieda looked fiercely at Ostvald and said, "Oh, *you!*" in a way she had never said it before.

The Princess Cerise caught up with Robert well before he even sighted Prince Reginald.

He turned at the sound of hoofbeats behind him and saw her pounding after him with her red cloak and her uncombed hair flying alike. He swore silently and reined up to wait for her.

She was shouting as she rode, but she was breathless by the time she reached him, and Robert was able to speak first. "Princess, this is mine to do. We both know that."

"We know nothing of the kind!" The Princess was flushed with indignation, and her nose was shiny. "Reginald has gone back where—where *it* happened, to prove himself worthy of me, and it is incredibly, incredibly stupid of him, and if anyone needs to go and fetch him before he gets eaten by dragons—"

"It's me," Robert interrupted her; and then, "Sorry—it's *I*," for Odelette was a stickler for proper grammar. He said, keeping his voice as calm and reasonable as he could, "Your Highness, I do not believe that the Prince is on another dragonquest, nor would he find any if he were. Unless I am greatly mistaken, he seeks an old man we both think may be a wizard, and who may have some connection with the dragons you and I still see in our dreams every night." He paused, watching the Princess's eyes and waiting until she nodded slightly before he went on. "I hope to bring him safely back to you, but if he will not come, for one reason or another—"

"Then he should not be alone. Yes, I understand." She was calmer now, even making a vague gesture at smoothing her hair. "We both know what he is, but he yet feels that he has to show me, the dear silly." There were sudden tears in the corners of her eyes, even as she forced a laugh.

"Yes," Robert said, after only an instant's hesitation. "Yes, of course."

"So you see why I must come with you. You do see how it is?"

"Yes. I do." Robert cleared his throat and picked up the reins. "We should go quickly, then. He cannot be that far ahead." As they set off, he added, "The King and Queen—won't they be anxious about you?"

"My father will be. My mother . . ." The Princess Cerise's dark eyes grew briefly warm with wistful affection. "Nobody ever thinks so, but my mother is *very* romantic."

"So is mine." They smiled at each other for a moment; then the Princess kicked her horse into a gallop and was off down the road, with Robert a length behind. Now and then she looked back at him, and when she did so, it was always with a curiously puzzled air, and once with a slight unconscious shake of the head. He wondered whether he was looking at her in the same way.

They did not catch up with Prince Reginald that day. The people in the village they arrived in at noon told them that a handsome rider had indeed been seen galloping through the town square an hour or more earlier, but had stopped for neither rest nor conversation. Robert and the Princess hastened on similarly but had no more success in the next hamlet, reached just before sunset. Yes, the Prince had passed through here as well, had stopped to eat, and to water and rest his horse and himself, but he had gone on long since. A nice-looking young man, but a bit preoccupied.

There was no going farther that night. Princess Cerise and Robert dined in the village's one inn, where she would spend the night while he slept in the stable, caring for their weary horses. Over dinner they spoke primarily of Prince Reginald—or at least the Princess did—as little of dragons as they could, and somewhat of the old man whom Robert's intuition told him the Prince was seeking. "He was in the hayloft—he must have heard me talking with Mortmain about the wizard. I mean, if that's what he was. The old man, not Reginald." It occurred dimly to Robert that his difficulties in speaking directly to the Princess were not lessening.

Princess Cerise leaned forward over her forgotten meal, staring at him. "And you think he really *was* a wizard?"

"Mortmain asked me that too." Robert slapped the table with the flat of his hand. "I told him what I'm telling you—I don't know, I don't have any idea. It was just the way he kept turning up, and kept staring at Prince Reginald each time. As though he were really angry with him—"

"Because he destroyed the dragons!" The Princess meant to hit the table as he had, but only destroyed her dessert. She hardly noticed, no more than she paid attention to the dry mud spattered on her riding dress, or the tangled hair falling across her eyes. "Well, actually, that was you—but he helped." Robert did not answer. "He was trying to help. Almost the same thing, really."

"The dragons killed each other," Robert said. "I don't know how it happened. I don't know if I had anything to do with it. Maybe it *was* Prince Reginald." They regarded each other in silence across the table. Robert said, "Maybe that old man thinks it was."

"The dragons." Princess Cerise's voice faltered, though her gaze did not. "You think a wizard made them? Bred them?"

"They shouldn't exist," Robert said flatly. "They don't make sense. They're bigger than the Kings—much too big to get off the ground—but those wings obviously work. The fire they breathe is white-hot, you saw that?" The Princess nodded. "No dragon in the world can brew that kind of flame in its body—or could live with it if it were possible. They're flesh and blood, whatever else they are. My father was always saying that."

"Your father," the Princess said thoughtfully. "I remember your father coming to the castle. A very tall man—or maybe he only seemed so because I was a child. *Was* he tall?"

"Yes, he was. Taller than I'll ever be." It was the first time they had spoken of any family but the Princess's—or of Robert's life at all, for that matter—and it put both of them somewhat off-balance, half smiling awkwardly. Robert said, "Another thing about dragons. They're smart. Nobody ever thinks so—they always think the big ones are just mean and stupid, and the little ones . . . well, those are just nasty little bugs—spray 'em, skin 'em, sell 'em, and be done. But they're smart, and they have *feelings*, and they—" He suddenly realized that he was half out of his seat and that his voice was loud and angry enough to have attracted attention from other diners across the taproom. Looking at the table, he mumbled, "Sorry . . . I'm sorry," and sat down fast.

The Princess said quietly, "You have feelings too. You care about them."

Robert still could not look at her. He said, "The ones we . . .

the ones who attacked us—they're *too* smart. When it comes to mealtime, it's pretty much every dragon for himself—they don't cooperate naturally." He thought of Adelise, Lux, Reynald, and the others making the beds at home and herding the chickens into their coop, and repeated, "Not naturally. But these . . . these waited in ambush for us, and then they came at us from three different angles, to make sure we couldn't escape. Even my father wouldn't have known what to make of that."

"You care about them." Princess Cerise rested her elbows on the table, her chin in her cupped hands, and regarded him out of the dark eyes that had no counterpart in her family. "You think about them."

"I'm an exterminator," Robert answered harshly. "I'm supposed to know about dragons." He tried to match the directness of her gaze, but failed.

"But you hate it. You really hate it. You hate your job."

"It's not forever. I'm not going to spend my life spraying walls and hunting nests and eggs. Mortmain's teaching me to be a valet."

He had thought that he wouldn't mention Mortmain's opinion of his body-servant potential, but he might as well have, for the Princess burst out laughing. "A valet? You couldn't . . . oh, you could never—"

Laughter kept her from finishing; laughter, and Robert's outrage. "Why not? Because I'm not good enough? Not smart enough? Not well-born enough? Not mannerly enough? Not *clean* enough? Would that be the problem?" His eyes were wide and white-rimmed.

The Princess met him head-on, shouting back across the table, "No, of course not! I wasn't saying that at all! You couldn't be a valet because you're better than that! For heaven's sake, don't you know"—she faltered momentarily—"don't you know you're a hero yourself? Just like Reginald, practically? Don't you have any idea?"

This time the landlord came over to the table, apologetic, because of the presence of Princess Cerise, but firm. They paid their score and left the taproom. Robert did not speak until they were standing at the foot of the stairs, about to separate for the night. Then he said quietly, "I don't want to be a hero. Heroes kill things. I want to be *ordinary*—never mind Vardis, never mind my mother. I just want to have an ordinary life."

"Well, you don't get to. No more than I do." The Princess's voice was no longer combative, but as subdued as his, and her face in that moment was beautiful in a completely different way than Robert had ever seen before. She said, "I've tried disguising myself, the way princesses do all the time in fairy tales. I'm good at it. I've dressed up like an old beggar lady—like a farmwife—like a street girl—all to get away from what I am for a day, for even a few minutes. It never works, no matter how I try—people always know. The same way they'll know what *you* are if you spend the rest of your life pretending to be somebody's valet. Take my word for this, Robert. I know."

It was the first time she had ever called him by his name. They regarded each other without speaking for what seemed to Robert a long time. Then he said, "We should start out early tomorrow. Very early," and the Princess Cerise said, "Yes," and went upstairs.

Robert watched her until she turned out of sight at the landing. Then he shoved his hands into his pockets and walked slowly toward the stables. There was no moon, and the warm night grew increasingly dark as he moved farther from the inn; by the time he heard the two horses nickering to welcome him, he could barely make out the groom asleep with his head on a grain barrel. Robert groped his way to their stalls, made sure that both were dry and warm with full mangers and new straw; then found an empty stall for himself, found a few armfuls of reasonably fresh hay, and was about to lie down when he heard the grass rustling just beyond the door. He saw nothing in the entranceway, but he heard the rustling, and he flattened himself against the stable wall, picked up a pitchfork leaning nearby, and waited, breathing as shallowly and silently as he could.

No one entered. The whisper in the grass continued, but what alarmed him more was the fact that the horses made no sound. They were sociable animals who enjoyed human company; either they were deeply asleep, or whatever was outside . . . He took the thought no further. After a time, growing impatient with immobility, he began to sidle along the wall until he was near enough to the door to make a sudden rush that took him out of the barn in one bound, to crouch and turn in every direction, jabbing at the night air with his pitchfork. "Reginald?" he asked the darkness. His mouth was almost too dry to make a sound. "Prince Reginald?"

The rush came so swiftly that he never saw or heard it coming, and so hard that he never remembered much about it. There was an instant when something slammed into him with overwhelming force, lifting him off the ground—he did recall that, and he also remembered landing on the far side of the stable with the wind knocked completely out of him, barely able to breathe. Then, without a pause, there was Princess Cerise's face, taut and white and almost old with anxiety as she leaned over him, her hands cautiously probing for broken bones. He tried to say, "I'm all right," but could not get the words past his throat. She read his lips, however, and smiled with relief.

"I came back down," she said. "I wanted to remind you not to give Mistral too much hay—she's such a little pig, and then she bloats. And I saw you. Can you sit up? I'll help you."

With her arm around his back, Robert first sat and then, after the nausea and dizziness passed, stood up and stayed up—anyway, the second time. The Princess said, "It was the wizard, wasn't it? He attacked you with . . . with a spell or a thunderbolt or something. The wizard did it."

"I suppose," Robert said weakly. Then he said, "No—no, it wasn't him," because a new memory was slowly swirling to the roiled surface of his mind. *Smell of cold smoke . . . power beyond power, lapping around me, surging under me like the sea . . . great green eyes knowing me . . .* But for Princess Cerise's support, his legs would have failed him again. He said, "It wasn't him."

I'm still alive. Why am I still alive?

FOURTEEN

Ostvald could not sleep. This was more than unusual for Ostvald; it was epoch-making. He was capable of falling asleep anywhere and anywhen, under any circumstances; more, within certain limits, he was equally capable of sleeping while he worked, and performing the task at his normal level of efficiency. Both Robert and Elfrieda had seen him doze off while repairing farm wagons, making hay, or even plowing a field, while his spokes remained perfectly identical, and his rows continued straight and clean. Teased about this, he would grunt in embarrassment, "Y'ought to wake me when you see me drop off like that. Might do someone a mischief, and not know."

"But you look so *sweet* when you're asleep," Elfrieda would say. "Working away, snoring away." Ostvald was never sure whether this came exactly to a compliment, but he cherished it as one, since Elfrieda offered him so few. The only other one he could remember was a moment out of their childhood when he had clumsily patched her lone pair of real shoes, and she had kissed him quickly in gratitude and run off to dance around Robert in her mended shoes. Slow and absent-minded as he was, Ostvald remembered, awake or asleep, the summer taste of her lips.

But tonight, three days after the consecutive rapid departures of Prince Reginald, Robert, and the Princess Cerise, there was too much to think about, and it all hurt Ostvald's head. He put his shirt and sandals back on (he usually slept in his trousers, because you never knew), and wandered aimlessly down the road he usually took to meet Robert for work. The night was warm, with the scent of the flowers his midwife mother gathered daily for her remedies and birthing spells; the moon, rising slowly over the distant peaks that gave Bellemontagne its name, seemed to Osvald to have a smell of its own, sharp and elusive as the mountains. He wished Robert and Elfrieda were with him: having thoughts like that on his own worried him.

Passing the crossroad, he drifted on toward Robert's house, on the vague off chance that his friend might have returned in the night. A light in the kitchen gave him a moment's hope, but when he knocked at the door, it was Odelette who answered, fully dressed and wary until she recognized him. She said knowingly, "You couldn't sleep either." It was not a question.

Ostvald shook his head. "Did he come home before he left? Did he—you know—say anything?"

"No. But I know where he's gone—Elfrieda told me." Odelette stepped back to let him in, wrapping her arms around herself, as though she were suddenly cold. "I don't think I'd be quite so nervous, except . . ." Even Ostvald could not have missed the abruptness with which she stopped speaking. She made tea for them both, while he fidgeted uncomfortably in the silent house, being much more accustomed to it aswarm with Robert's brothers and sisters. Once, turning toward the back of the house for a moment, he thought he glimpsed a flicker of green between a chair and a coal scuttle, but he blinked weary eyes and it had never been there. *I'll have the tea, and then I'll go on home and go back to bed. Not getting nearly enough sleep, with him gone.*

Odelette asked as she worked, "Is Walter still angry about Robert taking his horse?"

"Well, I told him it was in a good cause. I don't think he believed me, though."

The tea was as strong and sweet as Odelette always made it. They sat together in the kitchen and made fitful conversation. Ostvald said, "I'm really pretty sure he'll be all right. Them too." Odelette said, "My boy has the heart of a dragon. I'm not worried about him in the least." They drank more tea, as the silence stretched between them.

"He went after Prince Reginald," Ostvald said for either the fourth or fifth time. "And the Princess went after *him*. So they'll all be safe, and they'll all come home together. Safely."

"Of course they will. No question about it." Odelette went to the sideboard and came back with a flask containing a deeply amber liquid. She poured a generous dollop into her teacup, hesitating before offering it to Ostvald. "You're a little young." Ostvald silently held out his own cup. "Well, it'll help you sleep. My Elpidus made it himself."

Ostvald only coughed a couple of times. "It's . . . very good, Ma'am Thrax." When Odelette turned away for a moment, he reached behind his right shoulder, trying to thump himself on the back. He said, a bit weakly, "They'll probably be back tomorrow. I bet they'll all be back tomorrow."

Again the green flash, in and out of a shadowy corner, too swift to focus on. Odelette turned quickly, saying, "No. Not tomorrow, Ostvald. A mother knows these things."

Ostvald took a second sip of the enhanced tea. It did grow on you, somewhat, if you were reasonably vigilant. He said, "Elfrieda will be sad. She likes Robert."

"Yes, I know." Odelette came closer, pointing a finger directly at his chest. "And you like Elfrieda, very much—you always have done. Tell me I am wrong." She was smiling a little, as though happy to be diverted from fears for her son.

"I like her." Ostvald swallowed heavily. "Sure, I like her. She's . . . she's Elfrieda."

"And she is in love with Robert, I could see that when you were all children. But he is all wrong for her. She would never be happy with him."

The heaviness had reached Ostvald's chest now. He said, "How could she not be? He's very smart, and she's very smart, and he's really handsome, and she's . . ." His mouth dried up completely at that point, and he took a large gulp of Odelette's tea. "And besides, they're both . . . they're *quick*, and I'm *not* quick, I never will be. I'm just . . ." He shrugged, almost dropping the teacup. "I'm me. Big old Ostvald. Slow old Ostvald. Me."

Odelette smiled affectionately. "You are what Elfrieda needs. Whether you will have the courage to tell her so, that is another matter. Not everyone gets what they need." She patted his shoulder, at the same time—he could not help noticing—positioning herself between him and the corner of the room where he had seen, or thought he had seen, the scurry of green. "But I think you are much braver than you imagine. A mother knows these things. Go home now. I promise you will sleep."

When she had closed the door behind him, she said loudly, without turning, "Adelise, for goodness' sake, go to bed! The lot of you—go to bed!" With Ostvald gone, the dragonlets were all in the kitchen, perched variously on chairbacks, shelves, and pots, plainly waiting for something: whether it was Robert himself or word of Robert from her, Odelette could not tell. She said, "You have *got* to stop coming out when there are people here." And then, more gently, "I don't know any more than you do. But he will be all right—he *will* be. Sleep now."

They began finding traces of Prince Reginald's passage along the road as they journeyed on. Here he had made a hasty meal and not buried his fire completely; here he had halted to drink at a stream and unknowingly dropped a worn neck scarf, which Princess Cerise snatched up and treasured in her bosom; here his horse had cast a shoe, and he had led it limping to a blacksmith in a nearby hamlet. "So like him," the Princess sighed. "He would never, *ever* ride a lame horse."

"The horse isn't lame. It just needed a shoe."

"You know what I mean. It's a sign of his character."

Robert looked at her but said nothing. The Princess said, "What?"

"Nothing. I don't think it's worth going into the village. We won't find him there."

"We're getting close. I'm sure we are. He might be just a few hours ahead of us."

"Do you know why that shoe came off?" Robert took gentle hold of her arm. "That happened because he's pushing the horse more than we are. We've been stopping to rest, while Prince

Reginald's hardly stopping at all. He's farther ahead of us every day. We're not going to catch up with him unless—"

The Princess reined in her horse and turned to challenge him. "Unless he's wounded or . . . or dead. That's what you're saying, isn't it?"

"No, I didn't say that—I wasn't saying that at all! Unless he *wants* us to catch him, that's all I was saying!" But it wasn't, and Robert knew the Princess knew it. He said quietly, "We have to be ready."

Princess Cerise pulled her arm away from him and spurred ahead. Over her shoulder she said wearily, "I have planned all my life to love a perfect knight, a champion—a dragonslayer. Now I'm coming to think that I don't want anything to do with heroes, ever again. They're stupid, and they're pigheaded, and you can't tell them anything, and they run off to do heroic things, and then you have to go and"—she gulped or hiccuped or sniffled, and Robert almost missed the last words—"then you have to go and bring them home . . ."

Robert fell a little way behind her, deliberately, for the rest of that day's ride; nor did she look back until they were camped beside a purple, star-crowded pond, with Robert feeding dead branches to their cooking fire, and the Princess turning a spitted rabbit, which she had killed with a thrown rock, over the flames. To Robert's surprise at her accuracy, she remarked, "My father taught me. Daddy wasn't always a king, you know."

They were near enough to the village the dragons had destroyed to smell, even now, the ashy desolation and the lingering chill of the creatures' presence. The ground here was too hard and rutted to show even the faintest hoofprint, and there had been no further sign of Prince Reginald all that day. The rabbit came out somewhat singed in some areas, tough and raw in others, but they left nothing but fur and bones, hardly speaking while they ate. Robert fetched water from the pond afterward, so cold that it made their heads hurt, and they laughed about this a little, which helped. The Princess said, "I feel that he is near us. There is no reason for it, none at all, but I just . . . do you know?"

"I know why you feel it," Robert said cautiously. "This is where he was bound, to find more of those dragons and prove that he can . . . I mean, instead of . . ." Giving up all hope for that sentence, he tried another tack. "I mean, to find out whether there *are* any more of those dragons. I told you, they're not like any I ever saw in my life, or ever heard about. We need to know where they come from, and if anybody's actually breeding them, we need to know that right away. I'm sure that's what Prince Reginald was after. I really am."

She lowered her head, looking not at him but into the fire. "When he said he was making a lie come true, he wasn't just talking about dragons. He meant himself." Robert did not know how to answer her. Princess Cerise said, "He meant that *he* was a lie—that everything about him was a lie, from the way he looks in armor to the way he sits a horse, to the . . . to everything, *everything*. And it's not true—I *know* it's not! He can't be a—a fraud, a counterfeit, he *can't* be! I don't care what he says, I won't *let* him not be real!" She was crying, doubled over herself: deep, shuddering sobs from the center of her body.

Robert—wishing desperately that he were somewhere else—put an arm around her shoulders. Princess Cerise did not appear to have noticed. He tried to speak, but his throat hurt. He coughed a couple of times and tried again.

"My mother," he began. "My mother, sometimes she says that everybody in the world is a donkey with the heart of a lion. Everybody. Only most people don't ever discover it—they don't have to, they get along all right just being donkeys. But it's there, always, if you really need it. If you really want to find it. If you look for it. I think that's what he's doing, Prince Reginald."

The Princess neither answered, nor looked at him, nor pulled away from his arm, but she did manage to stop crying. They sat together like that while the moon rose and their fire dwindled, and the frogs chunked out in the pond, from which a thin mist was beginning to rise. From their position they could see the road on which they had come to this place, running on out of sight toward the little wood into which their doomed and overdressed campaign had marched so bravely. Robert marveled at it: such a drab, spindly, *ordinary* road, after all, for the hope and foolishness it had carried, and the horror at its end . . . and the discovery as well. He stared down it through the darkness, smelling the Princess's hair.

Which was undoubtedly why he never saw the dragon rising from the pond until Princess Cerise screamed.

It was bigger than any of the three dragons who had so ravaged village and expedition alike, but it was clearly of the same viciously lordly breed. It lumbered up out of the pond it could not possibly have hidden in, and no water parted to let it by, nor was there any water soaking the dark garb of the man who sat astride the dragon's neck, commanding it forward with his staff. He was old, and looked gray all the way through, but his eyes were merry with such delight as Robert had never imagined, and was quite certain he didn't want to imagine, ever. The old man spoke, and his voice had a ring of bronze in it, alloyed further by the savage resonance that justified spite always lends a voice. "Tell her to stop that noise. Waste of time and effort, squalling at an illusion."

Princess Cerise stopped screaming abruptly, with a single sniff of derision. Robert said, "I knew you couldn't be real. Dragons don't like water."

"Oh, *my* dragons don't mind it at all," the old man replied cheerfully. "You don't know nearly as much about dragons as you think, Gaius Aurelius Constantine Heliogabalus Thrax. What a pity you won't live long enough to learn what you need to know."

"If that's a threat," Robert began, "my little sister Rosamonde could—" But the Princess, on her feet and with her fists balled at her hips, interrupted him. "What have you done with Prince Reginald? Illusion or not, I will kill you if you have harmed him."

"Oh, I like her!" the old man said to Robert. "Oh, I really do like her. *Much* too good for any son of Krije's, that's certain." The dragon, illusory or not, growled fire at the name.

"You're Dahr," Robert said slowly. The old man bowed deeply over the dragon's neck. "You're dead. Krije killed you. Long ago."

"Alas, yes. Alas, not well." Dahr sighed sorrowfully. "Krije was always, shall we say, inclined to be a bit slapdash about his epic combats. A redoubtable fellow in many ways, but not what you could call precise. But yes, he did kill me, yes indeed. Just not—ah—*properly*."

"Prince Reginald will finish the job," the Princess said fiercely. "As soon as he returns from . . . from wherever you have imprisoned him. Where is he?"

The old man chuckled in an infuriatingly avuncular manner. Robert noticed that his eyes were the color of his dragon's eyes: so black as to be almost purple. "One thing at a time, child, one thing at a time." He bowed courteously over the dragon's neck. "Princess Cerise of Bellemontagne, it is truly an honor to meet you. I know your parents well—a silly, weak-minded pair who will come to no hurt as long as they stay out of my way."

The last words snapped like pine sap in the fire. Dahr's chuckle deepened and darkened as he savored the fear on the Princess's face, but it stopped altogether when he turned toward Robert. "Well," he said softly, his voice caressing the one word until it hummed and rang like the polished edge of a wineglass. "Well," he repeated. "You."

"You won't know my parents," Robert said, holding his own voice as steady as he could. "I come of humbler stock than you would bother to notice."

The old man raised a long, admonitory forefinger. "Ah, now, you can never tell what might interest a wizard. But in this case, you are quite right. My sole interest is in you—*dragonmaster*."

That word came out in a chilling crack, and Robert recoiled from it as if from an unseen snake. Rising, he managed to respond, "I am no such thing, friend Dahr. I do indeed have some small knowledge of dragons and dragonlore, but I am no master, nor do I aspire to be. That honor is yours."

"Do not pretend to play with me!" The bronze purr had fallen away, like the rotting flesh of a corpse, revealing the long, naked teeth. "At your word, my dragons—my children!—turned from their rightful prey and destroyed each other. At your word! There was never a dragonlord who could command such a thing—never before, *never!*" Dahr controlled himself with an audible effort: Robert actually heard a choking click in the phantom throat. "Until now."

Robert's jaws hurt from the effort of keeping his teeth from chattering, and his legs ached with his determination neither to tremble nor to turn and run blindly into the night, abandoning Princess Cerise, his stolen horse, and his mother's prayer to bear a hero. He said in a small, clear voice, "I feel dragons. Perhaps I understand them as well, a little. But I am not their master."

The old man smiled then, once again the grandfather with a sack of sweets to parcel out. "A pity, that—a true pity. Because, master or no, I cannot afford you, Gaius Constantine Thrax. I cannot afford to let you live."

What Robert would have done or said, he never knew, because the Princess was suddenly in front of him, standing—with the fiery blue flash of a kingfisher—between him and the wizard Dahr. Her voice was astonishingly level. "You will not harm him. I am the Princess Cerise, and I will not have it so."

Robert had his hand firmly on her shoulder to put her aside when the old man began to laugh: genuine laughter this time, not the benign chuckle with the blood and razors just underneath. "My, I *like* her! I may have to remove her from my path, after all, but I certainly do like her." He bent his head ceremoniously to the Princess, his dragon-eyes actually twinkling. "Remember, girl, what you see is only a vision, a sending, without the power even to muss your pretty hair. I was merely curious to see you, and to meet your companion, who is neither what he thinks he is, nor what he dreams of being." He spoke to the spectral dragon, and it lifted great ribbed wings under him. "When we meet again, it will be a different story, I am afraid."

"Wait!" The Princess's voice was as commanding as Robert

had heard it arranging the order of march, a world and a life ago. "Where is Prince Reginald?"

Dahr blinked like any startled oldster. "Where? Why, child, he is on his way back to you, just as fast as his steed can carry him. Or he will be, I'm sure, as soon as he gets down from that tree." He smiled, blood and razors once again. "He's fast on his feet, your Prince, I'll give him that. He has climbed out of reach of the dragon I set to guard him, and he has very nearly stripped the tree of every fruit it bears—none quite ripe, alas—and if he takes proper care not to fall asleep and fall out of the tree—"

Robert said to Princess Cerise, "Get the horses." The Princess looked from him to Dahr and back; then ran off without a word to where their horses were tethered. Dahr said, "Well, now, a man who can speak so to a princess surely has an interesting future—"

"Where are you?" Robert demanded. "Say where you really are and we'll face you there, you and your beasts—"

"Ah-ah," Dahr chided, pointing the staff at him. "You, of all people? Who should know better than you that dragons are no beasts? Especially my children"—the wicked chuckle was back—"the slowest of whom is a scholar and a mystic, compared to your Prince Reginald. He may possibly have deduced by now that the dragon holding him in that tree is no more real than the one I ride—but then again . . ."

"Where are you?" But the old man was already fading with his mount, back into the real mist over the real pond from which their apparitions had arisen. Only his voice lingered. "Where are my children and I truly to be found? Ask King Krije—Krije will know. Oh, Krije will most certainly know."

FIFTEEN

They met Prince Reginald on the road, walking and leading his horse.

When Princess Cerise ran to him, while Robert inspected the mare's legs and feet for stones or strains, Prince Reginald waved them wearily away. "There is nothing wrong with her. I am ashamed to make a creature so much braver and more intelligent than I carry me on her back." He could not meet either Robert's eyes or the Princess's. "*She* knew the dragon was not real. She went on cropping grass and scratching herself against a tree—the same tree I was hiding in, eating green fruit and wetting myself with fear. And calling for you, begging you to come and rescue me . . . a girl and a lowborn peasant boy." He did look straight at Robert then, and managed to mumble, "Forgive me. It was my shame that spoke."

"No harm," Robert said. Prince Reginald abruptly collapsed by the roadside, and although he was not weeping, his shoulders were shaking uncontrollably. Princess Cerise looked at Robert, and then went to kneel beside him. Robert said stiffly, "He is a wizard. Deception is his art and his nature—it is what he is. He might have tricked any one of us."

Princess Cerise agreed volubly, but Prince Reginald was not to be consoled. "My father was right in his contempt for me. He knew from my birth that I would never be anything but the shadow of his shadow—and I rebelled and mocked him because he knew the truth." He pushed the Princess's comforting hands away. "It is not my fault that I am the son of a great king—it is not my fault that I look like a hero. But it *is* my fault that I am both a fool and a coward. If I had dared to face that false dragon, I would have *known*—"

"Enough," Robert said loudly. "Enough!" He could not believe his own words—*first I order a princess around, and now I am shutting up a prince*. He said, "Enough, Your Highness. Tell me about Dahr and your father."

Distracted from his misery, Prince Reginald looked up in surprise. "What? Well, I don't know what there is to tell you. Dahr was an evil wizard, and my father killed him before I was born. That's really all I know."

"He's alive," Robert said. Prince Reginald stared, completely uncomprehending. Robert said, "*Think*, my lord! What did your father tell you about him?"

"Was he a dragony sort of wizard back then?" Princess Cerise was alternately brushing off Prince Reginald's shirt and trying without success to get him to stand up.

"My father mostly told me about his own invincible courage and strength," Prince Reginald answered bitterly. "To hear him, not only did he destroy the wizard at the risk of his life, he foiled Dahr's plan for domination—whatever it was—and humiliated him utterly before his forces, in addition. He goes into great detail about that part."

"Tell us the details. On our way home." Robert pulled Prince Reginald to his feet and prodded him—none too gently—toward his saddle. When he hung back, Robert snapped, "Your Highness, the last thing Dahr said to us—the illusion of Dahr, I mean—the last thing he said was that King Krije, your father, would certainly know where he was. Which means to me that he is either in Corvinia right now, or on his way there."

Prince Reginald, halfway into the saddle, fell off. Robert caught him. The Princess said quietly, "The main road to Corvinia from here passes through Bellemontagne."

Her expression had not changed, and her voice was as even as ever; but Robert knew her face by now, and he could see that her lips had gone the color of old snow. He said, "The dragons would fly. They *can* fly, you've seen them. There would be no reason for them to set foot in Bellemontagne."

"My father," the Princess began. She faltered, then tried again. "My father did not get on all that well with . . . with Dahr. Either."

She swayed forward, catching herself with both hands on her horse's withers, but did not faint or fall. Robert helped her mount, watching her carefully. When he was satisfied that she could stay in the saddle, he mounted himself, riding a little way behind her, as they had come.

Prince Reginald at first moped along in the back, far enough to the rear that Robert finally summoned him close, saying, "Tell me more about how King Krije killed Dahr, Your Highness. Anything you recall—*anything*."

"I've told you what I know! I wasn't even there, and I haven't listened the last seventy-eight times he's told me that story. All I remember is him roaring how Dahr invaded Corvinia with an army of wizards, and how my father went roaring out to the field all alone—to hear *him* tell it, anyway—not paying any heed to the other wizards' 'little pissant spells,' as he called them, just heading straight for Dahr himself. And he always said—he *said* . . ." He stopped, looking suddenly puzzled.

"Go on, Your Highness," Robert urged him. "Go on."

"Well, he *said* that he took Dahr's staff away from him, and broke it in two, and beat him to death with the two pieces. And all the other wizards just looked on and didn't intervene, because if you break a wizard's staff, he's helpless—because he's *in* that staff, in a way. But he's got one now, I saw it! So that means . . . that means *what*? I don't understand anything."

"I don't understand either," Robert said. "All I know is that he's alive. And what he has is dragons."

Mortmain was pacing.

Mortmain was a very precise and economical pacer. So many steps to this corner of the castle courtyard, so many across to the curtain wall; so many steps along the wall to the blacksmith's forge and brazier, so many steps from there to the quintain where young knights practiced jousting, so many back to the original corner, and begin again. He could have walked it in his sleep—and often did in his dreams, in the week since Prince Reginald's disappearance.

This particular morning, he was joined, to his surprise—and to his annoyance—by a small, dark, somewhat grubby, disturbingly lively country girl who boldly introduced herself as Elfrieda-something-or-other, and whom he assumed automatically must be in quest of word of the Princess Cerise. The poor—this being as well known in Bellemontagne as anywhere else—lived their real lives through following the lives of the aristocracy as avidly as they had energy and free time to do. Mortmain said, politely enough, "Girl, she has not yet returned. The King and the Queen have not slept in days, and the entire castle is on the brink of complete hysterical panic. And I myself am not feeling all that well. You are at liberty to pass this news on to whomever you choose. Good day to you."

But the irritating child curtsied to him quite formally—*only the peasants keep the old style up these days*—and addressed him. "Sir, I seek news of a man—well, he's a boy, really, we grew up together—named Robert Thrax, only that's not exactly his real name, but that's what he likes people to call him. Anyway, he went in search of Prince Reginald"—on the instant, she had Mortmain's entire attention—"when he ran off, you know, and I just thought, maybe"—and here she showed welcome signs of running out of wind—"if you could tell me anything about him, that would be . . . any information, even a rumor . . ." Here she did falter, but it had more to do with imminent tears than air supply. "If you know . . ."

"The dragon-boy," Mortmain said softly. "The one who wants to be a prince's valet. Yes, I know him, but I didn't realize he'd gone . . ." He sighed and patted her shoulder awkwardly. "Dry your eyes, dry your eyes, he's not lost to you. He came back from that slaughter in the wood; I suspect he'll come back from this. Interesting boy."

"But what should I do?" Elfrieda-something demanded. "I can't just sit still at home and wait for him like a good girl—

I *can't*! I can't sit still anywhere! There must be *something* I can do!"

Mortmain regarded her: pretty, in a lower-class sort of way—even piquant, with a suggestion of real intelligence under the country accent, the country smock, the wooden country clogs. He said, "You can walk with me, if you will. That's what I do."

So Elfrieda joined him in his pacing: courtyard corner, wall, unlighted brazier, swinging quintain, the corner again. . . .

They spoke little, but each time they passed a particular arrow-slit in the curtain wall, one or the other of them—Elfrieda running like the child she was, Mortmain maintaining a certain dignity—would go to it and peer down the two main roads approaching the castle, hoping to see so much as a far-distant dust cloud on its way home. Elfrieda would actually turn around three times and whisper to her name-goddess, Elfrieda of the Teeth. Mortmain, more circumspect, merely muttered to the empty tracks, "*Get back here, you idiot, get back here. . . .*" After some hours, though, he started adding the word *safely*.

That was where Ostvald found them, still stalking the courtyard, plainly leg-weary now, but matching each other's pace almost perfectly, both taking an unvoiced, side-by-side pleasure in their own stubbornness. He spoke to Elfrieda, being far too shy, and too wary, to address Mortmain directly. "Your father wants you home right away. His bad toe told him there's rain coming, and he needs everybody to get the hay in. He says to say that's an order."

Elfrieda shrugged without breaking stride. "His toe tells him whatever he wants it to tell him. I need to be here."

"He says if you don't come, he'll beat you."

"It wouldn't be the first time." Elfrieda stopped walking then, smiling a little at the anxiety in Ostvald's face. "Robert could be back at any moment, don't you see? If I'm not here—"

Ostvald did not want her to finish. He said, "Well, I'll just keep you company awhile. I can get to work later." Saying which, he fell calmly into step with Elfrieda and Mortmain on their absurd and patient round of the castle courtyard. At first he made an effort to keep up a conversation, but his companions were too silent and his surroundings too noisy, what with the blacksmith hammering dents out of armor and the quintain ringing as it swung round to knock another fledgling knight off his horse. He tried whistling then, loudly and off-key, but Elfrieda only spared him one quick glance of irritation, and Mortmain did not even bother to do that. In the end, he fell as mute as they, though lacking their mutual obsession with the arrow-slit and the two roads. Once he diffidently took Elfrieda's hand: she neither resisted nor responded, and he soon dropped it.

The three of them had been marching together for a good hour, when a single rider on a lathered horse appeared, racing toward the castle; but as he was alone, and coming down the less-traveled of the two roads, they took only a glancing notice of him. He clattered through the gateway, leaped off his mount, tossed the reins to a groom, and disappeared into the castle at a stumbling run. Elfrieda said, "It's not Robert," and Mortmain said, "Wrong direction," and Ostvald said, "My feet hurt."

They said nothing further, but went on walking until—Elfrieda first—they slowly became aware of the susurrus within the castle: whisper atop whisper, soft still, but definitely rising in volume and intensity; seemingly coming from everywhere, as though all the stones of Bellemontagne's ancient fortress had decided to tell all their stories at once. Activity in the courtyard gradually came to a halt: the blacksmith's hammer fell to his side, like that of a clockwork figure striking the hour; the laundresses and scampering squires dodging the young knights' practice charges moved steadily slower—even the dogs and ravens underfoot were standing still, heads tilted attentively, listening to the murmur of the stones. Elfrieda said, "It *is* Robert."

King Antoine and Queen Hélène emerged from the castle door into the sunlight, accompanied by the messenger. Both of them looked older than they were, and their royal robes seemed suddenly too large for them. The King's eyes were dry but red; the Queen kept pressing the knuckles of her right hand against her mouth. The messenger hung back, dusty and embarrassed.

King Antoine raised his voice, to be heard in the silent courtyard. He said, tremulously but clearly, "My people, we have received word that our beloved daughter, the Princess Cerise—" He broke off abruptly, turned his head to meet the Queen's eyes, and then with an effort resumed speaking. "Our daughter, together with Prince Reginald of Corvinia and—ah—Thrax, the dragon person, I know his mother, a fine woman . . ." Queen Hélène whispered sharply in his ear. "Yes. All three of them have gone on to Corvinia instead of returning home. Because Dahr—the wizard Dahr, who's supposed to be dead—ah—he's *not* dead, and Prince Reginald's father, King Krije, Krije killed him—only it seems not enough—and Prince Reginald thinks Dahr is on his way to Corvinia, to kill Krije, so *he's* going there right away, because . . . because he's a hero."

He suddenly took a faltering step back and leaned against the messenger, as though his legs were giving way. Queen Hélène patted his arm and stepped forward herself. She said, "Our daughter has gone with him, because she too is a hero." She paused. "This young man says that he guided them to a more direct route to Corvinia—the Pass of Maedchensflucht, south of our southern border. He left them and the dragon-boy there, and made all speed here, at their instruction. This is what we know."

It seemed to Ostvald that Elfrieda had grown as unsteady on her feet as the King as she listened to the news. He put a supportive arm around her shoulders, just in case, but she shrugged it fiercely away without looking at him. King Antoine, still leaning on the messenger, found the strength to announce, "We know one thing more. There are dragons."

Abruptly Elfrieda turned away and, without speaking to either Ostvald or Mortmain, began walking briskly toward the postern gate of the castle. Ostvald stared in dismay, called to her—she never looked back—and then ran after her, clumsy and clattering in the boots he wore for hod-carrying. Mortmain, himself white with shock, never noticed that they were gone.

She was moving fast, almost running, by the time Ostvald caught up with her near the stables, where Prince Reginald had slept. Nor would she turn, however pleadingly Ostvald called her name, until he finally caught her shoulders with both hands and turned her to face him. "Where are you going?"

Elfrieda, for once, did not say "Oh, *you*!" Ostvald could have wished she *had* said it instead of answering, almost gently, "Even for you, that was a stupid question."

When he could not speak, Elfrieda gave him the long, pitying look he knew so well. Carefully, precisely, as though speaking to a child, she said, "You heard the King. There are dragons. Robert will need me."

"No," Ostvald said. "No, Elfrieda." It sounded like someone

else talking far away, and he enjoyed the strange sound of it. "Elfrieda, you are not going anywhere alone."

Elfrieda stared at him in shock almost as great as Mortmain's. "Ostvald, I've made up my mind. You know the way I get when my mind's made up."

"I know how you are," Ostvald said firmly. "I know how you've been all your life—all *our* lives—telling Robert and me how you wanted things to be, and the two of us just as happy as sandboys to do what you wanted, to make sure we'd done it the way you wanted. Not this time." Elfrieda was gaping at him, a sensation he enjoyed immensely, whatever it might cost him later on. "Not this time. If you want to go after Robert, that's your business, that's fine. But I'm going with you."

"Oh, you are certainly not! Not a chance in the *world!*"

"Robert is *not* your stupid property—"

"Not yet, he's not—"

"And if I choose to go with you to bring him back—"

"Not a chance!"

"You're no rider, you never have been—"

"That is *not* true! *Not* true—"

The Pass of Maedchensflucht was not only as steep and exhausting as that frightened boy had warned them it would be; it was also as barren a piece of landscape as Robert could remember enduring. Even before they reached the timberline, there was nothing to divert the journeying eye but a handful of scrawny pines scattered over a balding carpet of sphagnum mosses and patches of gray frost. The two days it took to travel the pass held a certain thin warmth, but the nights were wickedly cold, cold enough that the three of them slept in their clothes on the hard ground, close together, with the Princess Cerise in the middle. During the day she likewise rode between them, with Prince Reginald in the lead, and Robert as rear guard, alert for either of the two species of predators that competed for dominance in these mountains. He never saw any, but the horses constantly winded them, which often made it necessary to dismount and lead them until they calmed down. Robert and Prince Reginald both got nosebleeds.

Nobody spoke much during the day; but at night, with Prince Reginald snoring on her left, the Princess murmured to Robert, "He *is* doing better now, don't you think?"

"Well, he's going home, going to his father's aid. That does tend to make you pay attention."

The Princess smiled tolerantly. "Ah, now you're making fun of me."

"No, I'm not." *Yes, you are*. But the smile lingered.

"It doesn't matter—I'm sure I deserve it. But the important thing is that he will be showing King Krije that his son's as good a man as he, and that will make *such* a difference in the way he sees himself, I know it will. I'm sure that's the entire key to Reginald, that relationship with his father. Don't you agree?" When Robert did not answer immediately, she nudged him half-playfully with a sharp elbow. "Robert, I've come to value your opinion quite highly. I really do want to know what you think."

Robert, curled into a ball against the cold—he could not feel his feet at all—was trying to take shy advantage of Princess Cerise's body heat, without doing anything that might possibly be construed as snuggling. He said, "I think Prince Reginald is much more courageous than he knows. Most people are." He wrapped his arms around himself, tucking his hands into his armpits. "But they don't all get the chance to show it. I guess that's a good thing, when you think about it."

"But he *has* to get to show it! Otherwise he won't know, and his father won't either, and he'll just go on being so ashamed of himself. . . . Oh, he *has* to have a chance to find out how brave he really is!"

Prince Reginald's mare whickered in sudden terror, pulling strongly against her picket rope. Robert said wearily, "She's smelling the wolves again. I'd better see to her." He stood up, shivering and stumbling in the cold, and made his way to the horses, where he attended carefully to all three stakes and tethers before he made his way back to the dying fire—he put the last of their wood on it—and the thin summer blankets. The Princess said drowsily, as he lay down beside her again, "Is everything all right?"

"Yes," Robert assured her. "Everything's all right."

Princess Cerise smiled with her eyes closed. "I knew it would be. Thank you, Robert." The last few words trailed off into a mumble, and then into a delicate snore. But Robert lay awake for some while, because there were green eyes restless beyond the firelight, and his mind was unquiet with images and possibilities, none of which he liked much. He wished with all his heart, and without the slightest shame, that he were home with his family, in his own bed, with a dragon on his pillow, and another one trying to paw his eyes open in the morning. *I don't belong in stories with heroes—that's for princes and princesses. I just want to be a valet—is that too much to ask?* The wolves prowled and waited, and the horses whinnied their fear, and Prince Reginald and Princess Cerise snored peacefully, and Robert thought, *Yes, yes, it is. . . .*

◆ ◆ ◆ ◆

"He is *not* a donkey! He is a *mule*!"

"*You're* the mule, to keep saying that! Of course he's a donkey! Look at his feet!"

"Look at the size of him! He's too tall to be a donkey!"

"Size? My feet are dragging on the ground! He's a tall donkey, that's all!"

"He *is* a mule! A small mule—that's all they had in the stable, I told you!"

"That's all you could ride, you mean! Me, I feel like a criminal, making the poor thing carry me—"

"Then walk, why don't you? *Walk!*"

Ostvald promptly slipped off the small animal that was carrying him and Elfrieda into the mountains of Corvinia. "See, I'm walking—there!" In frustration, he slapped the beast hard on the rump, and it promptly bolted up the road, taking a wailing Elfrieda with it. Horrified, cursing himself, Ostvald ran after them, and caught up in time to keep Elfrieda from toppling to the road, and simultaneously to calm and scold both her and the unconcerned creature. "Woman, for the love of God, what possessed you? Raised on a farm, like me, don't you know a donkey when you see one?"

"He's a small mule," Elfrieda insisted stubbornly, but her eyes were damp. When Ostvald looked into them, he saw a rumpled, glittery image of himself that touched his heart, greatly to his own annoyance. He said gently, "He's a donkey, Elfrieda, and you know it. Why could you not say so?"

"Because he was all I could find—well, he was!—and he's ever so peaceful and tractable, and I really thought he could carry us both. All right—a mule would have been better, I'm *sorry*! Are you happy now?"

"No," Ostvald said. "I'm not at all happy. I'm going to have to walk over the pass, to help you rescue your darling Robert—"

"He's *not* my darling Robert, I *never* said that!" Elfrieda was blushing fiercely, as furious at herself as at him. Ostvald settled her in the saddle and carefully prodded the donkey onward.

Elfrieda said, after a time, "I just think that we ought to be there when he . . . when he meets the bad wizard and the dragons and all. To help him."

"And how are we going to help him? Or that Prince, or the Princess, or anyone? By screaming very loudly until they come and rescue us—"

"*I* won't be doing any screaming! I can't speak for *you*—"

"We'll just be in the way, no use to anyone, and most likely put them in more danger because they'll have to be looking out for us." He drew a deep breath. "We can still go home, Elfrieda."

"No, we can't." Ostvald mouthed the words along with her. She said doggedly, "They'll need us. I don't know how or why, but I know they will."

Ostvald grunted without answering. Elfrieda looked down at him, lightly patting his hand where it rested on the stirrup. "I'm not going to ride all the time—we'll trade off every mile or two." Something large and winged passed high above them, blocking the sun for an instant, and she cowered in the saddle. *"Dragon?"*

"Mountain eagle. A lot of help you're going to be when there *are* dragons." She was plainly hurt, and Ostvald was instantly sorry. He said so, but Elfrieda only rode on without another word. Nevertheless, after they had traveled a mile or so, she dismounted and directed him with a curt nod to climb into the saddle. When he demurred, she shoved him—hard—and he climbed. She walked silently beside the donkey until it was her turn to ride again.

SIXTEEN

It was not a dream. King Krije knew it was not a dream. True, he was in his great bed, wearing his light bedtime mail, snug and secure under his usual blanket of Corvinian hounds: each the size of a calf, uniformly faithful and ferocious, and all of the unique fawn color, verging on violet, that marked them as Krije's. They woke when he did, rumbling concern, smelling fear in his sweat, sensing it in his rigidity as he sat up against the skull-shaped headboard, staring straight before him. Crowding close, they turned as one to follow his gaze but could not see what he saw, though they growled at it anyway. Then they all settled back into sleep.

The old man sitting in the air, just beyond the foot of the King's bed, smiled with lingering mockery. "Wonderful beasts, those, Krije. Fearless and murderous, and absolutely loyal, and not in the least handicapped by anything like intelligence. I've often thought the same of you."

"You're dead," King Krije said. The words caught in his throat and were barely audible.

The wizard Dahr shook his head, never ceasing to smile. "I can't hear you, my friend. Like everyone else, I was always so used to your brainless bawling and bellowing that when you speak like a normal human being—"

"*You're dead, damn you!*" Krije's howl woke the dogs, who fell to snarling and snapping at each other all over the bed, until he cuffed them silent, waving his arms furiously. "I beat you to pudding with your own staff and threw your body to my hogs!"

"Yes," the wizard responded thoughtfully. "Yes, I remember you did that. Well, I certainly wouldn't ever do anything so rude and vulgar to you." He beamed benignly, still floating slightly above the king's bed. The bedroom was dark, but there was a strange light around him, though it illuminated nothing else. Dahr said, "I have much more interesting plans for you, dear old Krije."

Whatever other qualities he may have lacked, no one had ever accused King Krije of wanting courage. Snatching up the dagger that spent every night under his pillow, he lunged from bed, brandishing it at the glowing image above him. "Come ahead, you milk-livered coward! I've never known a wizard who had the guts of a codfish, a bloody mud turtle! Come on ahead—I'll be waiting for you!" He was panting like one of his own dogs with rage and frustration.

"Oh, I will be coming, never doubt it," Dahr continued, barely sparing the King a glance. "But I do so enjoy taking my time, studying the scenery, thinking pleasant thoughts of you thinking about me." The bright rift in the air widened as he turned his head to peer over his shoulder, and King Krije saw the dragons. They were red and black and green—a number were somehow all three colors at once, depending upon how the light fell on them—and they were vast as cathedrals to Krije's sight, and there were far more of them than he could count. Dahr turned back again, and this time when he smiled, his teeth glittered like dragons' teeth. "The last time we visited together, I had wizards at my back. These may be a trifle more steadfast, perhaps . . . don't you think?"

He was gone then, and the dragons with him, and old King Krije clutched his hounds around him and bayed as they did, until guards and servants came running frantically with swords and torches and hot-water bottles in their hands, to find out what could possibly be tormenting their monarch. Krije was decidedly unclear on the cause of his distress; but for all the differing interpretations they made of it, each of them agreed on one astonishing point. He was actually calling for his son.

It was only on the way into Corvinia that the Princess Cerise finally yielded to temptation and drew her writing materials out of her saddlebag. The maneuver was a tricky one, because she had never let anyone see her struggling to teach herself to read, and she had no intention of starting now. Prince Reginald already knew, of course, but somehow that was different, because he was royalty like herself, and therefore illiterate. But Robert plainly *could* read, and the Princess felt distinctly shy—more than shy—about studying in his presence.

So she worked at night, by moonlight or firelight, and only after her companions were asleep. Sometimes her fingers would grow too numb with cold even to pick up the cold stylus, but she did her best as long as she was able. Then she would carefully pack stylus and wax away, along with the ancient poem she had been copying for so long, and slip back between the slumbering, snoring men, drawing what warmth she could from their larger bodies. Without snuggling.

Inevitably, because that is the way with such things, it was Robert who discovered her at her lessons. Apart from the practice it gave her, the poem itself was absorbing enough that she often got lost in the flood of it, completely unaware of what might be going on around her. It happened so on the last night of their descent from Maedchensflucht Pass, when she looked up and whirled to see Robert squatting comfortably on his heels behind her, his eyes friendly but his face without expression. Caught between alarm, discomfiture, and anger, she stammered, "I—I didn't know you were there."

To her surprise, she realized quickly that he was more embarrassed than she. "I'm sorry—I didn't mean to be spying on you. You learn to be really quiet when you do . . . what I do. But I just got caught up admiring the way you were teaching yourself. I couldn't ever have figured it out alone, reading. If it weren't for my sisters . . ." He shook his head, smiling now. "That's amazing, what you're doing."

The Princess blushed, which always annoyed her. She said shortly, "Anyone can do it. I think everyone should. Princes too."

Prince Reginald belched gently in his sleep, and both of them used it as an excuse to look over at him, and not at each other. Robert asked, "What are you copying? It looks crumbly."

"It is. I have to be very careful with it. It's the *Chanson de Jeannot et Lucienne*. I stole it from my father's library."

Robert's eyes widened. "The one about the boy and the girl who run off because he's accused of killing a bailiff—"

"Who was about to evict this poor old man—"

"Right, only he didn't do it, it was someone else—"

"Don't tell me! I haven't gotten to that part yet!" The Princess sighed, suddenly downcast. "It goes so *slowly* sometimes—and you probably know it all by heart. . . ."

"Well, my mother read it to me. Before I knew how." Robert was standing up slowly, stretching his cramped legs, when something occurred to him. "I could help you, if you like, Highness. Might make the learning go a little faster."

Princess Cerise considered the offer, plainly tempted, but finally shook her head. "No, I have to do this by myself. I don't know why—that's just how it is." She began replacing her kit back in the saddlebag. "Best sleep now, both of us."

They spoke no more of her studies that night; but as she lay half-awake on the mountainside, looking up at the cold, freckly stars, the Princess thought drowsily, *Prince Reginald hates his father, but he's running to save him anyway. I love* my *father, but I'm driving him mad with fear, putting myself in peril for strangers—for Reginald and King Krije. And Robert . . . did Robert love his father, or only learn from him? I wish I could ask him that, right now, that little boy in my bedroom, hanging on to that dragon for dear life. . . .*

"You have to ride. We'll never get *anywhere* with one of us always walking!"

"I've told you over and over—he's a donkey, he can't carry us both. You ride on ahead if you're in such a hurry. I'll catch up with you."

"I can't, I'm scared! He always runs away with me—he wouldn't if you were riding with me."

"Aha! So I'm useful for *something*, anyway!"

Stung, Elfrieda looked down at Ostvald from her tentative perch on the donkey's back. "Of course you are! You're good for plenty of things!"

"I am? Name two."

They might not have been squabbling in this fashion every step of the way from Bellemontagne; but if there had been a peaceful hour, neither of them remembered it. Now, however, Elfrieda fell silent at this challenge, long enough to wound Ostvald more than he thought he could be. He had just opened his mouth to say the most bitterly triumphant thing he could think of, when she answered him quietly, "You keep me from being afraid."

Ostvald stared. "I do *what?*" Elfrieda repeated her reply. "That's nonsense! You're scared on the donkey, like you just said—you're scared all the time at night, when you hear any noise anywhere—"

"Maybe I am. Maybe I'm just a big coward—all *right*! But I know you won't let anything bad happen to me—I've known that all my life." She glanced sideways at him and smiled for what seemed to Ostvald the first time in a very long while. She said, "How stupid do you think I am, anyway?"

Ostvald was having trouble breathing. Being Ostvald, he broke out in a pink sweat and prayed that Elfrieda wouldn't notice. He said thickly, "Robert . . . Robert wouldn't let anything bad happen. To you. Either."

"Oh, I know *that*," Elfrieda said impatiently, and nothing more for a while. Presently she demanded, "So? Are you going to get up with me or not?"

"Yes . . . well . . . I guess so. But if I'm too heavy . . ." It was almost possible for him simply to swing a leg over the donkey's back as he walked in order to mount up behind her. Both of them had been washing in whatever streams they encountered along the way, but they smelled of the journey even so, and of the donkey. But all Ostvald smelled was Elfrieda's hair, never for a moment noticing what might be tangled in the curls. He put his hands on her waist, lightly and very carefully . . . then withdrew them . . . then put them back where they had been. Elfrieda said, "Oh, for all the gods' sake!" and patted his hands, once.

By and by, he said, "The donkey seems to be doing all right."

"Told you."

"But we're still not going to catch up with them. Not in time."

Elfrieda turned her head sharply to look back at him. "In time for what?" There was a distinct quaver in her voice.

"I don't know." Ostvald shrugged helplessly. "For whatever's going to happen, which we probably wouldn't be any help with anyway. You heard what the King said about the dragons. You ever see a really big dragon? I mean, *really* big?"

"Yes," Elfrieda said boldly; and then, "No. Not a *big* one."

"Well, I've seen wyverns. With Robert. They can be nasty, those, but I don't think that's what that wizard's got with him. I think it's going to be much worse than wyverns. Bound to be."

"We're still not turning back. We *can't*, Ostvald!"

"I know we can't—I didn't say that. What I'm saying is . . ." In a lifetime of fumbling for the right words, or anything halfway resembling the right words, Ostvald had never fumbled quite this desperately. He said finally, "When we *do* get there, and it's all going on—I mean, whatever *it* is—I'd really feel better, be happier, if you'd sort of stay a little out of the way. I mean, just maybe don't go rushing up to rescue somebody, or fight somebody . . . you know? At least *think* about it?" Elfrieda did not respond, or turn again to look at him, and he cried out impulsively, hopelessly, "Damn it, I'm just asking you to take care of yourself, if . . . if I can't! That's all."

They jogged slowly on, hardly faster than Ostvald's own walking pace would have been, and still Elfrieda remained silent, and did not look back at him. When she did speak, he almost missed it, so low her voice was. She said, "You're sweet."

"No, I'm not," Ostvald said. "I'm big and thick and gawky, and Robert does everything right, and so do you—practically—and I've never understood why you two have always let me be your friend. All these years, I've never understood." He realized that he was shouting, and lowered his own voice until it was almost as soft as hers. "I'm just . . . thankful."

Abruptly Elfrieda slipped to the ground, to continue walking beside the donkey, looking straight ahead. When he got over his astonishment, he mumbled, "Why are you doing that? You don't have to do that."

Elfrieda did look up at him then, and the black eyes were a thunderhead of anger, the irises hardly visible. "I'm doing that so I can hit you better!" She pounded his thigh hard with her clenched fist. "So I can *hit* you better . . . so I can *hit* you better . . ."

"Ow!" Ostvald protested. "*Ow*, quit it!" The blows hurt—small or not, Elfrieda was a good deal stronger than she looked—but the only way to avoid them would have been to kick out at her, which was simply not in him to do. Instead he kicked the donkey into a kind of ambling trot, so that she had to run alongside him, still pummeling his leg and gasping, "So I can *hit* you better—idiot, idiot, *idiot!*" What with the pain, and the embarrassment, it took Ostvald some while to realize that she was crying.

He slid from the donkey's back himself and walked on her far side, watching her hands at all times. He said, when he judged it safe, "Don't cry. Please, Elfrieda."

He reached for her hand, but she pulled it away. "You're right, you *are* thick—*so* thick—and I don't know why anybody bothers with you, and walk on the other side if you're going to walk." And that was how they passed the rest of the day, speaking hardly at all, even when he built their fire and made a stew of roots she had never imagined might be edible, let alone surprisingly tasty.

But in the night, though she never knew it, she rolled over to sleep with her head on his shoulder. Ostvald gathered her in, as gently and carefully as he had ever done anything, and lay looking up at the strange stars of Corvinia, thinking thoughts just as high and foreign. He did not think he would ever sleep again.

He did, of course, weary as he was, but not before he saw the first great shadows passing over. The moon was half-hidden by clouds, and at first he took these for more of the same, until it became obvious that they were moving far too fast for that, and looked far too similar. Then it was that his gift for resignation served him well, for he said aloud, "Tomorrow. Tonight is mine," and sank into a tranquil doze.

SEVENTEEN

Robert knew the instant they crossed into Corvinia by the nearly immediate change in the terrain. Bellemontagne took its name from the rich hills and peaks he and his companions had crossed on their way; Corvinia leveled out within his sight into flat, hard country, suitable for marching large numbers of troops around, but as far as Robert could see, unwelcoming to any but soldiers. Even color seemed to leach out at the frontier: it was a pale, sandy land under a pale sky. Robert said aloud, forgetting Prince Reginald's presence, "No wonder Krije keeps snapping up other people's territory. Who wouldn't, living here?"

Strangely, it was Prince Reginald who chuckled, for perhaps the first time since they had met him on the road after his encounter with the wizard Dahr. "Corvinia might be the only thing in the world my father actually loves. He's convinced everyone else loves it too, and they're all plotting to steal it from him, so he has to take their land first. What else can he do?"

Robert and the Princess Cerise both looked at him in some astonishment; it was as much as he had said at one time on the entire journey. Maddeningly, to Robert, the Prince's accumulated grime and general grubbiness managed to make him look even more craggily valiant, valiantly weathered—something on that order, anyway. Yet he continued quiet, helpful, yielding leadership completely to the two of them, behaving neither like Robert's superior nor even his equal, but more like a willingly docile servant. Robert found this increasingly unsettling, especially since he himself had not entirely given up his vision of one day serving as Prince Reginald's personal valet. Dream or not, it was still more real and much more attractive to him than any notion of heroism. *Heroes kill dragons. I don't want to kill dragons. Heroes marry princesses. . . .*

The Princess asked, "How far is your father's city? What is it called?"

"Haults-Rivages," Prince Reginald said, "A day's ride if we push the horses. A day and a half or so if we don't."

"And a good bit less if you fly." Unlike Ostvald, Robert had not seen the dragons passing over, but he had no doubt that they were on their way, and that Dahr might already be savoring his revenge on King Krije. "Highness, what size of an army does your father maintain?" He could not keep from asking, lower but yet audibly, "For what it's worth."

Prince Reginald did bridle slightly at the implication. "The largest and best-armed by far in this part of the world. We have a saying in Corvinia: 'We grow soldiers as others grow grains of rice.' Alas, you can't eat soldiers, but my father doesn't appear to have found that out."

"He may," Robert said, still quietly. "He may."

They tried hard not to push the horses, but restraint was impossible for any of them. Alternating between a strict trot and an easy canter, inevitably one or another rider—usually, but not always, Prince Reginald—would urge his mare into a gallop, and inevitably the others would follow on at the same pace. This, in turn, would lead to halting altogether to rest and water their mounts, costing them, in the end, more time than they gained. But all three were remembering a wood in another land, and the dragons devouring horses as greedy children gobble gumdrops and peppermints, and there seemed no other way to treat their three.

They spoke little, each straining eyes and mind ahead, expecting every moment to see the horizon splintered with fire, the sallow, empty sky clouded with greasy black smoke. Ironically, the land itself was growing oddly appealing, to Robert's eye at least: flat still, flat in every direction, but laced with subtle, shadowy hints of real color, and dotted with actual trees and bushes, tracing the courses of real streams. Nor was the countryside as totally uninhabited as he had first supposed—he caught sight of rabbits, and of deer colored like smoke over a winter landscape. There were ducks as well, and something like a short-legged flamingo; and he began to see, at least a little, how someone like King Krije might imagine other rulers lusting after his realm as much as he did.

There was still no sign of dragons' presence in the land when they camped that night in a grove of tall, thin trees that Prince Reginald directed them to, saying that he had played outlaw there with his friends many times as a boy. His spirits seemed to have improved steadily through the day, as he recognized favorite landmarks and told stories out of his childhood about almost every one. His long-exhausted charm reasserted itself in full force, and he dominated the conversation effortlessly, riding stirrup to stirrup with Princess Cerise to point out this or that historic location. Most of them commemorated one or another of King Krije's famous victories, or those of his ancestors. As Prince Reginald said, in some embarrassment, "It's what we do, my family. Fight people. We've never been good at anything else."

"But you're good at other things," the Princess said. "Lots of other things. You're a *very* good cook—I'd never have thought to do what you did with those squirrels. And you're a *much* better rider than I am, and . . . and you have *such* a nice speaking voice. I'll bet your father doesn't have a voice anything like yours."

"No," Prince Reginald said quietly. "Just a really good collection of heads on spikes outside the castle gates."

In the morning he and his mare were gone. Robert and the Princess hunted for him in increasing alarm, both making wider and wider casts in every direction. When Robert said in frustration, "A note—why couldn't he have left a note?" Princess Cerise reminded him tartly, "Because he can't read or write. He's royal."

"But you can write," Robert protested. "You teach yourself every night—maybe he could have—"

Both saw it at the same time: the corner of the Princess's wax tablet protruding slightly from her open saddlebag. She seized the block, held it up in the dawn light, and slowly read it. *FOGIVE GO. MI DA MI FITE*. In place of a signature, there were only the two words, *MI FRENS*.

Princess Cerise dropped the tablet. She did not cry, but she put both hands to her mouth.

Robert said the bleakly obvious. "He went alone. He went off to face Dahr and the dragons alone. To protect us."

"He went alone because he's stupid!" the Princess responded furiously. "He wants to rescue his stupid father all by his stupid self, to prove he's really brave, really a prince. . . ." She was literally turning in circles, unable to contain her anger. "I am so *sick* of heroes! I don't want anything to *do* with heroes—I wouldn't have one if you gave him to me with half a pound of tea!" Startled, Robert laughed in spite of himself, and she promptly wheeled on him. "And that means you too! Definitely you too!"

The two of them stood staring at each other in a moment suddenly different from any since he had burst into her room at the age of nine. Robert felt overheated, and more than a little dizzy; but one part of him was entirely aware that in the books and ballads that had begun to take up all of his sister Rosamonde's free time—Patience being still too young to be interested in such things—at this point the boy usually swept the girl up in his arms and practically devoured her with flaming kisses. But the moment passed in mutual confusion. He said only, "Well, if you don't think it's being too heroic, let's go get him. Again."

The Princess nodded. Robert joined her in cleaning up their camp and repacking their saddlebags and blankets, all without a word on either side. But when Robert put a hand under the Princess's foot to help her into the saddle, she touched his hair, so lightly that he thought he might have imagined it. She said, "I am glad you are with me."

They set a quicker pace this time, but there was no sign of Prince Reginald anywhere ahead. What both of them did feel was a darkening: an intense awareness of shadows on their road heralding a coming storm; of the air drawing tighter and tighter around them until they could almost see the strain in the fabric of the sky itself, and sense it in their own drumhead skins. The horses seemed to be breathing with difficulty, and they themselves could only bow their heads and struggle on, wanderers helpless against a rising wind. And yet the sky was clear, the sun ripely warm, and it was absurd for Robert to envision the two of them as a pair of skeletons jog-trotting to nowhere on dead horses. Yet he did see them so, as though from very far away, and the image would not leave him.

"Hurry," he said, more than once, and they did press the horses; but even when the towers of Haults-Rivages began to show their tips on the horizon, Prince Reginald was nowhere in view. They scanned the roadside for any sign that he might have been injured—or worse—but saw no hoofprints leading away, nor any shrubbery suspiciously bent or broken. Prince Reginald might as well have turned into one of the stumpy-legged flamingos of this land and flown away.

"He had two hours' start of us, no more," Robert said through his teeth. "I woke before dawn, and he was still there, still asleep. He must have driven the mare to death to have already reached Haults-Rivages."

The Princess was—unconsciously, Robert thought—bending more and more over the neck of her horse, urging it on like a jockey. Speaking in short, breathless bursts, she said, "If I were Dahr . . . if I were a bad, bad wizard, with a score to settle . . . with a score to settle with a king who killed me . . . who *destroyed me . . . I* would go after his son before I ever touched him. . . ." She suddenly flashed a conspiratorial smile at Robert, such as he had never seen before. "Of course, Dahr may not be nearly as mercilessly vengeful as I am."

Very quietly, so low that Princess Cerise had to lean from her saddle, straining to hear him, Robert said, "I think he might be. Look behind us."

Seemingly between one minute and the next, the sky was full of dragons. Red, black, and green, for the most part—though Robert noticed an ice-white one to the rear, and another almost turquoise—they swarmed over the horizon, a dozen at a time, a score at a time, with the abandon of kittens scrambling up the sky. Horrifying visions out of the oldest nightmares, with their long jaws stretched wide and their great wings thundering, there was even so a ravenous joy about them, as though they could only barely contain their pride and pleasure in being what they were. And Robert, fleeing before them, as the Princess did, could not pretend not to feel the fearful surge of wonder in his heart, and his own strangely insistent sense of being one, somehow, with these terrible creatures. He felt himself glowing with it, in the midst of his dread, and was actually surprised that the Princess failed to notice.

Drawing a little ahead of him, she called back, "We must get to the city! Reginald *must* be there, somehow—and Krije will surely have his defenses ready—"

"Defenses? *Defenses?*" Robert could feel the first warning lurch in his horse's gait, and yet did not dare to slacken the pace. "How do you defend a kingdom against all the dragons in the bloody world?" He could not remember ever having felt so utterly lost and helpless; yet at the same time his entire body was thrumming with the equally helpless passion of being close to monsters, cousin to monsters. "*What* bloody defenses?"

If the Princess answered him, Robert could not hear her reply over the frenzied clamor now almost directly overhead. The unforgettable reek of cold ashes filled his nostrils, so that he seemed to be inhaling the dragons themselves: half choking on their ancient rage, halfway yearning to surge up out of his saddle and fuse with their pride and their power. His horse was plainly on the edge of foundering; only terror kept it on its feet, lunging along toward the approaching walls of Haults-Rivages. Princess Cerise, looking back, reined her own mount in sharply, slapping the animal's rump to indicate her intention. Robert took the deepest breath of his life, apologized softly, but aloud, to his horse, and leaped as strongly as he could to land behind the Princess, clutching her waist desperately to keep from toppling under flying hoofs. The horse staggered momentarily at the impact, but kept galloping as Robert righted himself. The Princess's hair smelled like warm wild honey, and he had not the courage to turn and see what had become of his own horse. Ahead of them, the gates of Haults-Rivages were swinging ponderously open to receive them.

Disoriented as he was, Robert could not help being impressed, less by the size of the place than by its massive fortifications. Krije, or some ancestor, had plainly decided that its walls were thick enough and its dominance of the surrounding landscape complete enough that it could have held off an army without ringing it with a moat or any stake-studded ditches. Against a normal army, he would have been quite right.

The walls were filling up with archers and crossbowmen, all with weapons cocked toward the dragon-cluttered heavens. Some novices were already loosing off—Robert could see their shafts clattering futilely off bony crests and naturally armored bellies—but most were professionals, waiting the command to let their first volley fly. Most of those undoubtedly knew, with Robert, that their arrows would be useless, but they held their positions all the same, and they waited as the dragons neared.

Robert saw a crowned man on the castle walls then. He seemed huge, even at a distance: wide-shouldered and deep-chested, and he strode from one group of bowmen to the next, brandishing a great shining spear, his purple cloak flaring out constantly with his movements, his bellowing voice audible as he rallied the castle's defenders. "Courage, you Godforsworn drunkards! We'll make pincushions of them all for our ladies' embroidery! Courage, I tell you! Who wants to live forever?"

He held them back dramatically with one upraised hand for an endless moment, until the vast, blazing flight seemed to hang motionless above the walls and the towers and the bright banners. Then he roared, so that every one of the dragons must have heard him, "*Now!*" and the arrows flew by the hundred, one whistling flight after another. And even on the ground, passing through the gates, with his own heart and the Princess's wildly pounding heart and her horse's stumbling breath the loudest sounds in the world, even so Robert could hear the shafts rattling futilely back to earth. Not a single dragon so much as veered or faltered before the barrage; rather, they banked as one to circle the castle—then, as one, settled themselves comfortably on the roofs and parapets, suddenly silent, folding their wings and cocking their heads attentively like so many parrots or canaries. King Krije's men, courageous as they were, scrambled away from them, dropping their weapons and clustering together, clutching one another for comfort. And even Krije himself, suddenly standing alone on the walls of his besieged castle—King Krije, whose overwhelming presence made Robert understand a great many things about Prince Reginald—Krije himself lowered his spear and his voice. "Dahr? Here I am, Dahr!"

Robert, sliding sideways off the lathered horse, caught Cerise as she tumbled out of the saddle. She ran instinctively toward the battlement stairs, with Robert following. Winded and panting, they reached the huge castle roof just as the uncannily white dragon opened its icy wings, allowing the wizard to step from their shelter. Robert thought that he had never seen so grandly commanding a figure. *He looks more of a king than Antoine, or this one either. Anyone who didn't know . . .*

"Well, Krije," the wizard said. "Well. Here we are."

The King's voice was like the first slow grumble of a landslide. "Here *I* am, anyway. Are you sure you're not another of your own filthy illusions?"

"Quite sure. Touch me if you doubt."

Dahr opened his arms invitingly, as though to embrace Krije. Even from where he stood, Robert could see the King rising to the bait, literally licking his lips. "If I ever do get my hands on you . . ."

"It should be interesting," Dahr replied thoughtfully. "Let's try it, shall we?"

King Krije took a single stride forward. The dragons lining his battlements never moved, but their long, angled eyes came wide open, making a sound together that licked pins along the back of Robert's neck. King Krije did not take a second step. Dahr said, "Perhaps not."

"What do you want?" Now Krije's voice had a hoarse, hesitant quality, as though he were strangling on his own rage. "Foul thing, what do you want of me?"

The wizard looked mockingly reproachful. "Oh, that is *not* nice, old friend. Do I call you names because of what you did to me? Do I so much as raise my voice to you? No, instead I go out of my way to prove that I hold no grudges, bear no ill will—more, I even rescue and shelter someone mightily important to you. At least, I assume he is—"

The Princess drew a single breath, and Robert whispered, "Oh, dear gods . . ."

The King said, "Where is he?" Robert thought he had never heard deeper despair crowded into three quiet, toneless words.

Only Robert saw the change in Dahr's eyes. But a second dragon unfolded its wings, with a sound like sails filling in the wind. Prince Reginald tumbled out of the freezing embrace, face forward, and lay where he had fallen.

King Krije did not move or speak, but only looked toward Dahr. Not until the wizard's eyes had cleared, and he nodded graciously, did Krije go to his son, kneeling beside him, the purple cloak trailing over Prince Reginald's body. Robert and Princess Cerise could not hear the king's words; nor could they tell whether the Prince was alive or dead, until the hoarse cheer—half cry of joy, half defiant growl at the fangs and wings that hemmed them in—went up from Krije's men, and several, valiantly ignoring the dragons, ran to assist Prince Reginald. Dazed, unable to rise without support, he seemed otherwise unharmed.

No one, including Prince Reginald, took any notice of either Robert or the Princess. All attention was focused on three figures: the Prince himself, the plainly anguished and helpless King Krije, and the wizard Dahr, looking on placidly. Clearly enough for all to hear, he said, "There, Krije. Bear witness how *some* people return good for evil."

Prince Reginald was on his feet now, standing alone, except for his father's powerful hands on his shoulders. Krije inquired, his voice uncommonly gentle and concerned, "Boy, how do you fare? Can you stay up if I take my hands away?"

Prince Reginald's voice was barely audible. "I think so, Father."

"Good," King Krije said. He stepped away then, drew his arm back deliberately, and slapped Prince Reginald across the face hard enough that he would have fallen again, had not several onlookers leaped to support him. A shocked gasp went up all around the scene, but it was drowned by Krije's bellow of contemptuous rage. "*Idiot!* Only an idiot like you—if there could ever be such a thing—only a stone-headed *idiot* like you could get himself captured by my worst, my most evil enemy in the whole world! Now I suppose I'll have to ransom you back, when what I really feel like doing is throwing you from the topmost tower of this castle. Bloody *idiot*—I might have *known* it!" He wheeled to face Dahr, who was laughing softly, almost silently, to himself. "All right, then, you. How much?"

With no eyes on them, Robert and Princess Cerise had inched their way close enough for Prince Reginald to see them. His eyes widened slightly, but he gave no other sign of recognition. Dahr did not reply immediately—so visibly was he savoring the situation—and King Krije repeated, louder, "How much for the idiot?"

For all the terror that the dragons and their lord woke in him, Robert found a strange and paradoxical comfort in observing the great creatures perched on the battlements, so motionless that they might have been stone gargoyles, except for their eyes. His glance passed over them slowly, one by one—raw-red, storm-green, deep sea-black, glacier-white—and each, as he studied it, turned its terrible gaze on him and saw him. He felt them seeing him, and he should have been frightened—and he *was* frightened . . . only not as he should have been.

The wizard Dahr, still chuckling, spoke kindly and patiently, "No, no, my good Krije, you mistake me. The boy is not for sale." And there was something in that warm, amused voice that chilled Robert far more than the piercing glares of all the dragons.

"Not for sale." King Krije scratched his head, then folded his arms belligerently. "Not for ransom, you mean? Nonsense—anybody can be ransomed!"

"Not this one, I'm afraid." Dahr moved closer to the king, patting his shoulder—almost caressing it, as one might do with a cherished friend. "No, my question regarding your son is whether I ought to have these colleagues of mine roast him crisp before your eyes, or simply take him up to rather a height and leave him to find his way back down. It's a delicate decision, as I'm sure you'll appreciate"—the amusement turned as hard as the walls of Haults-Rivages itself—"having made so many, many similar choices in your time. I would greatly value your opinion—perhaps you can advise me?"

The gasp from the onlookers this time was of horror, mingled not only with tears, but with cries of outrage and protest as King Krije's soldiers moved to their Prince's defense. But the dragons stretched themselves lazily on the parapets, rumbling so deeply that the sound was less heard than felt in the stones underfoot. People looked down, looked anywhere but at Krije and his son, looked desperately ashamed of their fear; but Robert felt nothing but sympathy for them all. *I can't help any more than they can. Prince Reginald's going to die, and Krije too, and maybe everybody up here, and there's nothing in the world I can do.*

In the silence—a sad abyss of shuffling feet and wordless mumbling—King Krije said calmly, "Take me."

EIGHTEEN

Just for that moment, caught completely off guard, the wizard Dahr stared blankly. Krije repeated—and this time it was a defiant roar to overwhelm all his other roars, "Take *me*, what do you want with him? He's done you no harm, but I have, and proud of it, and I'd do it again! *Me*, not the idiot!" He spat at Dahr's feet.

A very young woman standing next to Princess Cerise began to whimper and tremble and the Princess drew her close, all unaware. The silence on the castle rooftop was broken only by the deep wintry breathing of the waiting dragons, and Robert found his eyes once again drawn irresistibly to them. They looked back at him, every one, feeling him as he felt them. *But what do you want? What do you expect of me? Dahr is master here, not I.* He thought of the dragonlets at home—Adelise and Lux and shy Reynald—and tried to see them in the magnificently menacing forms towering all around him. *What is it we know about each other?*

The wizard shook his head slowly, in something like

admiration. "There's gallantry, Krije, no question about it. No king, at the last, but only a father willing to sacrifice himself for his son. But how can you know that I will let him live after I've avenged myself on you? What reason would I have to keep my word to one who murdered me?"

"Reason?" King Krije laughed then, for the first time. "Reason? You forget that I know you, Dahr. There wouldn't be one minute's pleasure for you in killing that poor fool—aye, or my people, either, or burning down this castle—if I weren't there to see it." He lowered his voice slightly, pointing a sausage-sized finger at the wizard. "And if you try that now, if you or your pets make a move toward the boy—why, then you'll *have* to kill me straightaway, *old friend*, because I'll come for you. And I *will* have my hands on you, whatever you do, and this time I'll take that staff of yours and I'll shove it—"

Dahr, his poise restored, waved him grandly to silence. "Never mind, never mind, most articulate Krije, it shall be as you wish. You are quite right, I have no interest in your son or your servants. Your castle, yes—it will suit me splendidly, for the time being—and your ill-gotten little empire, entirely. And I have certain plans, certain visions . . . but really, I came back for you alone. The rest is . . . incidental."

"Honored." King Krije sketched a clumsy, uncomfortable-looking bow. "So. It's settled, then?"

"It is settled."

On the word, there came a rasping downrush of air, as the six largest dragons took wing from the battlements, surrounding Krije, who stared only at the wizard Dahr. The dragons craned their necks to consider the King. Some even ran out their flame-red tongues, as though to taste him.

Prince Reginald found his voice, gritty and raw. "No. *No*, bloody hell, absolutely not! Take me, if you're bound to kill someone—take me, by all the gods! Live out my life with his sacrifice, his martyrdom, hanging around my neck forever? Thank you very much, I'd rather die! You'll take *me* and like it, do you hear?" Lurching, he thrust himself between his father and the nearest dragons.

Dahr cocked a sardonic eye at Krije, his smile a razor slash. "A certain family resemblance there, I think?"

"Aye, to my disgrace!" Krije thundered, shoving his son forcibly aside. "You'll die for no one, boy, it's not in you to do! You'll live a long, useless, namby-pamby life and die in bed—your own, more's the pity—with priests and women all around you. Out of my way now, and see how a *man* dies! And tell your children, if you should ever somehow manage—"

Prince Reginald hit him. It was no open-palmed slap, but a powerful punch with a shoulder as broad as Krije's behind it. It landed squarely on the king's mouth, and Krije dropped his spear and went over like a bowling pin. He was up almost on the instant, crown gone, spitting blood and lunging for Prince Reginald's throat. They rolled together at the dragons' feet, while Dahr the wizard stepped back, laughing truly for the first time. "At it, go to it, by all means!" he cried. "Settle your score—if not now, when, after all? But don't damage your sire overmuch, good prince—he's mine!"

In the midst of the thundering insanity happening all around them, a small motion drew Robert's eye: the girl slipping free of the Princess's sheltering arm. Cerise looked like every day of their journeying: sweaty, dirty, straggle-haired, bad-tempered, with several broken fingernails and a bruise on her left cheekbone.

Robert thought he had never seen her so beautiful, and the realization terrified him. *Please, no. I'm a dragon-exterminator. I'm a dragon-exterminator with visions of being a valet. Please.*

King Krije's soldiers, however cowed, had remained with him to a man; but most of the servants and other castle folk were slipping away on every side, with no hindrance from the dragons, or from Dahr himself. The wizard was clapping his hands slowly and deliberately, letting the sound echo over the castle roof. "Entertaining," he said. "For a time." He nodded once to the dragons, but spoke directly to Robert and Princess Cerise. "I would stand no closer, if I were you. There is often a certain back draft to the more complex spells." His white hair and beard glowed richly in the light of the descending sun.

"Wait," Prince Reginald said. "Wait." His voice was different, the voice of a child. "*Wait*, what are you doing? That's my father."

"Be still, boy!" Krije's growl was low and strangely calm—*dignified*, Robert thought wryly. To the wizard Dahr he said, "I wouldn't come too close to me either, if I were you. In case of accidents."

"Indeed." The wizard studied the King meditatively, as though they two were the only beings anywhere under the peach-colored sunset clouds. "Your pardon," he said with all apparent sincerity. "I have been anticipating this precise moment for so long, in this world and elsewhere, that I begrudge every instant of my vengeance, every least drop of it. You will understand better than most, I think."

"Indeed," Krije mimicked him. "Just get it done with, will you? How much longer must I listen to your yammering?"

"Not long," the wizard answered softly. "Not long at all." He raised his hands before him, framing King Krije between them, like an artist shaping an unpainted portrait in the air. Prince Reginald cried out desperately once again, "That's my *father*!" and Krije had just time to rumble, "Be *still*, damn you!" before Dahr brought both hands down and spoke. Where King Krije had stood there remained a golden statue, its arms folded and a ferocious scowl on its gleaming face.

Prince Reginald jumped for Dahr's throat with the same savage abandon that his father had leaped for his own, but was brought up as brutally short as though the air between him and the wizard had turned to glass. A dreadful groan went up from the onlookers, and even King Krije's soldiers scattered for the stairways and passages that led to the ground and escape. From where he stood, Robert could see them tumbling onto their horses or simply fleeing blindly across the lean landscape, constantly looking up and back as they ran, for fear of pursuit by Dahr's dragons. But there was none.

Prince Reginald gathered himself for a second futile assault on the wizard Dahr. He was raging and crying together, and the others tried not to hear anything he shouted, because it felt too shamefully like eavesdropping.

Robert shouted, "Highness, *no*, you can't help him that way!" The Princess herself was in tears, sinking under a wave of helplessness, a sensation as unfamiliar as it was infuriating.

Dahr ignored the struggle. He was admiring his handiwork, prowling around the golden Krije, considering it from every angle. Robert heard him sigh, "Simply beautiful—haven't lost the old touch," and then, "Such a pity . . . I could almost wish . . ." The statue of King Krije reflected the setting sun off the dragons' scales, in fire.

"*Enough.*" Dahr spoke no charms, made no visible gesture, but Prince Reginald abruptly fell silent and still. Dahr said, "There is no more time for foolishness. What I do now needs sunset to be effective. Say your farewells, if you will, and stand away."

Robert felt a sudden chill on his skin. The statue's eyes were King Krije's eyes, frozen in golden fury. Dahr followed the direction of his glance and nodded serenely. "Yes. He is there. He will always be there."

"What are you going to do?" Princess Cerise's voice was unnaturally even as she fought to keep it from trembling.

The wizard Dahr looked first at the red and pale green bars ribbing the horizon, then turned slowly back to her. He said, "Great monarchs of the past have often made royal thrones of their enemies' skulls and skeletons. I've always found that sort of thing vulgar in the extreme." The slow, closed-mouth smile seemed to slither across his face. "Krije entire will be my very throne, my golden seat of power and majesty, and not only will everyone who kneels before it know this, but so will Krije himself." They stared at him, sickened with understanding, and Dahr nodded amiably. "Oh, yes. His form may change, but his consciousness—that unique perception that made him the Krije we all know and love—that will remain. I'm sure Krije would have it no other way. *I* certainly wouldn't."

Prince Reginald remained mute and motionless, whether through wizardry or simple shock Robert could not tell. He himself stayed rooted where he was, without thought or hope, and so without words. The Princess Cerise, however, was not, and Robert stood in awed admiration of the words she proceeded to employ, for three-quarters of which Odelette would still have sent him to his room. The golden King Krije appeared to be listening with practiced interest, and even Dahr cocked an ear and chuckled appreciatively. "You'd have made a splendid witch, my dear," he observed, with apparent sincerity. "There's real power in you, real flair. A pity there's not the time to take you in hand."

"If I *were* a witch," the Princess began, but Dahr stilled her with a gesture; he was looking not at her, but at his waiting dragons. In the silence, Robert heard inside what no one else on the vast roof could hear: the wizard was addressing them by name. *Just as I do, back home. Is Dahr my kinsman, then? Is that what I'm feeling here?*

The six dragons who had first encircled Krije—Robert provisionally identified two of them as the biggest *snap-so's* he had ever seen; the others were completely new species to him—drew in even closer around the golden statue, positioning themselves as precisely as though they had been rehearsing the process—*and maybe they have*, Robert thought. With one hand on Cerise's shoulder, he could feel her trembling with . . . what? Robert wondered. Fear—confusion—anticipation? *I know less of this woman than I know of these dragons*.

"Gold is a comparatively soft element when it occurs in nature," the wizard Dahr informed them, placidly professorial. "The gold I make, however, is of a rather different spirit. It is so hard that nothing in this world can melt it—nothing, that is, except a dragon's fire. And not *all* dragonfire, but only that of certain beasts born with the gift of shaping, which is the rarest and wildest of traits among their kind." He nodded proudly toward the six dragons. "I think of these, you might say, as my goldsmiths. Watch now."

He spoke, and the dragons responded.

It began far down in the deep, swaying belly of the largest *snap-so*. Beyond simple sound, it came first as a shuddering in the great stones beneath their feet, and built to the roar of an avalanche. It was joined by successive mounting rumbles as each of the remaining five dragons joined in turn, until Krije's fortress shook to its bedrock roots. The impossible fire from the leader's mouth was white as a lightning bolt, nuzzling the golden King as affectionately as a house cat in a genial mood. Krije showed no effects at all; if anything, his defiant sneer seemed to grow more contemptuous. *It'll take a volcano*, Robert thought.

But it took only six dragons, six flames of what sometimes seemed a dozen different hues, to lick and caress and lovingly erode the great statue down to a bubbling yellow puddle with soft golden lumps in it. What came next would color their dreams.

Frozen cold to the core by horrified fascination, unable to turn away from the terrible remaking, Robert and Cerise looked on as the dragons went to work. They employed their fires like tongues and tongs and sculptors' chisels, swiftly rolling, molding, and smoothing the melted gold until it began to rise out of itself in a new form . . . that of a massively magnificent throne: but wondrous to Robert's eyes, who had never seen anything remotely that grand in Bellemontagne. *Even Krije would have liked it*, he thought in his dazzlement. *I'm sure he'd have been impressed.*

The dragons stood back from the golden throne, and it blazed atop the castle like a beacon of wicked triumph. It should have been unbearably hot to the touch for at least a day, born of such fires, but Dahr stroked and petted it, in the way that one pats the head of a child, or of a helpless enemy. "There," he said to it, "there. You have at last become what you were always meant to be, my dear Krije—the seat, the footstool, of one infinitely greater than yourself. And you shall commence your new career immediately—when I dine this evening with your son, with the charming Princess you planned for him to marry, and with their nameless but interesting servant. So glad you could be with us, old friend."

His eyes met Robert's for a moment, and Robert felt his stomach shrivel. *What does he see of me? What do he and his dragons know of me that I don't?* Speaking for his companions, he kept his voice timid and humble. "Sire, Majesty, we may not stay. We must away on the road to Bellemontagne this very night, to restore the Princess Cerise to her home, her anxious parents—"

"But this is Prince Reginald's home." The wizard sounded distinctly wounded. "Or it was, and it would be ungracious and unmannerly of me not to allow him to display its lost grandeur to his fiancée—"

"I am not his fiancée," Princess Cerise said quietly.

"Ah? Well, in any case, I cannot permit you young people to set off in the dark on such a long and undoubtedly perilous journey without at the very least seeing a proper meal into all three of you. No, no, certainly not—what sort of a host would I be? If you will please accompany me—"

"I wouldn't take food from your hands if I were starving to death in an *oubliette*." Prince Reginald's voice was as bleak as old armor, and as hoarse and rusty as though he had not spoken for years.

"You would if I insisted," the wizard Dahr answered him. "And I do insist."

NINETEEN

King Krije's dining chamber was different from the great hall of Castle Bellemontagne. There were no family portraits on the stone walls, for one thing, but they abounded in souvenirs of Krije's numberless conquests and victories. The customary swords, spears, shields, and pieces of armor that any king worth his crown will exhibit for his dinner guests were accompanied, in Krije's hall, by the very hand and arm bones that had brandished or shouldered them. For another, there were no dragons scurrying in the walls. They were crouched ringing the huge room, which already reeked coldly of their presence. Robert could not escape the sense that every one of their glinting diamond-shaped eyes was watching him.

He and the Prince and Princess were seated at the far end of a long, wide table, while the wizard Dahr presided at the other, begging forgiveness earnestly and often for the lack of other guests and the presumed spareness of the banquet. "When you've just taken over someone's castle, it's so difficult to know where things are. And as royalty yourselves, you know how hard it is to find good help." With a small shrug of apology, he indicated the servants coming and going around the table.

The servants handled their tasks with faultless efficiency, laying the table and setting out the meal—actually lavish, and quite good—but Robert found them almost as disturbing as the stares of the dragons. They were utterly silent, which is not the same as not speaking: neither their feet nor their breath made any sound, and their eyes were of a uniform pale yellow, never meeting the eyes of the three they served. There was a tallowy softness about them, as though they had literally been shaped out of candle wax. Unlike the dragons, they had no smell at all.

Robert turned from studying them to see Dahr smiling down the table at him. "Yes, you have it right, young sir, you do indeed—and quicker than your betters, to boot. These poor minions, I am shamed to confess, are neither human nor even animal, but were created for this single festive occasion from such scraps and leavings as I could find in King Krije's kitchens. That chap there"—he pointed—"was, earlier today, an honest loaf of brown bread, and will be again, once we are done here and the table cleared. That other began life as, I believe, a potato, or it might have been a turnip." He frowned slightly, trying to remember; then grew cheerful once again. "Actually, at this stage of my life, soldiers and servitors weary me. I find that the root vegetables in general make perfectly adequate human beings, as required. Animals—mice, dogs, goats, pigs—they don't do nearly as well. Curious, that, don't you think?"

He turned his head, to gaze with obviously genuine fondness at the vast creatures looming against the walls. "Of course you could never make a dragon out of any of them, not the best of them. No one can *make* a dragon." He paused for a moment. "Only I."

Robert stood abruptly, looking left and right, seeing his own feelings echoed on his companions' faces. "It is late, and a long road home awaits us. We must go."

"Ah well. If you must." He turned to Princess Cerise. "Give my most sincere regards to dear old Antoine, and tell him that we will surely meet again before too long."

To Prince Reginald he said with every evidence of sincerity, "I do hope you won't hold my somewhat strained relationship with your father against me. Considering that he destroyed me completely, after all, I rather think that I have been quite forbearing in my treatment of him. Believe me, he will come to be quite content in his new role as my seat of power—there's never been a throne that didn't have its own opinions." He peered shrewdly up at the tall prince, who avoided his eyes. "And whether you will admit it or no, you have choices tonight that you did not have this morning. Tell me I lie." Prince Reginald did not answer him.

He said no word to Robert as he escorted the companions out to the warm, heavy dark. The dragons came after, in a procession half-menacing, half solemnly comic. Dragons are not made for much walking: certainly not in line, like circus elephants clinging to each other's tails. Yet so they came, at Dahr's wordless direction—or was it Dahr whom they followed? Robert continued to avoid the diamond eyes.

Prince Reginald had already mounted, and Princess Cerise had calmed her own horse, unnerved by the nearness of the dragons. She had one foot in the stirrup, ready to mount, when the wizard spoke.

"I fear that your young servant will not be able to accompany you on your journey home. I must request that he remain with me—on a purely temporary basis, of course. He shall be returned to your employ shortly, I assure you."

If King Krije had been transformed into a golden statue, Robert felt himself turning to ice. As though from a great distance, he saw Prince Reginald turn inquiringly in the saddle, while Princess Cerise wheeled to confront the wizard Dahr, saying, with the full royal hauteur that Robert had heard before, "That will not be possible. I require his services."

"Ah, but so do I," Dahr replied regretfully. "Alas, Highness, what a poor sort of host you must think me, to guest you and see you to my gate, and to the right road—and then to snatch your servant bodily from your side. I can only beg your forgiveness, promise to make the inconvenience up to you, as I may, and repeat that I will not keep him long." Without seeming to move, he had nevertheless somehow interposed his body between Robert and his companions. "Not long, my word on it."

"You will not keep him at all." The Princess's voice was very quiet, but it held a quality to it that Robert had never heard from her, and that he would have been very happy to hear at his back forever. She said it again. "I am the Princess Cerise of Bellemontagne, and my servant goes where I go."

She said, "Where I go." She didn't say, "Where Prince Reginald and I go." Why am I even thinking *about this right now?*

The Princess's dress sword, meant only for occasions of state, would have been as much practical use in difficulties as a stick of candy. But Prince Reginald, swinging grimly down from his horse to stand behind her, had slipped the daunting *Doppelhänder* from its saddle scabbard, holding it at his waist with no apparent effort beyond a bit of heavy breathing. Robert edged away from her, silently pleading, *Stay back. Mother, make her stay back.*

Dahr shook his head. "To end such a delightful evening in unpleasantness—what a pity. Is there nothing I can do to avert your vexation?"

The Princess Cerise said, "You could tell us why you want to keep Robert prisoner. It will make no difference, but you could tell us."

The wizard's head shake this time was one of genuine—and only slightly mocking—admiration. "I certainly hope old Antoine and Hélène appreciate their daughter properly. If there were anything in me that might respond, even in the least, to a human relationship . . ." The Princess shuddered visibly, and Dahr smiled. "Yes. Well. Why do I want your Robert? I will show you."

Before any of them could move, he seized Robert by the arm and dragged him to face the largest of the six dragons. Robert struggled in his shockingly strong grasp, but Dahr forced him so close to the fanged head and bright, merciless eyes craning down at the end of the long neck that he could see the blue-green-blue ripple of the creature's scales, and taste the familiar scent of cold ashes. The dragon's gaze held him in a grip far more powerful than that of the wizard, and once again he cried out—or thought he did, *"Who am I? What do you want of me?"*

He was answered by a rumble he never really heard, but only felt; and not even in his bones, but absurdly through the soles of his feet and the tingling roots of his hair. Dahr said something in a language he did not know, and released him, shoving him toward the dragon.

Somewhere very far away, in time and in distance, he heard a woman's scream and a man's shout of rage. But there was nothing in his ears but the dragon's deep, jagged breath, and nothing to be seen in all the world but the blazing red gullet over him. Too frightened to feel fear, he thrust out his arm and cried directly into the monstrously wise face, "Back! I know your name! Back from me!"

And he did know the dragon's name. He knew the names and thoughts of every other of Dahr's creations, and knew that he was as safe among them as he would have been romping at home with Adelise, Fernand, or dear, clumsy Reynald. The dragon rearing above him bent its neck, low and deep, until the great head rested on the ground at his feet. Robert said, as formally as he knew how, "I greet you, Grand-Jacques."

And the dragon made a sound in answer.

So.

This is what I do.

This is who I am.

"You see, do you not, why I cannot let him leave?"

Behind him, Dahr spoke in the same dangerously quiet tone with which the Princess Cerise had spoken. "Your 'servant,' as you call him, is a dragonmaster born, as I am. I have met exactly two others in my life, which has been quite a long one, allowing for a somewhat unusual interval. Both are dead." He patted Robert's shoulder, almost affectionately. "This one . . . this one might be the most powerful yet. Too early to tell."

"And if you have your way," the Princess said, "we never will. Is that not so?"

Dahr spread his hands plaintively. "You continue to wrong me, child. Why would I seek to harm the first person I have encountered in more years than you or he have been alive who might be my equal—my superior, even? Princess"—his voice dropped into a lower range, and he spoke more slowly—"believe of me what you will, but it is lonely being who I am. I wish only to study your servant's ability for a while, and perhaps—I say *perhaps*—to be of some minor assistance in the ripening of his mastery." After a moment's silence, he repeated, "It is lonely, being who I am."

Princess Cerise did not answer him, but instead spoke haltingly to Robert. "I did not know . . . I mean, sometimes I thought . . . Robert, is this what you want to—?" when Prince Reginald interrupted her.

"No," he said. "Never." His own voice sounded like two millstones grinding together, and he held the *Doppelhänder* poised as if it were a club. He said, "You will not trust this man. Not ever, not in anything."

The wizard Dahr sighed. "Ah, again the business with your father, of course. What can I say to you? Krije and I understood one another perfectly—I so wish you could—"

Robert cut him short. He had been gazing from one of Dahr's dragons to the next, meeting their eyes now, his face showing nothing, betraying nothing. But he turned abruptly and was close enough to Dahr in two quick strides that the wizard actually took a step backward. The Princess put her hand on Robert's arm, but he looked only at Dahr.

"No, we will leave," he said, "all three of us. Your dragons will not hold me here."

Princess Cerise became aware that she was trembling: not from fear of Dahr, or even of the dragons, but of the pallor of Robert's face. His eyes and mouth were steady, but his face was the color of the old ice on the highest crags of Bellemontagne. She drew her hand away.

Robert said, "You're a fool, Dahr. A great wizard, perhaps, but as great a fool. If you had simply let us go home, it would have been a long time, if ever, before I recognized myself in Grand-Jacques's eyes. But you hoped he might devour me on the spot, and save you the bother of killing me." He was the one who smiled this time, and the Princess shivered again. This was not the shy, half-embarrassed smile she had come to know. Dahr was staring, his eyes shifting rapidly left and right, his own mouth slightly ajar, as though he were about to speak. Princess Cerise heard Prince Reginald chuckle.

"We will leave now," Robert repeated. "The Prince and I will be back for King Krije shortly, so I'd advise you to treat him very well. Polish him regularly, and do make sure his lining is kept clean—that sort of thing. Your dragons will teach me how to return him to his human form when we come again." He laughed suddenly, the sound almost luminous in the night.

"It's a strange thing, Dahr, when you think about it," he went on softly, "but you and I are the only two here who will never have what they want. All my heart's desire, always, was to be some lord's personal valet—I couldn't imagine any greater leap for a poor dragon-exterminator. I still can't." The sad, shining laughter came again. "As for your dream, was it merely to revenge yourself on Krije and rule Corvinia in his stead, in his castle? Such a small dream, really, but it won't happen either, Dahr, none of it. No more than my dream."

Dahr said nothing. Robert mounted his own horse swiftly, and Princess Cerise and Prince Reginald followed. Robert looked past Dahr toward the dragons and spoke to them silently.

"Dahr made you—made all of you—so you must all be evil in your natures. I have seen your brothers, red and green and black, do terrible things for the pure pleasure of it, as my dragons, my dear vermin, never would, even if they could. And still . . . still . . ." He raised his hand to the dragons, and heard the answer in his mind. Then he turned his horse and rode out through the castle gate, and the others followed.

They cantered three abreast where the road was widest, none of them speaking for a time. The moon had not yet risen, and it seemed to Princess Cerise that the only brightness in the night came from the white rims of their horses' eyes and the glimmer of the *Doppelhänder*, now hanging at Prince Reginald's hip instead of his saddlebow. She heard strange night birds calling, and once a wolf.

After a while Robert said quietly to Prince Reginald, "We will return for your father very soon, I promise. And we *will* find a way to turn him back to himself again."

"I know that," Prince Reginald answered. He laughed outright, loudly enough that his horse nickered in startled response. He said, "It won't hurt him to be Dahr's throne for a while. Do him a bit of good, I should think."

"*I* would like to know," Princess Cerise announced to no one in particular, "where it is written that I will not be among the rescuers of King Krije. Who was it who made that decision for me? He and I need to talk."

"You will be at home being a princess," Robert answered without looking at her, "and there is a really good chance that your father and mother will not let you out of their sight again until you're . . . oh, say, thirty-six." His voice was resolutely light and humorous. "In any event, I doubt they'll look kindly on your rushing straight back into dragon country a second time. Can you tell me otherwise?"

"What I can tell you," the Princess said through her teeth, "is that my parents are my own business, mine to deal with. Dragonmaster or no, you will not presume to inform me of where I can or cannot go. That is understood?"

"Entirely." Robert kicked his horse into a gallop, still without once meeting her eyes. The Princess followed suit and kept up with him, continuing to expound on her independence from her parents, him, and everyone else, with the conspicuous exception of Prince Reginald, which did not escape his notice. She had rounded into full cry concerning everyone's protectiveness—for which she had previously known no better than to be grateful—on the occasion of Dahr's conquest of King Krije's forces and the capture of his castle, when Robert jerked the reins and brought his horse to an abrupt stop.

"Listen!"

The Princess was silent, hearing nothing but the hoofbeats of Prince Reginald's horse drawing up to them. The Prince himself, however, had clearly caught a sound, for the *Doppelhänder* was out, and he was looking back over his shoulder as he rode. He said simply, "It cannot be wings."

"It is wings," Robert said.

Twenty

The sound was oddly musical, like the deep chiming of vast icicles in the dead of winter. None of them had ever heard a sound like it before, but none of them was in the least doubt as to what it must be. Prince Reginald said, "Stay on the road. It can't get down to us, the trees are too thick."

But the Princess Cerise whispered urgently, "*No*—we need to get off the road right now and cut across the fields. Because that's just what it wouldn't expect us to do."

Robert considered for only an instant before he nodded. "They don't see all that well at night—there's a chance it might not even notice us. Let's go."

They walked the horses, guiding them in single file down the low embankment into a stubbly field apparently left lying fallow for the season. The rhythm of the wings behind them did not change; whatever was following was not yet aware of the new tactic. The Princess was afraid to look back, but she looked back anyway, seeing only an owl in a tree, and the upper curve of the half-moon just beginning to show above the horizon. But the soft, chill chiming continued.

They did not dare to speak, but their thoughts were loud enough that each was privately certain they must be heard by the others, or by something worse.

When this is over, I am going to ask Mortmain if a dragonmaster can still be a valet. . . .

When this is over, and my father himself again—all in good time, that—I am going to go very far away and get very, very drunk, and I'm not taking Mortmain. Then I'm going to lie in the grass and look up at the sky.

When this is over, I am going to scream. I am going to scream and scream until I have no voice left. No—no, I can't do that, not if I'm . . . with Reginald. He wouldn't understand. I could scream with Robert. Robert wouldn't mind. Wouldn't care, more likely, the selfish pig . . .

They were halfway across the field, aiming without consultation toward a covert that looked more sheltering than the trees along the road. Robert reached back without turning his head, found the Princess's hand resting in her horse's mane, squeezed it very lightly, and let go. She had only an instant to register the sudden startling comfort, when a shattering screech raked the black sky to shreds and replaced it entirely with fire.

The three horses screamed almost as loudly, reared as one, and galloped frantically off into the wood, leaving Robert, Prince Reginald, and the Princess Cerise to stare up at what was circling overhead.

A dragon, certainly, but a dragon like no other that Robert had ever seen. As golden as the half-moon, as golden as the throne of the wizard Dahr, it was more than twice the size of any two of his creatures together—Robert could not imagine how it got off the ground, and less how it maneuvered its vast body in flight. Nor did it husband its flame, as all the fire-breathing species do, but continued to light the sky with it, so that the moon turned gray and Robert could feel the heat in his chest, as the air burned around him. The Princess was already staggering from the lack of oxygen, and Robert and Prince Reginald moved close on either side to support her.

Prince Reginald had the *Doppelhänder* out, its hilt tucked hard against his body as though he actually knew how to use the great sword, its point following every move of the dragon's approach. His eyes sought Robert's eyes in mute question, and Robert croaked, "A King. That's a King." Prince Reginald simply nodded and turned back to bracing himself for the coming charge.

It's beautiful. It's the most beautiful, magnificent thing I ever saw, and it's going to kill us all.

No.

I'm a dragonmaster. Whatever that is. There has to be a way.

He called out to the dragon first. The King answered him with its sky-rending shriek, breathed out a blast of fire that turned the entire field to noon, and stooped at him. Robert had just time to notice that it fell, not straight down, like a striking falcon, but at a deepening angle, as an eagle skims the water's surface to snatch a fish. Then he hurled himself to one side, as the gale of the King's passing set him rolling violently over and over on the damp earth, among the sharp stalks of whatever had been growing there. Prince Reginald caught him before he slammed into the wild-apple tree.

The dragon swung away, climbing again, scaling the moon, turning to hover. *So big, how does it* do *that?* To Prince Reginald he gasped, "Move, move, get away, it's after me. Get away!"

"Not bloody likely," the Prince said quietly; and in the midst of terror and confusion, Robert had to gape and stare to make sure of the man. Prince Reginald was standing almost astride him, the *Doppelhänder* still pointed unwaveringly at the golden flame wheeling high above them. He said, "You are the one who must stand away, my friend. This is the moment I was born for."

"Actually, it's not," Robert said apologetically. He pushed himself to his feet, touching the Prince's arm to urge him to lower the sword. "It was sent for me. Dahr sent it. I really don't think anyone else can kill it."

"I can," Prince Reginald replied. "This is the one dragon I will ever kill." He grinned at Robert then, a hero's grin. "The rest are all yours—you can spare me this one." He strode out into the center of the field, threw his head back, and shouted up at the King, "Here I am, worm! Crown Prince Reginald Richard Pierre Laurent Krije of Corvinia, at your service. Do not keep me waiting!"

The dragon took him at his word.

It came gliding in at the same high angle, astonishingly swift, the curious chiming of the wings now all but silenced. Robert and Princess Cerise both cried out as it seemed to home in on Prince Reginald, who stood his ground with the same triumphant smile on his face and the *Doppelhänder* braced and pointed just as it should have been. But at the very last moment, with no more than a flick of a wing and a bare flirt of the crested golden tail, it veered in flight to head straight for Robert, catching him completely unprepared for the onslaught. He turned to run and promptly tripped, which spared him the full power of the King's strike. Even so, the impact came as though the night sky had caved in, burying him under shards of stars and the moon. He was unconscious before he hit the ground.

When he came to himself, the dragon was on him.

The crushing weight was unbearable. He struggled under it, not to escape, but to find some way of softening the cold earth, making it cushion him even a little, squeezing his eyes tightly shut against the pain. The oven-breath on his neck set his body praying for a quick death; but his mind—or something that said it was his mind—called out, "*I am a dragonmaster—obey me! I know your name!*"

The pressure on his back and legs did not lessen, but for a blessed moment, the breath stopped. Something was tugging at him, a sense of enormous curiosity tugging at his entire being, like Adelise determined to get the coverlet off him in the morning. But Adelise had no such voice as the one that sounded inside him, deep and very clear, and terrifyingly amused. "*Indeed? Tell it to me, then. Tell me my name.*"

The name was in Robert. He spoke it.

The King did not respond in any way. Robert lay motionless, still dazed, flowing so easily in and out of consciousness that the state seemed to him entirely natural. Far away, he felt the huge, cold mind methodically ransacking him, turning his soul and spirit upside down and shaking them to see what dropped out.

This should be leaving me in madness. Why does it feel as if it's all happening to someone else?

One thing he did understand, disoriented as he was, was that he could have closed his own mind as securely against any other sort of dragon, even Dahr's rapacious creations, as against Lux or Fernand. Not this one. Not against a King.

The voice said, "A *dragonmaster.*" It came as a long, slow sigh, not friendly, not quite menacing either. "A *dragonmaster . . . Is that what you think you are? Master know I none.*"

All that Robert could feel beyond the pulse of the dragon's voice was the body-shaking pounding of his own heart. It was all but impossible for him to draw a deep breath, but he did the best he could. "*None? Then how is it that Master Dahr may snap his fingers and set you pursuing me like any paid assassin? Fit work for a King, that?*"

For a moment he not only thought but *knew* that he had gone too far. The immense body crushing him to earth seemed to double its weight, the difference being made up entirely by a rage that kindled every inch of Robert's skin as surely as if he had been caught in a full incinerating blast of dragonfire. The voice along his bones dropped so low that he felt it more as a wordless crackle that, somehow, he understood. *I serve no one.*

"*No?*" *In for a sou, in for every franc in your purse*. "*Your word that you were not sent to kill me? I will accept the word of a King.*" He closed his eyes against the sharp, damp grass and waited.

The dragon did not answer him. Emboldened, Robert spoke again. "*And if you are not planning to kill me, might you consider letting me up? I am only a small human, and there is no way I can harm you.*"

The weight eased, just enough for him to turn his head and shoulders. He was in time to see Prince Reginald, poised with the *Doppelhänder* swung high in both hands to sever the glittering golden neck. His eyes were shut tight, he had risen on the tips of his toes, and he looked very much like a little boy straining to reach a sweet on a top shelf.

Robert screamed, "*No!*" and the King wheeled, far too

swiftly for any creature so massive, to swing the endangered neck and head into Prince Reginald so hard that he careened halfway across the field, spinning as crazily as a poorly struck croquet ball. The dragon was on him instantly, jaws wide enough to swallow him whole. Princess Cerise beat at it futilely with her dress sword, which promptly snapped, and Robert labored hopelessly after, knowing that he could never reach them in time. *In time for what? What could I do to save that fool who thought he was saving me? Nothing—nothing—but I have to think of something, I have to!* He ran, feeling as though he were getting not an inch closer, and as though his heart would burst. *Get back from it, get back, Cerise! Please, my love, get back!*

The King turned its head and looked at him.

The dragon's voice did not sound in his body, nor could he read anything in the scarlet diamond eyes—the only aspect of the creature that was not golden. But it was waiting, he knew that, waiting for him to do . . . *what?*

To dominate it, like a proper dragonmaster? He tried that, shouting at it as commandingly as his panting breath would permit, "Do not touch him—let him be! I order you to leave him alone!"

No response. The King did not close its jaws on the stunned prince's throat, but neither did it move away. Its eyes remained fixed on his own; for whatever reason, he had all its attention. *Damn you, anyway, what is it you want? You and the rest of them, big and little, vermin and Kings—what do you want? What is it you have always wanted of me?*

Something was happening within that huge golden body. Robert could feel it in himself, see it without questioning it. The neck that he had preserved from Prince Reginald's sword was arching increasingly to the side at an angle that looked painful, even for a dragon; the mighty front claws were dug into the earth, bracing the King against whatever invisible talons were clenching on it. Scrambling with Princess Cerise to drag Prince Reginald as far out of range as they could, Robert saw something that might have been an appeal in the scarlet eyes—something speaking to him almost as equal to peer. The King lugged its head from side to side, like a rebellious horse, and shrieked once again. In the distance Robert could hear trees wrenching loose in the ground.

He said to Princess Cerise, "Stay here with him."

Kneeling by Prince Reginald, who was just beginning to regain his senses, she only looked up and said quietly, "Don't be killed. Do you think you could manage that for me?"

Robert's breath did something odd in his throat. "I'll do what I can. You be careful too."

He walked back toward the King with his hands up and the palms facing forward, to show them empty. The moon had grown smaller as it climbed, its color fading to a tarnished silver, and the night grown so still—*even the wind is waiting, watching*—that Robert felt himself wading through the silence as though through waist-high water.

The King could not see him. If Robert could be certain about anything, it was that the dragon was in actual pain: locked in implacable combat with itself, and losing. The terrible head thrashed and lunged constantly from side to side; the wings flailed aimlessly—not chiming now, but rattling like a horde of armored skeletons—and the violent rippling along the golden sides made it look as though the creature were about to give birth, as did the sounds—both earth-deep and shrill—that battered Robert like physical blows. A *dragonmaster would know what this means. A real dragonmaster.*

Standing altogether too close, he said aloud, "I am human, and have no power over you." The King gave no sign that it had heard him, Robert said, "But I am a dragonmaster, and therefore you can do me no harm." He had no idea whether this was true or not. "What do you want of me?"

The angled scarlet eyes finally focused on him, seeing and knowing him once again. But the voice that he had first heard in his bones and blood seemed now to be two voices, split and disjointed, answering sometimes together, sometimes in jagged fragments. When Robert repeated the question, the response came with swift, gleaming ferocity. "*Your flesh . . . only your flesh . . .*" followed almost immediately by a faltering, barely audible "*No . . . not, will not . . . I am . . . am, am . . . what I? . . . what . . . am not . . .*" It was a lost and wandering voice, and Robert found himself more frightened by the splintered, stammering words than he ever had been by the menacing rumble of a wyvern defending her nest. "*What's the matter?*" he asked, as simply as he might have asked Reynald, had that smallest dragon caught a claw in a closing door, or slipped into the pantry and made himself sick on honeycake, which he loved. "*What is wrong with you?*"

The second voice answered more loudly this time, and more distinctly, but no more understandably than before. "*Not, not I . . . coming cold . . . who is cold? Where? No room, no room, no I, never . . . never I . . .*" There was a sound in it that would have been a whimper of fear in a human voice.

In the silence, the rustle of dry grass behind Robert might have been a roll of thunder. He turned his head to see the

Princess Cerise coming to join him, and Prince Reginald slowly sitting up beyond her. She was dragging the *Doppelhänder*, which was hampering her pace considerably. The moonlight showed up every tangle in her hair, every streak of mud and dirt on her face, every rent in her tunic, and every flash of stubborn resolve in her dark eyes. Robert reconsidered his earlier opinion of the most beautiful thing he had ever seen.

"Stay back," he said sharply. "Stay right there."

"Fat chance," said the Princess Cerise, and kept coming.

The dragon was now convulsively snapping at its own flanks, for all the world like a dog driven mad by fleas. There was blood striping the golden sides, and the deep, swelling moan of a mountainside shuddering down into the sea. The King reared and clawed at the moon.

Speaking deeply and clearly in his mind, Robert said, "*I am not your enemy.*" The dragon ran out its red-gold tongue like a lightning bolt, and Robert flinched away despite himself but went on. "*I may not be your friend, but I am a dragonmaster, and I wish you no ill. How shall I help you, say?*" The words came naturally and spontaneously, and he spoke them with a confidence new to him.

The two voices again answered him together, speaking over and under each other, so that it was almost impossible for Robert to distinguish between them. "*Far away, far away . . . gone where . . . fleshyourflesh, burn, burn . . . I who . . . I not . . . burnyou, tearyou . . . gone . . .*" One voice touched his heart, and one froze it, and neither made any sense to him at all.

Behind him he heard Princess Cerise's frantic command, "You will *not* do this! I am your Princess, and I forbid it!" *Sounds like Mother trying to get Patience down from the roof*, he thought absurdly. He had just turned to reassure her when she cried out in absolute terror, and he whirled again just as the King lunged. Even an ordinary dragon's fire would have charred him in an instant, at that range, but no flame lashed from the wide-stretched jaws. Caught shamefully off guard, Robert could do nothing but leap back, tripping over a root and falling flat on his rump.

The King roared and loomed over him. Its fangs were crimson with its own blood, and its scarlet eyes were the end of the world.

And Princess Cerise hit it on the head with the *Doppelhänder*.

How she ever got the great broadsword, almost as long as herself, off the ground, no one involved ever discovered. Nevertheless, she did, and with presence enough to aim for the dragon's neck, as Prince Reginald had done. But the *Doppelhänder* turned in her grip, so that she struck only a glancing blow with the flat on the side of the King's head, barely hard enough to bruise a scale. In the next instant, she was on her back, the sword was somewhere far away—*as far as my Bellemontagne*, she thought dreamily—and her own head was ringing so wildly that she had no particular interest in whether the dragon made a meal of her or not. Princess Cerise realized in a casual, matter-of-fact manner that she was weary of dragons.

She also became hazily aware that Robert was standing unarmed between her and the King. *That's nice. That's really nice of him, to do that.* Then understanding rushed back, and she was on her feet, screaming, as Robert charged straight at the oncoming dragon and threw his arms wide. The King's shadow devoured him.

Princess Cerise had been very carefully coached by Queen Hélène and an exhaustive (and exhausted) succession of tutors, but none of them had ever accomplished in teaching her that there are certain situations in which royalty—well-bred royalty, at least—is not only expected but strictly required to faint. The Princess had skipped her lessons whenever she could get away with it and gone off to teach herself how to build a boat, or brew beer. She did not faint now, but snatched up the nearest practical weapon—a rock the size of her two fists together—and headed for the King.

It was Prince Reginald who stopped her, by main force. Once—how long ago—his arms tight around her would have been wings bearing her up to palaces in the clouds; now she made every effort to hit him with the rock, but could never reach a vital spot. He yelped more than once, "Princess, you can't—*ow!*—help him! He's the dragonmaster, he's—*ow!* Stop *doing* that! He knows what he's doing. Will you *stop?*"

She did, finally. They stood together, with Prince Reginald's arm cautiously on her shoulder, while the King dragon roared and convulsed, and at times seemed almost to be eating itself. The Princess was praying, loudly and fervently, to every deity she thought might know her mother; the Prince was simply gaping like any peasant at the thrashing, tormented shadow where Robert had disappeared. Once he made as though to retrieve the fallen *Doppelhänder*, but Princess Cerise lifted the rock, and he stayed where he was.

For all its madness, for all the blood, the King still shone in the moonlight more brightly than the moon. Its wings whipped and pounded the air, blowing branches down like leaves and hurling leaves like thousands of tiny spears. For one moment the Princess thought she glimpsed Robert in the colossal shadow, not attempting to ride the monster like a hero out of legend, but clenched to it under one of the blurring wings with a ferocity equal to the dragon's, as though he were trying somehow to merge with it. And in that dream-moment, to the Princess's horror, it seemed to be *happening*. . . .

For Robert's outline was fading, softening, melting into that of the King, his skin matching golden scales, his long brown fingers curling into talons where he clung, his face lengthening and swelling with fangs, his eyes tilting and reddening . . .

. . . and then he was gone, if she had ever seen him at all—or if he really had become one with the King, lost forever, lost to her forever. She had never in her life understood the word *heartbreak*, for all that she had used it as freely as anyone; now she learned that it was not in truth a cracking, but a rending, and not as neat as a simple, tidy split, but a mess of bloody ribbons. She felt it go in her breast, and wept with the pain.

. . . hold on hold on . . . nothing to hold anymore . . . like falling through clouds hot clouds hot clouds Mother's laundry day . . . heart, the heart, THE HEART BEATS BEATS hammering hitting mace war club, clubbing me away, hold can't hold hurts hurts . . . THE HEART . . . no MY heart, my heart clubbing drubbing make me let go, won't won't . . . dragonme dragonme DRAGONME won't let, won't let go dragonme . . .

Lost in the great golden ocean of the King, battered beyond his own recognition by waves of stupendous anger and fearful confusion, strangling on understanding, he held on.

Twenty-One

The moon was long down, and the sky thinning green, and neither Princess Cerise nor Prince Reginald had stirred from where they stood watching the night-long battle—if it truly *was* a battle; the Princess was no longer sure. Not once had the King breathed fire—not at Robert, even when it had had the opportunity, nor at them, defenseless, within easy range. But there was no further glimpse of Robert: he might well have been swallowed, not by the dragon's jaws but by the power and mystery of its very being, while it raged so enormously against itself, hour after hour. The Princess was past tears, Prince Reginald far past fear or concern for his image in the world. They waited, and that was all.

Abruptly, between one moment and the next, the King was standing as silent and as unmoving as they. It showed no sign of exhaustion, neither panting nor staggering, and the only change that Princess Cerise could see was in a certain new stillness about the scarlet eyes. The Princess took an impulsive step forward, but Prince Reginald caught her arm. "No," he said, and his voice was firmer than she had ever heard it, almost harsh. "Not yet."

The Princess halted. The blood-streaked golden scales blurred, her tired eyes lost focus, and a figure rolled nearly to her feet. Heart and body leaped together: she was on her knees beside it immediately, but knew her mistake even before she saw the white hair and beard.

The wizard Dahr reached for her as she recoiled, but Prince Reginald stepped hard on his wrist. Dahr yelped in surprise and indignation. "You dare, boy? I can turn more than one royal Corvinian imbecile to furniture, if I choose."

"You needed your dragons for that," Prince Reginald replied calmly. "You don't have them with you now."

The benign smile returned as Dahr freed his wrist and sat up. "I have something better than that."

"Sending a King to hunt us? To murder a dragonmaster?" Even from his father, Prince Reginald had never heard such contemptuous disdain as the Princess put into her voice. "For such a mighty wizard, there seems little you can do without assistance, Dahr."

"You think not? You think not?" There was a distinct crack in Dahr's voice, the first suggestion of anger that he had yet shown. He rose to his feet, sweeping an arm toward the silent, motionless dragon as though showing off a prize stallion or heifer. "Do you know what I have done with this creature? Do you have any idea?" He reached both hands out to the Princess Cerise in a curiously supplicating gesture; he might have been attempting to take her face between them. The Princess backed away.

"What is a dragonmaster, after all?" Dahr demanded. "Someone who can walk safely among dragons? Someone who can make dragons do tricks? Fly them like kites on a string—have them destroy an invading army or serve him as one themselves? Fetch his bedroom slippers, perhaps?" His voice was rising, and Princess Cerise realized that his hands were trembling. He said, "You have seen me do all these things—"

"Not the slippers," said Prince Reginald, who was a literalist by nature.

"—and I tell you that this may be command, but it is not mastery, true mastery. Compared with what I can do—what I have done—these are children's games, these are but cat's cradles, no more. Attend me now!" Aware of the increasing shrillness of his tone, he paused, smoothing back his white mane and finger-combing his beard. The voice became calmer, but he could not quiet his hands.

Dahr said, "I am something more than a mere dragon-trickster. I am something that has never been before." A giggle slipped out of him then, but only a small one, and only once; it could easily have been missed. He said, "There are endless old wives' tales of people who were part-dragon, sired by dragons at a crossroads in some evil midnight—all nursery nonsense, nothing more. But *I* . . . only *I* . . ." He beamed with something oddly resembling innocence at their bewildered expressions. "When you look upon me, you see the scales that clothe the King, the flame we breathe, the teeth that await our enemies. For I am *of* the King, do you understand me? No *master*, but as much a part of the King as the wings that lift us to the heavens. No wizard before me could ever say such a thing—only I! *Only I!*"

His laughter did break loose then, but there was nothing

frenzied or maniacal about it: it simply kept going, soft and almost childish, on and on. *Is that what happened to Robert?* Princess Cerise wondered. *Has he merged with the King, too, become one with it? But Dahr is still here in his own body—where is Robert, then?* A starveling flicker of life stirred among the tatters of her heart. She said aloud, speaking very carefully, "How did you ever come to trap a King and train him to bear you on his back? I've never known anyone who could ride a dragon."

Dahr reacted with the exasperation she had hoped for. "Have you heard nothing, stupid girl? I do not fly *on* the King, like some flea! I fly *with* the King—*in* the King, if you will—matched to him, indistinguishable, atom for atom, not a particle of separation between us!" But the question itself piqued and inflated him. Glaring, he struck a proper wizardly pose, with his still-shaking hands tucked into the sleeves of his robe. With his splendid head outlined by the rays of the rising sun, he began to declaim. Prince Reginald went and got the *Doppelhänder* to lean on while he listened; the Princess Cerise stared past Dahr at the dragon, desperately willing the great creature to *open* once again. . . . And the King stood looking back at her, its scales seeming to shift and flow in the feeble morning light, the scarlet eyes telling her nothing.

"The last of the Kings," the wizard said. "I found it asleep in the depths of the cave where my spirit had dragged my body from the hogpen where Krije threw it. There we rested long, while I slowly—how slowly!—knitted self and soul together and the King dreamed a King's dreams. *I*"—he raised his head proudly—"I entered into those dreams by a path I know, and so I learned many things. The making of dragons was . . . only one of them."

"And you learned to join with the King," the Princess Cerise said slowly. Prince Reginald blinked back and forth between them in some confusion.

"To *unite* with it," Dahr corrected her. "Can you not yet understand that I *am* the King, as we stand here, no matter that I am smaller and go on two feet? Can you not understand that the King is *me*—that you are speaking with him at this moment? That there is no boundary, no border where one leaves off and the other begins?" As though to confirm their shared identity, the dragon reared its head high above his, making a low and wicked sound.

"No boundary," the wizard repeated. "Not between our identities, not between our powers. How could there be?"

"Can you breathe fire?" Prince Reginald asked with real interest. Princess Cerise kicked his ankle.

"Would you like to see that?" The wizard's glance was suddenly aglitter with malicious mischief. Prince Reginald considered and shook his head.

Princess Cerise said quietly, "I don't believe you."

Something was happening to Dahr's eyes, and Prince Reginald took a step backward. The Princess said, "I think you are no more a part of the King than you were of those dragons you bred, or created, or whatever it was you did to them. At least you could hold those to your will"—her dark eyes narrowed like those of a much older woman—"although in a little while they would have been Robert's as they were never yours, and you knew that then. But I have seen a King now, and I have seen *you*. . . ." She smiled and left the sentence unfinished.

Prince Reginald fully expected thunder and lightning on the instant, to be followed, quite possibly, by an earthquake or a hurricane. All those prodigies of nature were gathering in the strangeness of the wizard's eyes. The Princess said, "You might—I say you *might*—have learned a little from a dozy King in a cave, but you taught it nothing, of that I am certain. You might even have been permitted to direct it—once or twice, perhaps, for a short while. A very short while. But there was never a chance in the world that you could ever *join* with such a creature, as you claim. I think"—and here her voice shook, just a trifle—"I think that is forbidden, even to the greatest . . . I think even my Robert—"

Dahr pounced viciously on her weakness. "Your Robert! Your Robert got himself eaten for his temerity, as well he should have been. He dared challenge me, he dared rush in blindly where I had labored in the cold darkness of the cave—he thought to steal my glory, to mimic my triumph while evading the cost of it, the *cost*! The *cost*!"

Spittle was flying from his thin, bearded lips, and he was panting like a dog as he ranted on. "I paid for what I am—paid for it in hunger and loneliness, paid in the pain of healing from what your father had done to me." He glared at Prince Reginald out of eyes like rotting fruit; then his attention returned to Princess Cerise. "Your foolish Robert is no dragonmaster, not as I am. Never as I am. Nonetheless, he has a certain way, a certain *kindness* with them—call it what you will—that I, perhaps, have not, and cannot afford to have running loose in the world. And your other fool is stupid enough to come back for his father, and strong enough to make a bit of a nuisance of himself. So I fear"—and he bowed mockingly to the Princess—"I greatly fear that Your Highness will be the only one who is not a dragon to leave this place. Farewell, then, and do give my fondest regards to dear old Antoine." Absurdly, and rather horribly, he winked at her. "I don't think your mother really likes me."

Prince Reginald and Princess Cerise looked at each other. Prince Reginald said, "Since coming to Bellemontagne I have been forced to learn how foolish I am, and how slow to understand so much. But I do believe that I have just been insulted. Apart from being threatened with death."

"I believe so myself," the Princess replied. To the wizard she said, "I came here with two friends, and so will I leave. Step aside, sir."

And with that, addressing him neither as *my lord*, nor even as *Master Dahr*, she walked straight past him—elbowing him slightly, Prince Reginald thought—toward the King.

What the Prince saw, as she did not, was the sudden fear spreading across the wizard's face like a birthmark. Princess Cerise never looked back at him, but stood calmly in the dragon's immense shadow, her head tilted back to view the great creature entire. She was so fully taken up with regarding the King, and the King with studying her—and Prince Reginald with trembling for her—that none of them were paying any attention to Dahr, as he stepped away, bowed toward the sun over his crossed arms, and began mumbling inaudibly to himself. The air noticed—it twitched and dimmed for an instant—but no one else did.

Princess Cerise's voice was as clear and firm as it had not been only a moment before. "Robert. Hear me. Where you are, hear me, Robert."

The scarlet eyes narrowed to wary, gleaming slits, but the King gave no other sign of interest or recognition. The Princess said, "You know me. As I would know you if you were truly a dragon—instead of its soul." She hesitated then, suddenly uncertain of the gamble she had taken, but went on steadfastly. "I'm right, Robert. I know I'm right. What *he* pretends to be, you are. Look at me—talk to me. I'm not afraid."

As Prince Reginald could tell, she was very much afraid, as was he. Monsters tend to dwindle notably in the light of day, but the King seemed to have grown greater since dawn, the illusion perhaps born of the glitter of its golden scales in the sun contrasted with the dark swell of the ribbed wings, huge even when folded. The dragon bent its head down toward Princess Cerise, baring what looked to be an endless row of six-inch fangs and running out its red forked tongue. The Princess whispered, "*Robert?*"

What happened next happened very fast.

The wizard Dahr turned back to face the King. His uncrossed arms seemed to leap into the air like live things—wings at last set free—and he uttered a vast screech that could not possibly have come from a human throat. The two humans hearing it had heard it before, and knew it immediately for the hunting shriek of a King dragon with its prey in sight. The beast itself, in seeming response, snatched up the Princess Cerise in its mouth, lifting her to a height that made Prince Reginald shudder to recall how the wizard's own dragons had played with the soldiers of Bellemontagne, tossing them up and batting them back and forth like shuttlecocks. Sickened at the memory, he started forward, swinging the *Doppelhänder* far back over his shoulder, meaning to slash with all his strength at whichever part of the King came first within range. But the thought of the dragon, enraged, dropping the Princess—or worse—stayed his stroke. Instead, he wheeled in frustration and knocked Dahr down with the flat of the great sword. The wizard neither protested nor retaliated, but only lay on his back and giggled. Prince Reginald dropped to his knees and began to pray. He was no better at it than Princess Cerise had ever been at fainting . . .

. . . which she felt seriously aggrieved at not being able to do, even in this dreadful and certainly final moment of her life. And yet, just as her moment of captivity in Prince Reginald's arms had turned out an irritating disappointment, so being swept aloft in the dreadful jaws of a legendary horror was—to her own horror—not only exhilarating but alarmingly romantic. The immense fangs never touched her skin, even when she struggled; or if they did, it felt somehow more like a caress. The dragon's breath, while strong and hot, was not unpleasant: there was a meatiness to it, certainly, but there was the smell of lightning, as when a storm is approaching from the sea. The Princess liked storms.

A voice sounded in her head.

Princess Cerise was used to hearing voices in her head—most often the one of her mother, Queen Hélène, explaining once more (*and once more only, Cerise*) why it was bad form for a royal to throw spitballs at her tutor and teach the scullery maids to dance a schottische. But she heard this voice all around her as well, and jarring her heart, saying, "*I'm here, Princess. I'm here.*"

"Oh," said the Princess Cerise. "*Oh.*"

"*Don't be frightened.*" The voice was unmistakably gentle and earnest, unmistakably Robert. "*Please, it's just me.*"

The Princess, who had been lying more or less crosswise in the King's mouth, cautiously sat up, then managed to stand, clinging precariously to the dragon's right eyetooth. "I'm *not* frightened! I told you I wasn't." The sea-roll of the dragon's tongue under her feet made her queasy. She said, "I was right, then? You're the one who's—I don't know—*mingled* with the King, the way he said he had. You're it, and it's you, is that what's happened?" When he did not answer immediately, she pressed him, "Just *tell* me, Robert. It's been a very long day."

He laughed—*so near*—as wearily as she felt. "*No, I'm afraid it's nothing like that. No one can do that, join with a dragon, feel what a dragon feels, what a dragon* is. *No one.*"

"But you're a dragonmaster. You must be. Otherwise . . ." The Princess Cerise was suddenly very, very tired. "Otherwise, nothing makes any sense."

"*There's no such thing as a dragonmaster. I've spent a very long night learning that. Dahr is powerful enough that he can ride even a King—when the King permits it, as this one did, for its own reasons, its own amusement. But he's not . . . what I am.*" After a moment, he went on slowly, "*What I seem to be.*"

"What you seem to be," Princess Cerise repeated. "But what *are* you? *Where* are you?" When he did not respond for a maddeningly long time, she discovered that the inside of a King dragon's mouth serves excellently well as an echo chamber. "Robert, I am still your Princess. That may not mean very much anymore." In a quieter voice, she added, "I don't think it does." And then, more strongly, "But I am your companion, and so is Prince Reginald, and we three have endured much together . . . and are you alive, Robert? Are you even alive?"

The answer came quickly and warmly. "*Yes, I am, I promise. I haven't gone anywhere—I just needed to make sure that you were safe*"—a sudden chuckle—"*and the gods know you won't ever be any safer than you are right now.*" He paused again, but only briefly; she could feel him searching for words. "*I think what I am is some kind of . . . dragon* friend. *I don't know how else to put it. Likely enough, I should have known it long ago, even when I was no friend, nothing more than a butcher, a slaughterer—even then I should have known, I* did *know.*" He took a long, careful breath.

"*Dragons talk to me, Princess, they always have. It's just taken me a long time to learn to listen.*"

"Those dragons," she said slowly. "The ones that attacked us—you spoke to them. You made them kill each other. And then at Krije's castle, yesterday . . ." *Yesterday . . . but isn't this still yesterday? All one long, long yesterday, since we left Bellemontagne . . . one long yesterday . . .*

"*Dahr's dragons. They aren't like the others—in a way, they're not exactly real dragons. But they knew me, even so. I couldn't control them then, not in Dahr's presence. I could now.*"

The assurance in his voice, quiet as it was, was almost frightening. *Do any of us ever know each other?* She asked, "But the King?" remembering Dahr's boasts. "Can you control the King?"

"*No, of course not. Nobody does. I'm just . . . visiting.*"

As though it had been listening—*and how could it not be?*—there came a rumble under her feet and the great jaws widened, so that Princess Cerise, still hanging on to the eyetooth, went up with it, along with a startled yelp. "Stop that!" she demanded, without thinking. There came another deep sound, something that might in a human throat almost have been laughter, and the Princess found herself once again swaying almost as precariously on the dragon's tongue. She said politely—and only a bit unsteadily, "Thank you."

"*I don't think Kings understand gratitude,*" Robert's voice commented. "*They don't have much to do with human beings, except by accident. Stepping on houses and towns, and so forth.*"

"Dahr said it was the last. The last of the Kings."

"Dahr wants it to be the last. The same way he wants to believe that he is truly joined with it—that they are the same creature. It isn't, and they aren't. It followed us for its own reasons, not because he commanded it to, and it let him come along under its wing, like a—"

"Flea," said the Princess quietly. "Like a flea."

"Flea, then." Robert hesitated. *"Princess, I asked the King to take you out of harm's way, because I couldn't tell what Dahr was up to, or what Prince Reginald was likely to do trying to save you. He has courage, but I'd suggest you keep pointy things away from him when you . . ."* Princess Cerise drew breath to interrupt, but he let the sentence trail away. *"I can't give it orders, no more than Dahr can. But I think it will set you down, if I ask nicely. Courtesy does seem to matter."* He grinned at her—suddenly purely, heart-stoppingly like the boy she had heard in her parents' castle, several worlds and lives ago. *"A dragon's sense of humor is not like anyone else's. It's not human."*

"Robert, I'm not—" she began, but she could tell that he was no longer there, wherever *there* was. A moment later she found herself standing free on the morning grass, without having noticed her liberation, so slowly and gracefully had the King managed it. She turned and curtsied to it, as her mother the Queen had spent so much time and patience teaching her to do (*Because it's polite, Cerise! Because people will think you're a charming little girl if you do this, and only you and I will ever know the truth*); and it seemed to her that the terrible head dipped slightly in some sort of acknowledgment. Then Robert was stepping from the shadow of the dragon, and the Princess Cerise whispered his name and forgot about curtsying and most other things.

The first thing she said, the words muffled against his lips, was "Don't worry about my mother."

At the same time he said, vaguely trying to get her hair out of his mouth, "Your mother's going to have me absolutely hanged."

The second thing he said, looking over her shoulder, was "*Get down!*"

His violent shove flattened her to the ground as he dropped beside her, a split instant before a blast of fire so intense that it singed the ends of her hair passed over them, incinerating one of the few trees in the field. Raising her head—though Robert kept pushing it down—she could see the wizard Dahr rushing upon them, not merely breathing or spitting fire, but smiling it, singing it, screaming it, drooling it from the corners of his mouth. She and Robert were sprawled directly in his path, and the only thing between them and crisp, crackling death was Prince Reginald, held back by the flames from heading the mad wizard off, and reduced to repeatedly thrusting the *Doppelhänder* between Dahr's ankles in hope of tripping him up. It was not working.

"Run," Robert said.

"Fat chance," Princess Cerise replied.

She had immediate cause to regret this. Robert was on his feet, racing away across the field, shouting back insulting challenges that would have shocked his mother but would certainly have impressed Ostvald and Elfrieda mightily. Dahr came after him, burning through the field like fire himself, gaining as though Robert were standing still. His laughter hissed flame across Robert's back, and the Princess's body twisted with the agony of watching each lash.

But after them both came laboring Prince Reginald, slowed

both by weariness and by the burden of the *Doppelhänder*. Recognizing the absurdity of his pursuit, he halted abruptly and, with an effort that left him gasping and on his knees, hurled the great sword after Dahr. It turned over three times in the air and sank deep between the wizard's shoulder blades, knocking him flat with the force of its impact. He coughed fire once, and did not move again.

Robert was crouched beside him when Prince Reginald stumbled up, still wheezing for breath. Robert's tunic had crumbled almost entirely to ashes, and Prince Reginald could see the raw burn stripes. They looked at each other over the body. Robert said, "Thank you."

"Don't mention it," Prince Reginald replied. "Sort of thing we heroes do, you know."

His face was very pale as he stared down at the motionless wizard. The *Doppelhänder* had gone completely through him; they could see the tip jutting through his breast. Prince Reginald said, "Excuse me . . . I never killed anybody before," and threw up.

Remembering another field, and other flames, Robert remained, ignoring his own pain, until Prince Reginald had somewhat composed himself. He suggested, "We might as well bury him right here. I can't think of a reason not to."

"Except that we don't have a spade. We'd have to use my sword."

Robert shrugged. "Seems appropriate." They set the body down, and Prince Reginald, with a single swift pull, drew the *Doppelhänder* free. On an impulse, Robert turned the body over to study the dead face, now appearing almost tranquil, almost at rest. "A remarkable man," he said softly.

Prince Reginald snorted. "So remarkable that I won't feel easy until we get him under the ground. If then."

"Not without reason," said the wizard Dahr.

He sat up, eyes open, smiling and spreading his arms as grandly as a carnival player finishing a sleight-of-hand performance. "My thanks for pulling that skewer out of me," he said to Prince Reginald. "I could have managed it myself, but I'm not nearly as supple as I used to be."

The smile broadened as he regarded the two stunned faces gaping at him. He said, still addressing Prince Reginald, "Did you think I learned nothing from being beaten to death by your estimable father? There is dying, and then there is dying, and each time, if you keep your wits about you, you rise wiser." He stood up, stretching his arms and shoulders as though he had just awakened from a restful nap. "Unfortunately," he added, "this does not apply to either of you. But the principle is sound."

"I *knew* he could breathe fire," Prince Reginald mumbled.

The Princess Cerise ran toward them. Robert waved her back with both hands, and for once she actually heeded him, stopping where she stood. Her face was old with fear.

Prince Reginald had sunk onto his haunches and was aimlessly plucking grass blades. "It's true, all of it, about him and the dragon. It's all true."

"No," Robert said. "No, it's not true." He stepped closer to Dahr, standing so near indeed that it was the latter who moved a pace back. Robert said, "You're a very powerful wizard, friend Dahr. You can create dragons to serve you, and you can turn a man into a gold statue, and you can breathe fire. But you fought all night to make a King accept you into itself, a part of itself, and you lost. And you never had a chance—you *had* to lose—

because you haven't the least idea of what a King is, no more than I do." He was crowding Dahr even further now, tapping the wizard's chest gently but constantly with his forefinger. "You're a parasite, Dahr. We're all parasites to a King dragon, but some of us know it, and some of us don't. You never will, no matter how many times you die and rise. There is wisdom, and then there is wisdom."

Dahr was trembling visibly with the effort of maintaining control. "And you? You were there all night yourself, and you too struggled vainly to unite with the King. I felt your presence, and I felt your failure. Deny it if you will, boy, but even a *parasite*—"

Robert interrupted him. "No, I don't deny that, for it's no more than the truth. I leaped into the King's shadow with all my heart, wanting to know what a King knows, wanting to embrace the shadow and have it embrace me, wanting to be rid of my humanity—rid of bloody stupid *Robert*—just for once, and to be one with something splendid and magnificent and uncaring. Oh, I understand you, Dahr. I didn't yesterday, but I surely do now."

He was shaking himself, as much as the wizard, and his voice was hoarse with exhaustion and emotion. "But then I thought of Odelette. Then I thought of my sisters and my brothers, and Ostvald and Elfrieda"—he looked directly into Prince Reginald's eyes—"and I thought of Princess Cerise."

Prince Reginald nodded silently. Robert said, "And I thought, perhaps it would be good to . . . to settle for less. Better, even."

"I will never tell the Princess that you said that," Prince Reginald answered him. "There's my wedding gift to you." Robert smiled.

The wizard Dahr said, politely enough, "Excuse me. There

will be no wedding. Breathing fire is dramatic, but rather wearing, in all honesty. I sometimes forget how old I am." Prince Reginald made a frantic dive for the *Doppelhänder*, but Dahr gestured, as graceful as a dance movement. The sword flamed up all along its length, brighter than the King's golden scales, and then fell to ash, crumbling like a blackened fire log. Prince Reginald rolled to the side, blowing on his fingers.

"I must face facts," the wizard said sadly. "I am simply no longer in condition to go chasing people through the shrubbery. 'Simplicity' must be my watchword from now on—simplicity and 'vengeance,' for vengeance is the truest spice, without which mere action has no savor." Ignoring Robert, he regarded Prince Reginald thoughtfully, his mouth twitching as though he were lapping up the other's pain like blood. He said, "Your father killed me long ago, and I took my vengeance on him yesterday. You have just killed me today—what must I do to you to ensure that none of your breed ever trouble me again?" He acted a charade of pondering deeply, while Prince Reginald made a similar show of nursing his hand and braced his legs for one last doomed assault, and Robert set himself similarly to stop him. It occurred to him, in a distant, detached manner, that the Prince was actually an honorable person in many ways, and that it would have been nice to live long enough to get to know him better.

Dahr said, "I have debated simply turning the pair of you into furniture, along the lines of the late—yet present—King Krije. I also considered whether it would be more interesting to compel you to eat each other—untidy, that, obviously—or to summon insects to do the job. It would take longer, but they leave nothing. Perhaps if either of you expressed an opinion—"

"My own opinion," Robert said tightly, "is that you have fiendishly set out to bore us to death. It's working."

"Have mercy!" Prince Reginald chimed in. "Whatever you do to us, great wizard, we beg you—stop *talking*, and just get it over with. In a heroic lifetime devoted to slaughtering villains, I have never encountered one who *chattered* so!"

It was childish, purposeless baiting, and Robert, for his part, had no least notion of what it might possibly accomplish. It was merely better, somehow, than standing meekly silent, waiting to be magically murdered—or worse. And it was clearly making the wizard Dahr turn all sorts of unusual colors, which was a good thing by itself. The noises he was making did not sound at all like sorcerous incantations, and that was good too.

When words began to emerge and take shape, he was saying, "Very well—very well, excellent. You have decided me, and I thank you for it. You shall both join my dragons—the one to spend his days on guard behind the golden throne that was, until recently, his lamented father." Prince Reginald did leap at him then, and it cost Robert all his strength and a black eye as well to hold him back. Dahr looked on approvingly.

"Excellent," he repeated, "splendid. You will make a splendid dragon, constantly alert and attentive, with a double reason to be so. First, there will be the hope of somehow returning Krije to his former appalling self. Secondly, the eternal possibility of that one moment when I just *might* be thinking about something else." Poise swiftly restored, he beamed on them both. "Neither will happen, ever, but it is always important to have a dream, a deep wish, something to live for." He winked at Prince Reginald. "As I know myself."

Over his shoulder, Robert could see the Princess Cerise,

seemingly paying no heed to their plight, but standing almost in the shadow of the King dragon, as he had stood, as he had yearned for one night to be absorbed, enfolded, swallowed by power beyond his ability to desire. *Don't, Cerise—don't go where I almost went—it's so hard to get back, and I don't know whether you'd want to the way I did. Stay, Cerise. . . .*

The wings opened.

The risen sun brought out a curious sheen to the undersides—somewhere between deep violet and purple—that he had not noticed in the light of the half-moon. Wingtip to wingtip, fully extended, they seemed of greater length than the King itself, and Robert realized that what made them dazzle and confuse his eyes was the special glitter of the edges of the scales, razor-sharp and deadly as the dragon's fangs or blazing breath. *Cerise, Cerise . . .*

He looked away, instinctively not wanting Dahr—or Prince Reginald either—to follow the direction of his glance. He need not have worried: the wizard was embarked on a languorously vengeful fantasy of his own. "As for you—exterminator, vermin-chaser, ratcatcher—*you* shall have your dream almost entire. You may not be magicked into a King, as you have wished all your life, down in your deepest heart—am I not right about that, boy?—but you shall be elevated far above your betters, far above your deserving." He was stretching himself like a cat for the pure sensual pleasure of the motion, flexing his fingers as a cat does its claws.

Don't look, don't look . . . don't make him turn his head . . . The wings were lifting now, a wonder in the sun.

"You shall become my own personal dragon—my mount and my companion, my shield and my footstool. Always at my side (I must tell you, the others will hate you for it), guarding my sleep and my waking equally; always attuned to my call, my humors, my concerns, even my dangers. Rather like a dog, you say?" He reached out and patted Robert on the head, grazing him with his fingertips as Robert backed away. "Rather. Yes."

Keep control. Hold his eyes to yours. "And why would I be doing that?" *Hold his eyes!*

"Oh. A sensible question." The wizard mimed puzzlement, then pensiveness. "Well, perhaps because you feared, from experience, that something untoward might occur—oh, never to your Princess, but conceivably to her family—if you ever permitted yourself to think, even for a moment, about something that was not an immediate need of mine. That might be a good reason, wouldn't you say?"

Prince Reginald remarked to no one in particular, "The King's flying." His voice was conversational with disbelief. The wizard Dahr blinked, shook his head irritably, and swung round to see.

Ironically, Robert, who had been wondering from his first sight of the great dragon how it could possibly get off the ground, never got to observe that particular technique. He had been so intent on keeping Dahr from noticing the King's behavior at all that he was standing with his back to it, partially blocking the wizard's view, when the dragon presumably lumbered into the air. When he did turn himself, the King was already bearing down on them, gliding almost delicately, with hardly a wingbeat, more like a falling leaf than a monster the size of the Great Hall of Castle Bellemontagne. The scarlet eyes were half-closed—*the flying ones always do that when they strike, Father told me*—but the immense jaws where Princess Cerise had stood up were wide open, and Robert momentarily fancied that he could see down and down the red-roaring gullet to where the fire waited. He had one quick glimpse of the Princess, safe on the ground and clear of the shadow, before the King filled the sky.

The wizard Dahr said—quite mildly, considering, "No. Oh, no, I can't have this." The King shrieked, and both Robert and Prince Reginald fell to the ground, covering their ears.

They never saw the flames, but they felt them on their skin. It sounded to Robert as though the entire sky were whipping back and forth like a sheet on a line. It filled his head for days afterward; yet what lasted longer in him was the smaller cry of pained surprise that he kept hoping he hadn't heard.

Lying on his face with his eyes tightly shut for the next year or two seemed a fine practical idea to him, so it was Prince Reginald who saw the pile of white ashes first. It was still smoking—the Prince remembered similar smoke dreadfully well—and smelled slightly of hair pomade.

"Well," he said aloud. "I might be wrong, but you *would* think that would do it." But Robert did not raise his head until the Princess Cerise came to him.

Twenty-Two

Her name is Marie-Galante," Robert said to his sisters, as the ice-white dragon preened on his palm. "You must always call her by her full name, or she won't pay attention."

Patience bounced with utter delight at the pronouncement, but Rosamonde, always precise about such matters, frowned. "Marie-Galante? That's a princess's name!"

Even Odelette marveled somewhat. "Gaius Aurelius . . . are you certain? I don't think I've ever heard of a dragon—"

"*That is her name!!*" Robert was short with everyone these days, as he had been ever since he came home. "The others accept it already, so that's all that matters."

Patience was happily crooning, "Marie-Galante . . . Marie-Galante," stroking the white dragonlet's throat with a cautious forefinger. "She might even be a transformed princess herself. . . ."

"Girls, you are late for school," Odelette snapped at her

daughters. Usually Patience and Rosamonde would have gobbled their breakfast and been well out the door by now, but they were both caught up in playing with the little dragon, unlike their older brothers, who were most often too weary for such matters. (Caralos had lately taken to sleeping with shy Reynald on his pillow, whenever he could get away with it.)

For his part, Robert simply stalked out of the kitchen and upstairs to the room that had once been the quietest, safest place in the whole world, only a few centuries ago. Now it had become noisy with memories, cluttered with disasters that no one would ever stop celebrating him for. Most often since his return, he slept in his brothers' room, his moans and whimpers invariably rousing them. But they knew a hero's horrors when they heard them, so there was nothing to be done.

"Go away, Mother," he said, though she hadn't knocked. Odelette did not speak at all, but by and by he got up and opened the door for her. He said, "I'm tired, Mother."

"When you can't sleep, *I* can't sleep, Gaius Aurelius Constantine." She marched past him and sat down on his bed, firmly patting the blanket for him to sit beside her. She said, "Ostvald and Elfrieda were here twice yesterday. Looking for you." Robert did not respond, nor did he sit on the bed. "And Prince Reginald . . ." Odelette smiled fondly, as though at the pleasant memory of a relative in a faraway country. "The Prince was hoping to see you."

Robert looked sideways at her. "What did you say to them?"

"What I always say. As instructed." Odelette donned an air of slightly wounded courtesy like a favorite gown. "I told them all that you were properly engaged in the practice of your legendary profession—"

"I don't do that anymore, not ever again!"

"—ridding noble houses of their intolerable pestiferous infestations." As deeply as he knew his mother, Robert still marveled in the back of his mind at her way with a sentence. "Oh, and King Antoine sent two separate messengers—everyone saw them galloping to our door—"

"Dear gods, dear gods." Robert sat down slowly, barely aware he was doing it. "Did they believe you?"

Has she always done that thing of turning her head so that she seems to be peering at me around the corner? "Well, I can't be altogether sure, not altogether. You know what Ostvald says about kings. . . ."

"Mother." Robert made a particular point of keeping his voice low. It was not an easy task.

"But one thing I *am* sure about"—and it wasn't so much that Odelette *did* raise her own voice as that her eyes widened and darkened until they looked annoyingly like another pair of eyes—"what I *do* know is that I would be ashamed of you, ashamed of my son for the first time ever, if he dared to slip away from Bellemontagne without any proper farewell to Princess Cerise. I am sure I raised you better than that, Gaius Aurelius Constantine Heliogabalus. . . ."

Robert had never seen his mother cry before. Not ever, not in eighteen years of confusions, tender bewilderment, and maddened acceptance. The whole notion of Odelette Thrax in tears made even less sense than the memory of the wizard Dahr with a *Doppelhänder* still jutting through his body. But he saw the tears glinting in the twilight, and her hand furiously swiping at them to make them just *stop*, and he knew beyond doubt or language that he was a doomed man.

"Mother, tell me what Cerise and I could possibly have to say to each other? After everything we've been through together, we both know what we know. She can't change what she is, and I'd never want her to." He caught Odelette's hands, making her look directly at him. "And poor Reginald . . . Reginald would give anything he owns to be anyone but the King of Corvinia, especially now that he understands he's really the brave hero he just happens to look like. But sooner or later he and I will have to go to his home and free Krije from that golden throne Dahr stuck him into." He chuckled slightly, in spite of himself. "It won't do the old horror any harm, I shouldn't think—and it'll certainly do Prince Reginald a lot of good. How can you fear your father ever again, when you've seen him being a fancy footstool?"

Odelette managed to sniffle and giggle simultaneously. Robert went on, "And Cerise . . ." He said the name lingeringly, tasting it very slowly, "Cerise has to become the only Princess of Bellemontagne who ever taught herself to read and write . . . and may every single stupid god please bless her always. But she has no more choice than Reginald of Corvinia." He spread his hands out to his mother, almost pleadingly. "So you see, Mother? You do see?"

"What do you expect me to see?" Odelette stood back from him indignantly. "Gaius Aurelius, I am a silly old countrywoman who only knows how to milk a goat and when to call the chickens in for the evening—"

"Mother, don't you dare start—"

"But I *will* tell you, since you don't ask, that wherever in the world you go, all dragons will know you. There is not one of them—whether great or tiny, King or wall-scuttler, who will not know your smell, your heart—"

"It's not that simple! It's *never* that simple—"

"And as for the Princess . . ."

"Mother, I swear I'm warning you—"

Odelette gripped his wrists and shook him harder than she had ever done in his life, even the time he put that snapping turtle in his father's bed when Elpidus came home drunk and beat her. "And *I* am telling you that the Princess will follow you anywhere you go. Don't you know that?" *Gods, she's strong. I'd forgotten!* "Don't you *know*? Even *I* know, and I'm only a foolish old woman! If you leave without telling her, she will be on your track while your horse's shit is still steaming . . . don't you know that?" Now her eyes were again wet, but she paid no heed at all to the falling tears. "Because that's what *I* would do, and I'm no bloody princess. Because that's just what stupid people do!"

Doomed. Doomed. Completely doomed.

"I'll talk to her today. Before I go anywhere, I'll find her and speak honestly to her. Today, I promise! Will that content you, you terrible woman?"

His mother smiled suddenly and widely at him, waving away the quite clean handkerchief he offered her. "Oh, I'm easy, Gaius Heliogabalus. *I'm* the easy one."

He didn't even notice Ostvald and Elfrieda when he finally stumbled out of the house, and they didn't approach him directly. They simply walked beside him, as they had done on so many other occasions since their childhood. It even took him more time than it should have to become aware that they went hand in hand, and that when Ostvald dropped a coach spring he was awkwardly lugging along, Elfrieda stopped and waited for him to pick it up. Neither one spoke, but they smiled at each other.

Robert halted finally and turned to them. "I'm sorry, I really wasn't ignoring you." Then he said, "Yes, I was. I'm sorry."

"We kept each other company," Ostvald mumbled, a shade above inaudibly. Elfrieda blushed, but she didn't contradict him, and she didn't let go of his hand.

Ostvald added hurriedly, "I mean, while we were waiting. For you to talk, I mean."

"You brought us home," Robert said. When both of his oldest friends began shaking their heads vigorously, Robert continued, "You found us—Princess Cerise, Reginald, and me—lost and wandering as we were, and you brought us safe to our own doors, the two of you." He put his hands very lightly on their shoulders. "I knew you were there, you were with me all the time, but I couldn't hear you . . . not where I was. Do you understand me?"

After a small moment, Elfrieda ventured, "Reginald . . . he told us you were with *him*, with the King—"

"I was never once *joined* with the King," Robert interrupted fiercely. "I never became *part* of him—that was Dahr's dream, Dahr's poor vanity, not mine. Never mine. Not for a single moment. Do you understand me?"

He never knew truly whether they did or not, but both of them reached up to squeeze his hands. They walked on in silence, halting occasionally for Ostvald to readjust the coach spring on or off his shoulder. Only when Bellemontagne Castle came in sight did Robert veer aside, nodding apologetically. He said, "I have something to do. I'll find you later."

"She isn't there," Elfrieda said. Robert turned to stare at

her. His eyes frightened her, though she could not have said why. She said, "You know where she goes."

Robert turned without answering her. Ostvald cleared his throat. "Except . . . except only she isn't always there. Not always . . ."

For someone who had never once been where he was bound, Robert knew exactly how to get there. *Across the Royal Lawns . . . then straight past the Royal Croquet Grounds, left at the Royal Folly . . . up a couple of miles, until you get to the Royal Grotto . . . after that, it's all the Royal Woods, and in a while there's the clearing with the tree. . . .*

Her clearing. Her tree. Cerise's tree.

But only Prince Reginald was there. Reginald, sitting with his back slumped against the tree and his undeniably powerful chin cupped wearily in his long fingers. To Robert he looked like nothing so much as a lonely knight at arms, abandoned by a strange love and palely loitering in eternal despair. *I could go into a lifetime's training, study some special monkish discipline that enables me to walk up walls, and I could never, never look like that. Not a chance, Cerise.*

Prince Reginald scrambled to his feet when Robert walked into the clearing, even backing slightly away, as though he had been caught trespassing. "Forgive me, my friend," he muttered awkwardly. "I was just . . . I mean, I was thinking. *Thinking* . . ."

"Yes," Robert said. It was really a very small, ragged sort of clearing; hardly more than a thicket, not actually. "But she isn't here."

Reginald shook his head. "I waited most of yesterday. I thought . . . maybe, just for a while . . ." He kneaded the back of his neck helplessly, pointlessly, beautifully. "I don't know. I guess I'll wait a bit longer."

Robert nodded. He sat down in the grass, folding his legs under him, and after a hesitant moment so did Prince Reginald. They smiled briefly at each other, and then sat silently, both gradually leaning against the tree.

After a very long stillness, Reginald finally looked directly at Robert. "I meant what I said, the other day. That other day. About your wedding."

"Oh," Robert said. *That other day, when Cerise curtsied so elegantly to the King dragon, and I knocked her down.* "Yes. Well. That will have to wait for a bit, won't it? You and I will have to journey back to Corvinia, you know, to deal with poor old Krije." He found that he really liked saying that. "Poor old King Krije."

"Ah," Reginald said. "Poor old Father." He plainly liked the sound of it himself. "Actually, I was thinking, I might perhaps do a little more adventuring before then? Before quite then, you know? Just a touch of adventuring . . . and perhaps a bit of drinking, as long as I'm at it?" He grinned suddenly at Robert, and it made him look shy and joyous, and very young. "Perhaps a *lot* of drinking."

Robert grinned back at the Prince. "And Mortmain?"

Joyous or not, Reginald looked around the clearing hurriedly and cleared his throat. "Mortmain. Do you know . . . do you know, I was thinking about not telling him? Just . . . ah . . . being rather gone. I mean, I'd leave a note, of course. Certainly, I would."

Half closing his eyes against the morning sun, Robert remembered rather fondly his last encounter with Prince Reginald's spelling. "Um . . . I don't know whether you could get away with it for long. Mortmain's quick."

Quick enough to realize well before I did that I had no least interest in becoming a great lord's valet. All the same, the look of pained chagrin on Reginald's impossibly handsome face touched a thoughtful place in Robert's mind that it had crossed once before. He suggested diffidently, "Thinking about it, though . . . that is, really thinking about it, good old Mortmain might make a fairly good King of Corvinia himself. Just a thought, I mean—maybe just for the time being, until you returned. . . ."

He never really noticed the sudden brightening in Prince Reginald's blue eyes, because at that point his dearest friend in all the world stepped into the clearing, and he couldn't move, and he couldn't think, and nothing that mattered, mattered. One of the two people in the world said, "Well, it took you long enough," and the other said at the same time, "Oh, do be still, my darling," and neither of them ever remembered anything much beyond that.

Robert did manage to warn Prince Reginald, "When you go back to Corvinia, you will *not* go alone, my lord," and Cerise kissed Reginald quite chastely on the cheek. Then she threw her whole weight into it, kissed him fully on the lips, and held Robert's arm tightly as the Prince bowed royally and wandered off to get a jump on Mortmain. "I always wondered what that could ever possibly be like," she explained unashamedly to Robert. "How could you not, after all, really?"

Robert arched his right eyebrow—a trick he had finally acquired from his sister Rosamonde after endless practice—and the Princess laughed and promptly kissed it. "*Now,*" she said. "Wouldn't you think it's time we went to see Mother?"

"No, I wouldn't," Robert answered. His grip on the Princess's arm became slightly firmer. "Cerise. You're your parents' only child—even if they'd let you marry somebody just this side of a beggar—"

"Oh, don't you start *that* with me, Aurelius-smelly-us! You know you're part of a higher ancestry than my people ever bloody *imagined*—"

"Even if that were true—which it certainly isn't, believe me—would they ever, *ever* let you toss your crown over the windmill to run off chasing dragons on a moment's notice with someone who'll likely never know exactly who or what he is?" He covered her mouth before she could answer him. "Would *I* ever let you?"

She bit his hand.

Robert pulled his hand away and gaped at her, then at the blood. She had bitten him far harder than Adelise ever had, or even the new ice-white one, Marie-Galante. But her eyes were remarkably tranquil, as a dragon's eyes could never have been. Her voice was a voice he had never heard before, as she said, "Robert, my one companion, love of my life forever, 'let' is not a word you will use to me again."

Then she tore a strip off her silken petticoat and bandaged his hand while he stared. After which she smiled up at him warmly, delightfully yielding. "My father is the only one who knows this, but my mother is *very* romantic."

At least, he did say it aloud this time. "I am so doomed. . . ."

On the way down to Bellemontagne Castle, past the Royal Grotto, the Royal Folly, and the Royal Croquet Grounds, they met Mortmain walking alone. He greeted them pleasantly, asking if by any chance they had encountered Prince Reginald.

They told him they hadn't, alas, and went on their way together. But Robert did not have to turn his head to feel Mortmain looking after them: puzzled and wary and doomed, like himself and everyone else. The morning sun, as golden as the King dragon's scales, warmed the backs of their necks.

ACKNOWLEDGMENTS

As time passes, I'm increasingly grateful for those people who are dear and important to me, like Joe Monti, who cared for this book all its long way through, to Howard Morhaim, who fought for the manuscript with the single-minded ferocity of a ferret. And I shared my office with a ferret for some years, so for once I actually know what I'm talking about.

Deborah Grabien is the nearest thing I've ever had to a sister. I always wanted one of those, since I was little. She never changes a line or alters a character—she just nags me until I do it myself, the right way. A seriously aggravating woman, bless her forever.

Lauren Sands is my dear friend and tireless pusher. Every artist of any sort needs a few people he or she can truly trust. I've been luckier than most, luckier than I ever expected to be.

And then there are all those people I've worked with, even when I never got to meet them in person, because that's the incredibly cluttery way books actually get published. I have been extremely lucky to have Jéla Lewter and Caroline Tew on my side, contributing their painstaking devotion to detail to make the text as good as it could possibly be, as well as Christine Calella and Savannah Breckenridge, who helped to make sure that audiences knew that this book even existed. In addition to the gorgeous artwork by Annie Stegg Gerard and Justin Gerard, I'm grateful for the beautiful design work of Esther Paradelo and Lewelin Polanco, as well as for the amazing efforts of Amanda Mulholland, Lauren Gomez, Zoe Kaplan, Christine Masters, and Chloe Gray.

I thank you all more than you can ever possibly know.